THE SCOUNDREL'S DEADLY DEED

GRAVESYDE VILLAGE MYSTERIES
BOOK TWO

PATRICIA RICE

PLEASE JOIN MY READER LIST

Please consider joining my newsletter for exclusive content and news of upcoming releases. Be the first to know about special sales, freebies, stories from my writer life, and other fun information. You'll even receive a thank-you gift. Join me on my writing adventures!

To Join, Please Visit —
https://www.subscribepage.com/ricewebsite

AUTHOR'S NOTE

In the Gravesyde Priory Mystery series I introduce readers to the heirs of Wycliffe Manor, who turn a derelict manor into a home. Each of the couples have their own romance and mystery to solve and some of those couples will continue to appear in this spin-off.

In this new series, I'm writing about the people who bring Gravesyde Village back to life. The history of the village is wrapped around the manor, the ancestral home of the Earls of Wycliffe, built on a former priory. In the way of medieval fiefdoms, the earls resisted district boundary changes, so the estate, in 1815, is an exclave of Shropshire, although south of Birmingham and surrounded by Worcestershire, creating legal havoc when it comes to crime. As appointed executor of the trust operating the manor, Captain Huntley has been chosen as the local magistrate.

Due to various circumstances, the manor has been empty, or nearly so, for decades. The village has been left to die. With the return of the manor's inhabitants, spurred by the industrial revolution, the locals are gradually returning to their ancestral homes.

As the series continues, we can watch the village and its inhabitants grow and find romance—and solve a few crimes along the way. Each story stands alone.

As a side note, I have referenced the town of "Stratford" where the bankers and solicitors reside. Although there is a Stratford in London and the famous Stratford-on-Avon nearby, this Stratford exists only in my mind. Birmingham, however, is completely real, an industrial and technology center akin to today's Silicon Valley.

CHARACTERS

VILLAGE:

Damien Sutter: lawyer, son of shoemaker
(Harry Sutter: deceased, Damien's soldier brother)
Meg Sutter Butler: Damien's mother
Brighid (Brydie) Calhoun: spinster, neighbor of Sutters
Caitlin (Kate) Calhoun Morgan: widowed with three children,
Arthur age 14, **Rob** age 12, **Lynly** age 8.
Edward Evans: shoe factory owner
Zebediah Johnson: itinerant preacher
Thomas Butler: Damien's former neighbor, now works for Zeb
Elizabeth Butler: Tom's nearly blind sister
Verity Russell: teacher, Rafe's wife
Sgt. Rufus Russell (Rafe): retired army; innkeeper
Sgt Major Fletcher Ferguson (Fletch): retired army; Rafe's friend
Jacques Rousseau: Damien's French valet
Paul Upton: curate
Daniel Corcoran: curate's grandfather
Mrs. Hatter: one of Zeb's followers
Martha Mayfield: widowed camp follower
Harlan Terwilliger: financier

Mr. Oswald: mercantile proprietor and postmaster;
Charley Jones: church deacon

MANOR:

Captain Alistair (Hunt) Huntley: US Army engineer
Clarissa (Clare) Huntley: wife of Hunt and secret novelist
Arnaud Lavigne: Hunt's artist cousin, former French comte
Henri Lavigne: Arnaud's younger brother, tavern owner, peddler
Lady Elsa Villiers de Sackville: manor cook
Honorable Jack de Sackville: stable owner; Elsa's husband
Lavender Marlowe: young seamstress
Dorothea (Thea) Reid Talbot: haunted interior decorator
Sofia Lavigne: young cousin of Arnaud and Henri; perfumer
Daniel Walker: Hunt's friend, steward; Meera's husband
Meera Abrams Walker: physician/apothecary; Clare's best friend
Henrietta (Nettie) Upton: curate's stepmother; housekeeper
Patience Upton: Nettie's daughter and curate's stepsister;
gardener
Minerva Peniston: librarian
Duke of Castlefield: visiting manor
Montague Dacre, Earl of Weston: duke's eldest son
Gavin Smith: duke's investment advisor

MONDAY

ONE

DAMIEN

November 1815

"No room at the inn?" Damien Sutter asked in amusement, gazing around at the nearly empty, half-timbered lobby. A gray wolfhound sprawled in front of a coal grate, undisturbed by childish voices emanating from an area that ought to be a pub. Other than those limited signs of life, the deteriorating medieval inn echoed hollow—evidently inhabited by no more than ghosts.

The tall, carrot-haired man behind the battered counter shrugged his powerful shoulders. Behind him, Damien's valet whistled softly in admiration. Jacques would be exceedingly displeased if they didn't obtain rooms.

"Like everything around here, this place has been abandoned for half a century," the innkeeper said apologetically. "We're working on rebuilding and furnishing, but it probably won't be usable until spring."

"I see. What is considered *usable*?" Damien kicked himself for listening to Evans. After losing everything with the war's end, the former factory owner was desperate.

Damien had an alternative place to lay his head. He simply wasn't prepared to face real ghosts without a good night's sleep.

Before the innkeeper could explain, a dark-haired, raw-boned man of about thirty, wiping greasy hands on a rag, emerged from the corridor behind the desk. *Soldiers*, Damien began to understand, just back from the Continent.

At Damien's request to define *usable*, the newcomer smirked. "As in, we have no one to carry your water and slops or make your food. This is a luxury campground for us."

"Army?" Damien guessed. "I lost my brother at Waterloo, cavalry. I'm Damien Sutter. I grew up around here. I've come to look at the shoemaker's shop he left." He turned to Jacques. His valet was a slight man but reasonably strong. "Can you manage the water and slops?"

"And prepare light meals," Jacques said fervently, eyeing both muscled soldiers. "If you do not need me to clean and mend three sets of attire a day."

The red-haired innkeeper sketched a vague bow. "I am Rafe Russell. This is former Sergeant Major Fletcher Ferguson, but we call him Fletch. The manor will be happy to hear some of the original landowners are returning. Any other time, we'd have found a room for you up there."

The dark-haired Fletch didn't offer his grimy paw but gestured in the direction of the hill behind the inn. "The manor is full to overflowing. The curate is getting leg-shackled and all his bride's friends and family have descended for the occasion."

"And their retinues," Rafe added dryly. "Dukes travel with a blamed lot of people. But he's paying to stable their mounts and keeping Fletch busy, so we can't complain."

At hint of a need for cash, Damien removed his purse and set a sovereign on the counter. "We'll pay to stable ours as well. I have a friend arriving this evening, Edward Evans, so if you have three empty beds, we'll take whatever is available. I had no idea duke's daughters resided in the area these days. Which duke?"

He already knew which one, and that His Grace had no daughter, but he had reason to remain unremarked for as long as he could.

"Castlefield. It's not his daughter," Fletch explained. "Daughter of Colonel Peniston, the duke's steward. His Grace simply wants an excuse to raid the manor's library. The captain can hardly refuse him. The duke's book buying is paying to restore the old keep."

Rafe chuckled. "Our *curate* nearly refused His Grace when he offered to purchase a special license so the wedding could be held at the manor. He said he could feed the village for a year or build an addition to the chapel with the cost of the license."

"But dukes can't attend services in tiny public chapels," Damien surmised. "I remember Gravesyde's being as drafty as sitting outside this time of year."

"Once the inn is open, we hope to expand and improve the chapel next. Upton understands that the manor's great hall is more suitable for a duke. Our good parson simply dislikes the waste of all the fol-de-rol. He gave in when he realized a duke was the only way to entice his wealthy vicar into a day-long carriage ride to tie the knot, since he can't do it himself. But it took some fancy negotiation," Rafe said in amusement. "The duke's paying dearly to plunder the library. The bride is curating what she'll allow him to buy and demands high prices."

Educated soldiers, Damien concluded. But they hadn't reacted to his name, so they probably hadn't known the brother Damien hadn't seen since adolescence. He'd always thought there'd be more time. He should have learned that lesson by now.

Rafe spun the gold coin in his fingers, considering. "You'd be our first paying guests. I hope to set this up as a fancy establishment for business travelers. I don't want to develop a bad reputation before we even open."

"I can assure you, I will have nothing but praise for your hospitality. I am interested in setting up a business here, also, so it's in my interest to encourage visitors." Which was only half a lie. *Evans* wanted to set up a shoe manufactory. Damien never wished to live in this hellhole again.

Before they could accept his offer, a squeal followed by a howl rose over the piping voices in the room off the lobby. A marmalade kitten dashed out and attempted to scamper up the innkeeper's leather breeches. He scooped up the creature, placed it on his shoulder, and waited in expectation rather than rush to the rescue.

The shrill voices hushed as some miscreant shouted, "I didn't do nuttin!"

"We've told you to leave the girls alone."

Damien couldn't resist the urge to peer into the next chamber. As he'd expected, it appeared to be a pub, with huge mullioned windows—only the blackened bar was loaded with books and the trestle tables were filled with children.

"I just pulled her ribbon!" a lad of about ten protested, while dangling by his collar.

The woman hauling him from his feet stood a head above the bemused teacher at the front of the room. All athletic muscle and grace, the Amazon swung her victim off the floor and lugged him to the door. Ignoring their stares, she deposited the boy in the lobby. "Go home and tell your mother why you're not in class or I will."

She watched the boy scamper out the door. Then, unfazed by male stares, she brushed off her hands and marched back to the schoolroom.

In that brief moment when she had practically looked him straight in the eye, Damien's breath caught in his throat. *Surely not. . .* But the wild bush of auburn hair, the proud chin and haughty cheekbones. . .

As if his shock had hit her, she swung back around, wide-eyed. *"Damien?"*

6

"Brydie?" He hadn't seen her in fifteen years, but how could anyone forget a Celtic warrior goddess? She'd been all skinny awkwardness back then, but she'd filled out nicely. He'd thought her married and well gone from here by now.

"You bloody bastard." She reached him in a single step and smacked his jaw hard enough to spin his head.

TWO

BRYDIE

Brydie was still steaming hours later. She'd made her excuses and slipped out of the schoolroom after making the usual spectacle of herself. But she had to warn Kate.

To keep busy, she laundered the bed linen in the washing shed, where she kept the fire hot so as not to freeze. She had to wear gloves to hang them, though. Awkward, but she didn't want another case of chilblains and end up like her mother, her fingers crippled with arthritis.

Besides, from the washing line, she could see Kate approach down the wooded path from the manor. It had once been called Wycliffe Manor but the Wycliffe title had died with the last earl. Newcomers had taken to calling it the Priory, like the village and monastery that had once stood there. Times changed, but she'd never thought Gravesyde would.

Strolling down the hillside, her sister carried a basket of sewing work. They needed all the coins they could earn, but it was difficult to work and mind families too. While they were in the schoolroom, the children were out of trouble, and Brydie was there, if needed. But classes ended early so all the students might return home before dark and do their chores. Kate needed to be with hers.

"Don't go in yet," Brydie called, crossing the packed dirt of the inn yard.

Her sister glanced up in alarm. "Is Lynly well? Did she have another spell?"

Kate was a miniature version of Brydie, her auburn hair darker and straight enough to make a sleek chignon. She took after their mother's shorter, sturdier side of the family. Brydie had their father's height and distinctive angular features. On Kate, the angles were more rounded and feminine. Brydie had been called *handsome*, never beautiful, graceful, or delicate. Kate achieved a welcoming prettiness.

"Lyn and Rob are fine," Brydie assured her. "I just wanted to warn you that Damien Sutter is in town. He's staying here at the inn and not out at the farm."

"Damien?" Kate looked surprised, and then she remembered. "Oh, his brother died, didn't he? We read it in the newssheets. He was one of the cavalry officers who led the charge against the French."

Brydie frowned. "What if he sees Arthur? They look enough alike. . ."

Kate caught her breath and glared. "Don't you dare, Bree Calhoun! George is Arthur's father and I'll hear no more said of it." She marched off in a huff.

Lynly and Rob had none of the Calhoun traits. They were unmistakably George Morgan's children—at eight and twelve, they were small, dark, and sickly. Arthur, at fourteen, however, was as tall and healthy as Brydie—and had the same golden-brown hair as Damien Sutter.

She'd cuff the dastard again, but she couldn't afford to lose her position at the inn. Rafe was kind and generous, but he was also the town bailiff, and Damien was apparently a guest. Rafe's patience for her temper would only stretch so far.

Slapping linen on the line gave her over-active mind a chance to seek nefarious ways to make the scoundrel pay. He'd seduced and abandoned her sister that last summer and never returned—not even after his parents vanished. Brydie had always assumed the Sutters had run away to avoid responsibility for their son's behavior, but they'd never returned. Perhaps he knew where they were, but everyone else still gossiped about the mystery.

The village talked about poor Arthur, too, born months after the wedding, but George had given him a name and been a decent husband to Kate. Only, now that the consumption had finally taken him. . .

Arthur needed a proper education. And Kate deserved an easier life. Without George, they couldn't keep running the farm. There were only so many hours in the day. This winter. . . She shuddered to think of how they'd afford coal once the pile ran out. Maybe she'd chop down that forest springing up on the Sutter's abandoned land.

School over for the day, Verity Russell, the innkeeper's bride and the village's new schoolteacher, emerged to help pin the last of the linen. Sturdier even than Kate, but with soft feminine features and wispy brownish curls at her nape, she appeared motherly even if she'd only just married. "We need a drying shed. These are likely to be frosted on overnight."

Verity only expressed a slight curiosity at the odd hour for washing. Given the lack of staff, Brydie knew she wouldn't complain.

"Sorry, the stable is too full for hanging, and I needed to clear my head before I killed your first paying guest." Brydie stabbed a pin over the line, knowing she had to explain herself. She'd spent years doing so. She had a lot of practice.

"Rafe is still laughing. Mr. Sutter explained that you'd been children together and you carried grudges."

If she meant to make Damien pay. . . She needed to know more. "Why is he back?" Fifteen years he'd been gone—Arthur's birthday served as a reminder.

"Rafe says he mentioned a shoemaker's shop and that he

wants to start a business, but you interrupted before he could learn more. Wouldn't it be wonderful to have someone to make shoes right here in the village?"

Damien's father had owned the village shoemaker's business once upon a time. Damien had hated it. Brydie didn't express her doubts. "I'm sure we'll find out why he's here, sooner or later."

"He's very handsome for an older man, isn't he?" Verity hung the smaller linens.

Older? *Hmpf.* He was only five years older than Brydie. And she'd be thirty and well past her prime in a few months. Old, indeed, perhaps to Verity, who'd only just turned twenty-five and emerged from isolation to start living in the real world again.

"I didn't notice," Brydie said stiffly. And she hadn't. He'd always be that laughing, twenty-year-old lad who'd lingered at home one summer, then vanished, like his parents.

Leaving Verity feeding the chickens, Brydie cleaned up after herself, then donned a cloak to walk home. Rather than go through the inn where she might run into their guest, she skirted around the outside. Kate had taken the pony cart with the children, so it was a long hike.

Normally, she planned her evening during her walk, but she couldn't settle her roiling emotions. She hesitated on the main road through town. She was late enough that the mercantile had closed for the day, and The Monk, Henri's tavern, was full enough to be rowdy. Gravesyde had no other shops and many of the cottages were empty, but lights glittered here and there in the homes of older folk who never left. She couldn't see the far end of town, where the physician/apothecary and her estate steward husband were setting up housekeeping and a badly needed infirmary.

There seemed to be a gathering on what passed for the village green, past the mercantile. A man ranted at the top of his lungs, and people had gathered to listen. In her current humor, she'd most likely shout back. The sight was so unusual, she lingered.

Paul Upton, the curate, emerged from the parsonage gate. He

11

was about Brydie's height, with a sheen of red in his hair, darker than hers. He'd only recently learned about his parentage and that they were distant cousins.

Paul nodded at the gathering. "Zebediah Johnson. His followers call themselves the People, and they seem to appear wherever His Grace goes. Johnson is calling our poor chapel as heathen as the Papists' cathedrals and is raising funds for a *people's* church. I must assume Catholics are not people?"

"Or that he's *people* and he's raising funds for himself?" Brydie usually had a more optimistic outlook, but today's unpleasant surprise had left her cynical. "Most *people* barely have funds to feed themselves, much less build a church. A people's church ought to feed them, instead of taking food from their mouths."

"Gravesyde is an unlikely place for fomenting revolution," the curate agreed. "Captain Huntley fears they're here to cause trouble."

"We don't have enough *people* to cause trouble," Brydie scoffed. "Besides, we're all happily looking forward to your wedding. It might ignite all-out warfare if the outsiders try to interfere in our celebrations."

Mr. Upton bowed and grinned in acknowledgment. "My bride would most likely come after any rowdies with an ax should they attempt to intervene."

His bride was the manor's librarian and appeared as meek and mild as a librarian should. But Brydie had heard tales. . . Mostly descendants of the late earl, the manor inhabitants were eccentric. But remembering Damien commandeering a room at an empty inn, she had to ask, "Where is this Zebediah staying?"

"I fear my grandfather is at fault. He is renting them one of his fallow fields for their tents," he admitted.

Curious. "Your grandfather is Catholic, like mine was. He does not fear they'll burn him out? And I do hope he's charging them a great deal for the trouble."

Smiling, Upton shook his head. "My granddad is frail and can't work his fields, but he still has his money-making skills.

He's charging them a season's income for the sheep he can't graze after they've muddied the field. The sheep he doesn't have, mind you. And since the old heathen has not been to church since leaving the old country, they have no notion that he was born papist. They buy his eggs and pay for his water. He's quite entertained."

"Pity they didn't ask to rent from me and Kate. We have no means of planting the fields come spring either. Earning a bit of rent would have been useful." Brydie tightened the hood on her cloak. She'd take the footpath home. She didn't have any use for troublemakers.

"Whoever made the choice may not have known that your brother-in-law recently died and your fields are available. Makes me wonder who is behind this, but granddad dealt only with Mr. Johnson." He doffed his cap and bowed. "I trust we'll see you at our wedding breakfast then?"

She had been planning on it, until Damien arrived. "We'll have to see how my niece is feeling. Good day to you, sir."

Wondering who knew what fields might be available to rent but not realize theirs were fallow kept Brydie's mind occupied as she traipsed the two miles home. It was full dark, but she had walked these paths since childhood, lived in the same house all her life, and knew no fear.

Kate's husband, George, had been little more than a hired hand until their father died. The Calhoun farm would pass to Arthur when he came of age. Perhaps it was better if Devil Damien didn't know of his son. She really needed to think things through. . . should she ever have the time.

The aroma of roasting chicken filled the kitchen as Brydie hung her cloak in the mudroom. With its brick fireplace and flag-stone floor, the spacious kitchen boasted an ancient round oak table with room for ten. Their mother had died before Brydie and Kate had reached adolescence. Having lost both father and Kate's husband in these last years, they now set it for half that number.

Her eight-year-old niece was just placing the last glass when

Brydie stepped into the warmth. Small for her age, her thin dark face almost gaunt, Lynly flashed a smile that lit the already well-lit kitchen.

"Aunt Brydie, I've outgrown my Sunday shoes! Mrs. Russell says I am growing bigger every day!" She coughed after those breathless exclamations.

Brydie knew what that meant. Any other time she would be delighted to measure her niece for new shoes. But if Damien had come to inspect his father's shoe shop. . .

"That is amazingly excellent news, Princess." She hugged her niece and distracted her. "Did you make tonight's pudding?"

Lynly nodded vigorously. "I even cut up some of the apples."

Arthur clunked in as only an adolescent can, followed by Rob, his little shadow. Removing a pot from the grate, Kate cast Brydie a worried frown.

She shouldn't have said anything. Her temper had overtaken common sense. Unlike Brydie, Kate was all that was proper, except for that one unfortunate summer when she must have fallen for pretty green eyes and seductive flattery. Not that Damien had ever used fancy words on a carrot-haired giant like herself, Brydie remembered with rancor. Kate was cute and small, not nearly as big as a man.

"I can't be stealing leather from Sutter's shop while Damien is in town," she whispered to her sister, taking the pot from her hand.

"You could *ask* him if you might use it." Still in a snit, Kate slammed the chicken onto a platter.

Brydie would rather stab him through his pretty green eyes. That summer had ended both their childhoods.

THREE

DAMIEN

W<small>ATCHING</small> B<small>RYDIE STALK OFF TOWARD HOME IN THE DARK,</small> <small>WITHOUT</small> lantern or company, Damien frowned. But if the good curate thought it acceptable, the village must be safer than he'd heard.

He introduced himself to the curate as they headed down the road to the gathering—which now appeared to include a bonfire. Well, it was cold. Damien didn't think anyone was burning torches. Yet.

As if he'd been waiting for him, Lord Weston, the duke's eldest son, emerged from the manor walking path. "Zeb brought his own audience, I see."

Older than Damien, Lord Weston was far wealthier and more aristocratic than Damien, but they'd fished together as boys and Damien had tutored him at Oxford. They'd found each other mutually beneficial upon occasion.

Upton tipped his hat to the earl and continued on, as if they were well acquainted and didn't need to speak.

"He'd be talking to himself, elsewise," Damien said, lingering in the shadows. "How are you faring at the Priory?"

"All the ladies are already attached, more's the pity. His Grace is in a froth by the unwed states of his sons. Nuptials remind him of our existence."

"He has a point, you know." Enjoying their wealth and varied pursuits, none of His Grace's many sons had shown an inclination toward marriage. Damien halted just outside the circle of firelight. "If Zeb had his way, His Grace would lose his head, and your estates would go to his *People*. He might succeed if you have no progeny to inherit."

Lord Weston shrugged. "Men of his ilk talk big to rile the populace. They hide the fact that they take money from wealthy Cits who resent aristocrats and think *they* should control Parliament. The poor have very little to do with any of it. Is it His Grace's stand on Catholicism, slavery, or industrialization that's Zeb's target today?"

"All three, I believe, but here, industrialization is an odd choice, considering the only business is a band of seamstresses and the dream of a perfumery." No one needed to know about Evans' plan for the shoe manufactory until it was formalized. Damien feared the revolutionary fanatic had discovered the plan somehow, but he couldn't fathom how.

He searched the shadowy figures shouting and applauding Zeb's fiery speech. The loudest shouts came from his followers. Damien recognized most from their manner of dress. Camping didn't allow for a large wardrobe. The rest of the mob came and went as the fancy took them and weren't as easily identifiable.

"I'm going to mingle," Damien warned. "Go back and tell your father no one will be burned at the stake tonight. I have it on good word that the bailiff is here, and a few of the ex-soldiers the captain employs."

His lordship nodded. "No insult intended to you, Sutter, but the company at the manor is much more entertaining. Let me know if you require anything."

Damien didn't watch him leave. He eased his way through the crowd to the back of the circle, behind Zeb. He'd not worn his

London attire when he arrived. He knew how to look like the villagers. He was one, after all.

Besides, he'd seen Zeb and his crowd in other places, even recognized Tom Butler, Zebediah's right-hand man. Butler was from Gravesyde and the most likely source of Zeb's information.

Butler and Sutter lands had run together for generations, until Tom had been imprisoned for theft and his farm had been lost. Tom had to be near sixty by now. He doubted the avaricious scoundrel would notice him. Damien owned nothing—or hadn't.

"It's time we take the power back from our oppressors," Zeb shouted. "The nobles hold us under their thumb, refusing us the right to steer our own destiny!"

Well, if Damien understood Gravesyde's difficulty, it was the *bank* who held them hostage. But Zeb took his rhetoric straight from the history books—as if the French revolution had ended well for the peasants. Killing the lower classes with war was a tried-and-true method of ensuring the few who survived were too hungry to complain about returning to the plow.

He didn't entirely disagree with the rhetoric, just the manner of implementing it. Violence only accomplished more violence. After years of war, the country needed peace.

Wearing a wool cap even shabbier than Damien's, Edward Evans appeared at his elbow. Older than Damien, not as tall, he was broad through the chest he currently disguised in a loose jacket. His broad, smashed nose hinted at humble origins. "Am I one of the oppressors or is that epithet reserved for the aristocracy?"

"Since you haven't built your factory yet, it's a little harder to work you into the demagogy. To broaden his audience, Zeb needs to hit as many grievances as he can. Keep listening. He's almost at the good part. He's been waiting for The Monk to empty, so he has a fresh audience." Damien crossed his arms and continued scanning the crowd.

"Foreigners," the speaker shouted. "They're bringing in filthy

17

outsiders who work for nothing, taking our land and the positions we once held! It's a wonder we're not all begging in the street!"

"The bank took mine," some newcomer cried. "Ain't no furriners here."

Damien hid a grin. There were the locals he knew.

"The Irish, the Welsh, the papists, the aristocrats, the *banks,*" Zeb replied, skillfully working the local complaint into the tirade. "They all conspire to steal the rights of the working man. How can you feed your babies without a decent day's wage? Don't be fooled by empty promises. The duke, the banks, the industrialists all want us to be their slaves."

"And what can we do to stop them?" one of Zeb's followers asked.

"Take back the power!" Zeb cried. "Demand the right to vote! We need our voices heard in Parliament!"

"Does that include women? People who don't own land?" Evans murmured cynically. "The poor, uneducated folk who work in manufactories?"

"Wait for it," Damien murmured back.

"They gave the *Irish* representatives in Parliament!" Zeb cried in ringing tones. "Just think about it. . . the papist foreigners can tell us good Englishmen what to do! Who will it be next, the dirty Jews?"

"Bigot," Evans said wearily. "But no danger to my plan, I think."

"He's here for a reason," Damien argued. "And unless he's after the Priory's perfumery or sewing shop, yours is the only new project in town. It will take him time to go after you directly. He needs to work up a lather first."

"You believe someone has recognized me? How? I've never been in this part of the country." Evans had discarded his city top hat and frockcoat in an effort to blend in. But his polished boots and tailored tweed cost more than a working man's wages for a year.

"Perhaps His Grace is taking up industry and this is about

him. Give me time to find out. I'll take you to the shop tomorrow." Damien left Evans stewing and slipped into the growing mob.

Damien had escaped Gravesyde for many valid reasons. He had buried his tempestuous upbringing with education, learned to curb his frustration with boxing, and practiced control by rubbing elbows with the right sorts who expected civilized behavior.

Since university, he had spent his time in positions that allowed him to cultivate relationships with everyone from dukes to industrialists. If the army needed boots, Damien knew the men who could produce them efficiently and cheaply. Evans had been a supplier until the war ended. Damien had met the man through his father's shoemaking trade.

Bringing powerful men together was more interesting than sitting in a law office, writing wills. Creating wealth by employing those who struggled to survive pleased him more than fighting for justice in corrupt courtrooms. For a younger son with no expectations, he had done well.

But his brother's death had left him questioning his choices. He had a little land and money now. He wasn't a farmer. There wasn't much future in returning to this dismal village or his father's shoemaking. The days of handmade shoes were numbered. Soon, they would only be for the rich. But a manufactory. . .

As he worked his way through the crowd, he attempted to recognize faces he hadn't seen in years. Deacon Jones was fatter and grayer. Oswald from the mercantile seemed to have shrunk, but his bespectacled cynicism remained in his scowl. There were a lot of new faces, probably from the manor. The old viscountess had died shortly after he'd left. He knew the late earl's property had been abandoned until recently. He'd wrangle introductions to the heirs when he was ready.

Seeing Brydie again after all these years had unsettled him more than he'd like to admit. She'd only been a skinny fifteen-year-old when he'd last seen her, but he remembered her laugh, the way she had wielded a hammer in his father's shop with expertise. He'd missed Brydie, but she'd been better off without his family history of violence.

The city didn't have women like her —unbridled and unaffected by society's artifice. He hadn't realized that he missed that kind of raw honesty—although the devil if he knew what had raised her ire.

With his thoughts elsewhere, he thought he heard a woman whisper his name. He swung around, searching for the source, but only saw the back of Butler's coat as he made his way to the other side of the crowd.

Damien's anonymity might be over if Butler had recognized him. Best to settle his business with Evans and then decide what to do next.

He walked away from the loud altercation at the bonfire. Zeb's diatribes always ended in a brawl.

TUESDAY

FOUR

RAFE

Tuesday morning, Rafe added toast to a plate of rashers and eggs, pushed aside the kitten intent on hunting bacon, and picked up the teapot. "Keep an eye on the bread in the oven, please? I'm practicing my hospitality by taking breakfast to our guests."

The second businessman, older and more rotund, had arrived just before dark—another paying customer and gold coin in Rafe's pocket. And Mr. Evans had been agreeable to accepting Sutter's offer of his valet as servant.

If Rafe opened the inn now, perhaps he could seek some of his old messmates and see if they'd be interested in working here. Opening early had a certain logic. Winter business would be slow and give him time to practice being an innkeeper.

"Aye, aye, sergeant." His wife peered dubiously at the ancient oven. He loved that Verity was attempting to assist him in the kitchen, but she had been raised as a lady and was still new at it.

He squeezed his beautiful bride and kissed her caramel hair. He also loved having the right to do that. He loved it better when she snuggled against him and pressed kisses to his jaw. If he didn't have hot food waiting—after years in the army, he couldn't waste good food.

"But you're too late to carry it up." Verity stepped away and gestured at the wall dividing pub and kitchen. "The pretty one is already out there, prowling through my schoolbooks. You'll need to give him the keys to the upstairs library. He might dress like a countryman, but he's no such thing."

Verity had brought her father's library with her when she'd arrived in Gravesyde. They hoped to someday make it a feature of the inn.

"Said he once lived here, close enough." Rafe poured tea into their new mugs. They hadn't bought fine china. Men preferred solid mugs and he didn't anticipate entertaining lady travelers in this backwater. Not yet, anyway.

"If Mr. Sutter has Brydie slapping him before he's here a day, we'd better keep a watch on him," Verity warned.

His wife had learned caution for good reason. But Rafe's size left him more confident, so he had to practice listening to her words of caution. "He was at the bonfire with his friend last night. I have questions."

Rafe carried the overflowing tray into the pub. The children wouldn't arrive for another hour. "Hope you don't mind tea," he called to their prowling guest. "We're a little short on coffee until the wagon arrives."

In informal short jacket, breeches, and riding boots, Sutter appeared ready to go hunting with the Priory Manor crowd. He offered a genuine smile of appreciation at the food. "My valet was supposed to do that, thank you. I left him fussing over a missing button, smelled food, and followed my nose."

"A man needs a hearty breakfast, my mother always said." Rafe set the plates out on a table that actually had a chair with a back. "I need practice if we're to open in spring."

"Sit down, join me for tea, if you can. After last night's excitement, I'm eager to hear the latest gossip." Sutter settled into his chair and ripped at his toast.

Rafe had had every intention of joining him in one manner or another. He settled on a bench across from his guest with the second mug of tea. "Just some troublemaker set on annoying His Grace. He's entitled to his opinions, I suppose, but if I see them marching with torches on private property—and a great deal of the village belongs to either the bank or the manor—I have a veritable army prepared to drive them out of town."

"Good to know. I've heard the manor folk are attempting to revive the village. I have fond memories of the place, but there's not much reason to live here anymore, is there? Small farms barely put food on the table." Their guest dug into his eggs with what appeared to be appreciation.

"There's a lot happening that isn't visible yet," Rafe replied complacently. "The Reids have funds now, and powerful connections. It will take time, but it's good to be here at the beginning. A few decades down the road, this inn will be worth a fortune. Right now, they're practically giving the place away." Rafe sipped his ale. "What about you? You planning on selling your brother's shop?"

"Possibly. It's not my news to impart yet, though. I dislike troublemakers giving the place a bad name. Makes it harder to sell property."

"Not fond of them either," Rafe admitted. "I'm afraid they're here to cause trouble at the wedding on Sunday. Makes no sense. The curate and his bride aren't wealthy nobles. What is the point of scaring away their family and friends? I'm new in town. Did you recognize any of them last night?"

Sutter sipped his tea. "I know one of the main instigators, a man name Thomas Butler. His family once owned land near ours. . . and Brydie's. Is she still Miss Calhoun?"

Rafe hid a smile. "She is. She'll be in with her sister's children shortly. So, she knows this Butler also?"

Expressionless, Damien drank his tea before continuing, "She was only a child when Butler was sent away for theft, I believe. Creditors took his farm. Doubt she remembers him. But he worked for my father for a while after he was released. It's possible she met him then, when I was off to the city."

Rafe beamed at Verity when she carried in a tray of scones and jam and a fresh pot of tea. "Have I told you lately how much I love you?"

She blushed, rumpled his always rumpled curls, and fled back to the kitchen. He needed to pry as much information as he could from their guest before the wee ones arrived.

"I don't recognize your wife, either. Neither of you from around here?" Sutter broke open a scone and poured jam over it.

"Friends of locals," Rafe said. "We don't know the history of the place well. Heard your parents vanished sometime back without telling anyone they were leaving. What happened there?" Given the village's history of murder, Rafe was curious. He didn't want this city man here in pursuit of revenge.

His guest grimaced. "I wish I knew. If my brother did, he never told me. Back then, I was barely scraping a living, juggling a half dozen tasks at a time, establishing my reputation. I'd write occasionally to tell them I was alive, but I didn't want them having to pay too much postage, and I was young and heedless, thought they'd always be there. When I didn't hear back, I just assumed they were having a hard time of it after Lady Reid died, and the bank started foreclosures."

"And no one told you they had left?" Rafe had a hard time with that. He supposed, if his parents had disappeared while he was on the Continent, it would take a while to hear of it. But for no one to even question. . .

"I didn't have a fixed address. I traveled. My brother was in the military, on the Continent. Eventually, we received letters from each other, each of us asking the other if we'd heard from them. When neither of us knew anything, I rode out one winter. The place was locked up. There were still clothes in the wardrobe, old ones. They most likely had bought new since I'd seen them last. The carriage and livestock were gone." He shrugged. "It is not one of my fondest memories."

"Did you ask the neighbors? Surely, they left information with someone so you could find them?" This tale was taller than Rafe could swallow. He heartily disliked mysteries.

"As I said, Butler had lost his land to the bank, so he was gone. I checked with Brydie's father, and he claimed my parents up and left one day, and they hadn't heard from them since. There's no one else closer. The previous curate had left town by then. The manor was closed up. I asked Oswald and whoever I could find about, but they all said the same. I left my solicitor's address on the door in case they ever returned." Sutter rubbed his brow. "You have no idea what crazy things ran through my mind."

"I'm not a man of imagination, but I can think of a few. I'm sorry. I see why you'd want to sell the place. And why your brother didn't. He was hoping they'd return." Rafe thought he'd take a trip out there when he had a few spare minutes, have a look around. He didn't like the sound of this at all. But it had been fifteen years or so, after all—not exactly a priority.

"And after all these years, I'm afraid they won't return, that something dreadful happened. My brother convinced the court of that some years back, had the land put in his name, but he simply couldn't bring himself to sell it. It's small, but there's no reason for it to go to waste. I don't know if I can live in the house again. I'm going out today to have a look around."

Rafe exchanged a few pleasantries, then returned to his kitchen and the bread Verity was frowning at. "It needs to be nice and crispy brown on top or it will be soggy in the middle. This is almost there." He popped it back in the oven. "You'll recognize it after a time or two. I'm going up to have a word with the captain. Will you be all right with all the noisy brats?"

"Brydie will be here. Nothing frightens Brydie. I really hadn't imagined teaching children almost as large as I am. I suppose I should have." She dusted off her hands. "Go on with you. I'll clean up."

His wife might not be a cook, but Rafe had confidence in her level head. She'd once taught rowdy street urchins.

27

He let himself out the back. In the distance, he heard duck hunters out already as he trotted up the concealed path through the trees. Shots echoed from the misty river on the far side of the hill. Like the fortress both monks and the first earls had required, Priory Manor sat at the top with nearly inaccessible hillsides surrounding it.

He caught up with Upton going the same direction. "Thanks for keeping tempers under control last night. We may need to close The Monk while that scum is in town."

Dressed informally in tweed, the curate shook his head. "Henri can control how much they drink. He and Patience keep the locals entertained and happy. It's Zeb's followers who are the troublemakers."

"I want to visit their camp, but I'm not certain if that exceeds my authority." Rafe slowed his stride. The curate might be of humble origins and poor as the proverbial church mouse, but he had his hand on the pulse of the manor as well as the village.

"Captain Huntley was discussing that last night. Of course, he'd like to chase them off with shotguns. He resents them disturbing the wedding party. He had some notion that he could show the duke that we're quite civilized." Upton chortled at the notion.

"*London* isn't civilized. Men are animals and always will be. Although the ladies do try. Who is in the hunting party?" Rafe nodded in the direction of the noise.

"Weston, at the very least. He's known for his expertise with firearms. Should have been in the military but as the duke's eldest son. . ." Upton shrugged.

"Understood." Rafe waved off the curate as they reached the manor and went their separate ways.

The ex-prizefighter butler led Rafe to the library, where he found Captain Huntley, Walker, the estate's steward, and the petite librarian comparing maps.

"Ah, good, there you are, Sgt. Russell. Appreciate how you handled the mob last night." A tall man with a scar marring the side of his face, Hunt pounded Rafe on the back in greeting. "Now, if we can only force the riffraff to leave—"

"That's why I'm here. I never asked the boundaries of the estate or the extent of my authority." Rafe had only been in Gravesyde a little over a month and was still learning his duties. He bowed a greeting to the others present. He thought one was a banker. The rest were presumably guests.

Hunt gestured at the drawings on the table. "The large map shows the extent of the original Priory lands. The monks owned the village and the entire valley, as did the first earl. Subsequent earls had other properties and weren't interested in this rocky soil. They began selling off plots to tenants."

Before Rafe could work out the obscure details of the large map, Hunt threw down another, donning a monocle to study it with his one good eye. "We've been gradually working our way through all the deed files since learning the last viscount was a bit of a scoundrel."

The banker huffed and studied his nails. That viscount had— theoretically—mortgaged most of the village to the bank. The deeds were in dispute.

Rafe had never owned property, but the agreement he and Fletch had drawn up with the Wycliffe estate and Priory Manor owners had taught him a few things about surveys and boundaries. He studied the plot lines on the map, locating the village parcels first.

Hunt drew his finger along a line well outside the village. "As far as we can determine, the earl's estate no longer owns anything outside this boundary. Those outlying farms were legally sold to tenants over a century ago."

That left a great deal of land no longer belonging to the Wycliffe estate.

"Here's the interesting part—the *entire* original estate still remains as an exclave of Shropshire as it was in medieval times, while everything *outside* the priory's original boundaries. . ." He

29

produced the larger map. ". . .is now in the jurisdiction of Worcestershire."

"Which means Hunt, as magistrate, has authority over the entire exclave, whether or not he owns the land," one of the strangers concluded.

"Your only problem," the librarian reminded them, "is that Paul's grandfather owns the land the ruffians are renting, and he has not asked you to evict them."

"I don't mean to evict anyone," Rafe assured her. "I simply want to know if I have the authority to keep the peace if necessary."

As if to test his declaration, an anxious footman arrived at the library door. "Captain, sir, there's been. . . an incident."

Rafe grasped the unspoken message as quickly as the captain. Leaving the guests undisturbed, they followed the servant into the hall and closed the door.

"You wouldn't interrupt us for a quarrel in the kitchen, Adam. What is it?"

"Someone shot at. . ." The handsome young footman floundered, searching for a proper name. "The speaker, from last night, at the bonfire?"

"Johnson," Rafe offered. "Someone shot at Mr. Johnson. That was rather to be expected. I assume he's still alive?"

The footman nearly turned purple finding polite phrases. "He claims Lord Weston shot at him, sir!"

FIVE

DAMIEN

DAMIEN AND EVANS WERE ALREADY MOUNTED AND ON THE ROAD, when their host and his hound stormed down from the manor, shouting at them. They waited to hear what was wrong.

"You've not been to the other side of the village yet, have ye?" Rafe called.

"No, we're just escaping the hordes of youngsters gathering in the pub." Damien glanced toward the village but noticed nothing untoward.

"No one ride by in a hurry or anything like that?" The big man stopped at the end of the drive.

"Just the usual farm carts rolling in, not away. Heard some hunters while we were saddling up, but not nearby," Evans offered.

"Is there a problem? Might we help?" Damien inquired, although he was impatient to be off. He'd hated his home, but he hadn't remembered the village being much trouble—although there had been rumors of recent violence.

"Zeb Johnson is claiming the earl shot at him this morning.

Don't suppose you've seen Weston recently?" Rafe looked rightfully harassed.

"I did, actually." Damien didn't wish to mention their conversation in front of Evans, not until the earl's offer was firmer. He'd
kept an eye on Johnson for the earl over the years. Weston would
do whatever it took to protect his father from the troublemaker.
"Weston stopped by to discuss a bit of business." He pulled out
his timepiece. "About half an hour ago? He wasn't carrying
weapons that I noticed."

"Excellent," Rafe said in satisfaction. "I'll pin Johnson down
on time, but he's way out the other end of town. Can't think the
earl had time to be bothered with him. The fog this morning must
have fooled him." He saluted and jogged down the village's one
street in the direction of the green, the wolfhound on his heels.

"Why would the addlepate accuse an *earl*?" Damien turned his
horse to the hedge-lined walking path Brydie had taken last night.
The wagon lane revealed them to too many spying eyes and busy
tongues.

He had watched for Brydie's arrival, but she had eluded him.
He didn't dare ask if she came every day. He preferred not to
wonder why he wanted to know.

"We can hope someone succeeds at murdering Zeb," Evans
muttered.

"More likely to be one of his own misfits." Damien rode down
the once familiar lane. The village had been deteriorating since the
old earl's death, well before Damien had left home. People had
continued as always, buying his father's shoes, selling and
trading among themselves, hoping one of the noble family would
return and provide work again. They hadn't.

It had taken decades for the villagers to give up and go away.
He hoped it wouldn't take decades for them to return.

"You'll have difficulty finding workers," Damien warned.
"You'll have to house anyone you lure from the city."

"I can't expect to start an operation as large as I had during the war. If your cottage is as large as you say, I shouldn't have to build anything immediately."

"You're trading inexpensive land for expensive transportation," Damien warned.

"I'd rather own than rent in the city, if I can."

There spoke a man who wished to leave a legacy to heirs. Damien had rented all his life, not collecting material possessions, free to come and go as he pleased. But now, with no family left, he had to consider his future. Harry wouldn't be there to take him in.

At thirty-five, it was time he grew up and looked ahead.

The path led past the field where the Calhouns raised a few sheep. He didn't see any sign of the old squire or his sheep. No smoke rose from the chimney on the far side of the hedge. He hadn't sought out gossip yet, wishing to stay unnoticed until he'd settled business. Brydie's mother had been dead twenty years or so. Was her father still alive?

The path emerged on the tree-lined wagon road that divided the Calhoun home and farm from the Sutter manor and shop. Overgrown trees and hedges blocked more than a glimpse of both homes. Damien rode up to the drive where there used to be a wooden gate t0 keep in the animals. The remains hung from one hinge. Someone had pushed them out of the way.

The rose bed was a briar patch of fallen leaves from trees that had barely been more than saplings last he'd seen them. The goats had been gone when he was here last, so the weeds had taken over the yard. The place felt haunted.

"My word, this is what you call a cottage?" Evans asked, whistling in surprise.

The drive led directly to the tall stone house with its ambling wings to either side, then curved back to the shop and office. If it hadn't caved in, there should be a barn out back as well.

"It's hardly a manor." Damien couldn't very well turn back now. Reluctantly, he dismounted and tied his horse to a post. "It started as a traditional two up, two down. Local stones are inexpensive. It just takes labor and my family was once large. Most of Gravesyde was built using the quarry."

The original cottage had probably been built over a hundred-and-fifty years ago. As the family had grown, they'd added on. Damien had vague memories of doddering great-aunts and uncles occupying the wings, of aunts and uncles visiting. The sons and daughters had all left in search of their own places in the world, as he had. His father had been the heir and no one had been interested in going into shoemaking with him.

Very few had been desperate enough to even share the house with his father. Damien's childhood had been a series of final departures.

He stepped onto the porch and produced the key the solicitor had given him. He hadn't wanted to return here alone. The memories weren't pleasant.

He had to shoulder the door open. The stench of must and dead vermin hit him. They spent the next few minutes prying open shutters and warped window frames.

"Should have rented it out," Evans said. "Empty houses deteriorate."

"That was Harry's decision. He thought the war would end soon and he'd return here, take up where our father left off." Damien let the familiar pang roll over him. They'd both been young and stupid. He didn't have the excuse of youth any longer.

Evans wandered off, testing floorboards and admiring the size of the rooms. The furniture hadn't been covered. Dust and mice droppings littered the cushions. The colorful quilts his mother had hung on the wall to keep out drafts had vanished. Perhaps she'd taken them with her.

Their family had never been poor. They'd built to last, built for generations.

"The shop is out back, beyond the hedge," he called as Evans entered the spacious kitchen. His mother never had a proper stove. The enormous fireplace had produced adequate meals. They'd seldom kept servants for very long.

The place was too depressing for words. Damien prayed Evans would offer for it. If Damien wanted to settle down, he'd do it somewhere less haunted by his childhood.

Punching his father's nose had ended a long war that his father had won.

He followed Evans out to the shop. It offered a few happier memories. He and Harry had escaped here in the evenings, pounding their frustrations into leather soles. The Calhoun sisters had run in and out, bringing flashes of color and laughter. His father hadn't minded teaching the girls how to work the leather and sew slippers. They had been like bright flowers that last summer before he couldn't take it anymore.

"Good solid foundation," Evans said approvingly, walking around the shop interior. "Walls are solid. I'll have someone up to look at the roof."

"He had it tiled about twenty years ago. Should be sound for a while." Wanting to escape grim memories, Damien ignored the interior office door and returned to the open air. They'd owned a carriage once. He assumed his parents had left in it.

"Do you have the deeds or a survey map?" Evans came out to admire the graveled, weed-filled drive. "Good wagon lane, good drive, room to expand. I'll need to go above, see if we can set up dormitories, check all the roofs for leaks."

"He had an office behind the shop. Might be papers there." Damien went around the outside, checking shutters and over-grown shrubbery. Pulling out his keys, he sorted through for the office key. He hadn't had this ring when he'd last been here. He'd simply verified that everything was locked up.

Evans opened the outside shutters to let in light. Damien found the key and unlocked the door.

The gray November light fell on overturned chairs. A hurricane of paper caught in the breeze from the open door. All the drawers in the desk hung open.

Evans whistled. "Looks like you had thieves."

35

SIX

BRYDIE

Adding the final polish to the stove, Brydie heard the rise of excited voices in the pub, dodged the kitten dashing for its bowl, and knew lunch hour had arrived. She washed her hands and brought out the jugs of watered apple juice. Each child had their own tin cup. They clamored around her when she carried in the jug.

"Orderly line," she commanded, refusing to pour until they settled in place. She tilted her head at the kitchen as she spoke to the exhausted teacher. "I put together a lunch for you. Rafe had some official duty."

With a grateful nod, Verity took Brydie's place in the kitchen. It had taken them a few weeks to work out this routine. They were supposed to have more help, but so many mothers had babies at home, or worked elsewhere, that sharing work hadn't happened. With no children of her own, Brydie had to act as substitute for Kate. Since Rafe wasn't earning any income on the inn yet, she wasn't certain what fancy financial juggling paid her small salary for cleaning so Kate could pay Verity for teaching.

Something had to change if she and Kate were to dress the

children another winter. They'd outgrown almost everything. The farmhouse was large and drafty. Selling eggs and a few pigs barely put coal on the fire. Kate's husband might have been an uneducated hired hand, but he'd kept the farm producing even while ill. Kate and Brydie had been raised as the daughters of a wealthy landowner, not to be farmhands. It wasn't as if men took orders from women.

As she poured juice, Rafe stormed into the inn's lobby, followed by Jack de Sackville, the owner of a stable on the other side of the village. Jack's wife, Lady Elsa, even though she was an earl's daughter, cooked for the manor inhabitants. The couple lived up there. To Brydie, the manor folk had an easy life, but both Rafe and Jack were currently wrapped in thunderclouds.

"We are damned well not bringing in the earl for questioning," de Sackville shouted. "I'll haul Johnson in by his heels and let him explain himself! If Weston had shot at him, he'd be dead by now."

Brydie filled the last tin mug, and while the children tore through the lunches they brought from home, she stopped in the doorway to the lobby. "Do I need to bring you whiskey or ale?"

"A barrel of ale and a whipping post," Rafe said in disgust. "But we can fetch for ourselves. We'll go around back so as not to disturb your students."

"Verity's in the kitchen. Try not to shout too loudly. The little pitchers carry everything home."

They saluted and strode out the back hall. Before she could retreat to keep the wild ones from turning the classroom into a circus, Damien and his stodgy older friend stormed in, looking nearly as unhappy as Rafe and Lt. de Sackville.

"Sgt. Russell is the bailiff, is he not?" Damien asked. Before she could reply, he asked, "Is he around?"

"In the kitchen with Lt. de Sackville." Brydie wanted to escape to the safety of the classroom, but she had an uneasy notion that Damien had been out inspecting his father's shop. Surely, he wouldn't notice how much leather was missing?

"We need a room with a table to spread papers on. Do we have to wait until your students leave?" He'd removed his hat and now ran his hand through his thick hair, making a rat's nest of it. Silver strands gleamed in the golden-brown. The years had carved his jaw and cheekbones with maturity. He'd been a handsome boy who had made it impossible to look at another man since.

He was a more handsome man. She wasn't about to fetch and carry for him, no matter how good he looked, but he was a guest. She had to be polite. "The inn has a small library. Ask Rafe for the key."

She retreated into the pub, pointed commandingly at a boy dancing on the table until he climbed down. She waited to hear Damien's voice in the kitchen. When it became apparent he'd gone to his room first, she entered.

Rafe and Jack were shouting at each other while quaffing ale. Verity was no cook, but she was sawing at bread and had slapped cheese and pickles on the table.

And this used to be such a quiet inn.

"Your guests would like to use the library," Brydie said over the hubbub. When the men didn't immediately respond, she banged a tin pot against the iron stove. She hadn't learned to deal with Kate's three, plus drunken farmhands, by being polite.

Once she had their attention, she repeated her first request and added, "Mr. Sutter is looking for a bailiff."

Before anyone could react, Damien's fancified valet waltzed in from the schoolroom. "I am to prepare a light luncheon for the gentlemen, if I may. And if you have a stout whiskey, they will gladly pay."

Brydie didn't hold with drunkenness. Having said her piece, she swung around and returned to the classroom. Dancing Boy was now prancing around poor Lynly, who clung to her stuffed sock doll, terrified. Lynly was small for her age and had vapors that were enough to give the adults around her attacks of the heart.

This bully was too large for Brydie to lift by the collar, but she was still taller. She picked up Verity's pointing stick, came between the two, and shoved the stick at his midsection, pushing him back to the coldest corner of the pub. "Sit there this week, freeze your dancing toes a bit until you learn to treat others with respect." He protested. She crossed her arms and glared down at him from her greater height. He slumped on the bench at the pub's most dilapidated table.

Despite not being paid to monitor the schoolroom, she enjoyed doing it. Lynly flashed her a trembling smile that broke her heart. That poor lass had so many difficulties. . . She didn't need bullies pushing her round, not until Brydie could teach her to set their pants on fire.

Kate would probably object to that.

Verity returned just as Brydie was desperately ordering everyone to add two and two on their slates. Dancing Boy had lost his chalk and Lynly was offering one of hers.

"Show our guests to the library, will you, please?" Verity whispered, handing Brydie a key. "With any luck, that should lure their valet out of the kitchen where Rafe is likely to squash him like a bug."

"Are the stars in the wrong place in the heavens?" Brydie asked, taking the key. "What on earth is happening that everyone is in such a stew?"

"The troublemaker claims the Earl of Weston shot at him this morning, and Mr. Sutter says someone broke into his father's office." Verity added dryly, "Since that house has been empty for years, I assume that last happened before the stars shifted into wrong places."

Mr. Sutter's office? Brydie's throat dried, so she couldn't reply. That didn't make sense. The office had always been locked. Trying to work her head around that bit of news, she took the key and entered the lobby, where Damien waited.

He glowered at her as if the vandalism were her fault. She could have told him she only had a key to the shop. But he wouldn't like that news either.

Silently, she led him up the narrow wooden stairs to the

bedchamber floor of the old inn. Verity had stored the remains of her father's library up here in vague hope that she might someday open it as a lending library. For now, Rafe had furnished it with crude shelves and castoffs from the manor.

An interior room with no windows and the kitchen's heat below, it wasn't as cold as other areas of the old inn. Brydie lit a lantern and left it on the battered table she'd polished to a gleam. "There are candles in the box on the shelf if this isn't sufficient."

She turned to leave, but Damien blocked the doorway. "Have you ever noticed vagrants or anyone else lingering about after my parents left?"

"You are assuming I have naught better to do than stand in our yard, watching the road," she said stiffly.

"You once did," he replied with a glimpse of the old Damien's mischievous smile. "I suppose you've grown up since then."

He didn't take his gaze from her face but she was still very aware of their proximity. He was a tall man, topping her great height by half a head. He'd filled out in the chest and shoulders— as had she since she'd seen him last. In this narrow space, they were practically touching, but she refused to back away.

"We all grow up and have to do our share. If you'll excuse me, I have work to do." She eased around him as his friend arrived with a sheaf of papers.

"You still live with your family? May I call on them?" He relented and shifted from the door, holding her with his questions instead. He'd always been good at that.

"It's just Kate and me and the children now. No point riding all that way when you can greet us here in town." She fled before he could question more.

She almost ran into the valet coming up. Since he had a full tray, she pressed against the wall to let him pass. He smelled of French cologne, wore lace on his neckcloth, and a blue, superfine frockcoat so tight she could almost count his skinny ribs. He feigned a smile and swept past as if she were no more than a charwoman.

Well, she supposed that's all she was these days. The daughters of once prosperous squires were meant to marry well and take their proper places in the community. She'd shirked those duties, and now look where they were. Perhaps she should have gone to Bath to find a wealthy husband, as the baker's daughter had. But their father had died and Kate had her hands full with a toddler and another on the way. . . By the time she was eighteen, the chance had been lost.

Rafe and Lt. de Sackville had left the kitchen by the time she reached it. The valet had left a mess for her to clean. She wondered what was happening with the earl and the man Rafe had called a troublemaker, but the inn wasn't exactly gossip central. Lt. de Sackville had presumably become involved because his stable and training ground was out the river side of town, where the preacher's followers camped.

Brydie decided she'd have to wait until The Monk opened later to hear the story, but she wasn't in the habit of visiting the tavern, even though she loved listening to the curate's sister sing.

She was about to brave the cold to feed the chickens when Minerva Peniston and Clare Huntley rapped at the kitchen door. Minerva was Priory Manor's librarian and the bride-to-be who had brought a duke to the village. Mrs. Huntley, like Minerva, was one of the late earl's granddaughters and presided over the manor with her husband. Anywhere else in the world, gentry from the manor would not be sitting in a kitchen with a charwoman, but this was Gravesyde. They all had to work together.

Brydie ushered them in and set them by the fire. "What can we do for you?" she asked while putting leaves in the teapot and checking the kettle was full.

"We're worried this Mr. Johnson and his followers will disrupt the wedding trying to reach the duke," Minerva said bluntly.

"We can't order a duke and his son to go home." Clare accepted her teacup and sighed. "If they did, all the other guests would feel obliged to do so, too, and that includes Colonel Peniston, who works for him. Minerva needs her father to give her away."

"Archaic custom," Minerva scoffed, but she didn't argue the statement. "The gentlemen seem to have no understanding of why Mr. Johnson and his followers arrived in Gravesyde. Other than the myth of the missing jewels, there's no wealth here for them to exploit. There's barely enough population to convert."

Brydie set out a plate of bread and cheese. They'd run out of scones and biscuits until Rafe had time to bake. "Sgt. Russell has no suggestions? I should think he and the gentlemen could provide adequate protection if the duke stays inside."

"That's just it, His Grace *won't* stay inside. He's fishing with his son as we speak. The two never see each other, so they were hoping to have a peaceful opportunity to talk." Minerva cut cheese as if she'd like to use the knife on her nemesis—whether that was the duke or Mr. Johnson, it was difficult to say.

"So, no one is locking up the earl for shooting at an itinerant troublemaker?" Brydie asked dryly, taking a seat. The kitten jumped into her lap, and she gratefully stroked it, calming her overset nerves. "Shouldn't we wait for Verity to discuss this? What can I possibly do?"

"Verity will defend her husband's ability to be everywhere at once. Men prefer confrontation, and that simply won't do. You know this village as well as anyone. We wish to be devious." Clare nibbled delicately at her buttered bread.

"I don't understand." Brydie pushed her cup about. She'd worked with these women on church projects and in setting up the school, but she had no qualifications for much else.

"That's because you haven't a devious bone in your body." Minerva licked her fingers.

Byrdie leapt up to fetch napkins but the ladies waved her down.

"We want you to befriend some of Mr. Johnson 's followers, lure them here with tea and friendly gossip," Minerva explained.

"Find out everything you can about their reason for being here," Clare continued. "We'll pay you."

Brydie could not afford to turn down money, especially if she might be helpful and ease her curiosity all at the same time.

SEVEN

DAMIEN

"THEY WANT YOU TO DO WHAT?" RAFE WAS BELLOWING AS DAMIEN trotted down the stairs in search of writing paper. "I won't allow it!"

Brydie appeared to be the recipient of the innkeeper's bellows. Unless she had changed mightily—and Damien had seen no evidence that she had become a genteel, obedient lady these last years—Rafe might as well give up now.

"Unless you tell me you'll boot the children out of school, you cannot stop me," Brydie reminded him, reaching for cobwebs in the distant corners of the ceiling with her long-handled mop. "I've lived here my entire life. I know people you haven't even met. I will have plenty of company. All I want from you is your permission to use the pub after school lets out. I'll still put in all my hours for you."

By working into the night, Damien surmised. He strode into the lobby. "The village is overrun by Johnson's rowdies. You cannot be walking home in the middle of the night.

She scowled at him, her silvery-gray eyes darkening to thunderclouds beneath her sunset hair. "This is none of your affair, Mr. Sutter. Did you require anything?"

"I can fetch it myself." He turned to the red-headed innkeeper. Two tempers under the same roof were not conducive to peace and quiet. "Miss Calhoun is quite capable of punching noses. I don't mind escorting her, if only for the entertainment. I will not allow her to walk home alone in the dark."

"I only punched you once and you dared me to!" she protested. "It's not my fault you dodged the wrong way."

"You're right-handed. You hit me with your left! Quite unfair for a girl." Damien hid his grin at her reddened cheeks, indicating steam was building to a head. He still knew how to ignite her temper.

"You'll see my fist again if you don't go about your business, Mr. Sutter. Go fetch what you came to fetch and leave us be."

The large innkeeper sighed. "It's not just the pub. She wants to visit the camp. The women are up to something."

"If Brydie's involved, I'm sure they are. When is this visit to take place? Do I have time to fetch paper and ink from the mercantile?" Damien allowed the inquisitive wolfhound to check his scent, even though the animal's head was taller than his waistband. He scratched behind its ears and, satisfied, the hound returned to the hearth.

"There's writing supplies under the counter." Rafe produced a sheaf of paper, an ink bottle, and a pen. "A good inn provides for its guests." He threw a warning glance at Brydie. "We do not get said guests killed. Johnson is irate that we're not arresting an earl for missing a shot at him. He's a loose cannon."

Since he'd very much like to learn what Johnson was about, Damien shrugged. "You'll be taking your pony cart, I assume?" At Brydie's wary nod, he continued, "A harmless woman in a pony cart should be safe enough. I'll ride behind, make certain there's no trouble. Is there a goal to this performance?"

"Protecting the duke and the wedding from any retaliation,"

Brydie said stiffly, obviously unhappy that Rafe was listening to him and not her.

"I have men working around the clock to protect them," Rafe protested. "I know how to secure the perimeters."

"You cannot put everyone in a box and expect them to stay there," Brydie countered. "And on Sunday, you'll have the entire village in the manor's yard, anticipating one of Lady Elsa's celebratory feasts. Your men cannot keep out the camp followers."

She had a point. Damien waited with Rafe to hear the solution.

She sighed and lowered her voice so they could barely hear over the noise of the classroom reciting their multiplication tables —badly. "I will only speak to the women. I'll take them into my confidence, tell them the real wedding breakfast is to be held in the pub for the gentry, while the village eats in the manor's stable. If the duke is their target, they will come *here* looking for him."

"I didn't know you could be so devious," Damien said in admiration.

"It's the bride's idea." Brydie glared again. "So, you see, it's perfectly safe."

"Shots were *fired* at Mr. Johnson," Rafe protested. "The duke and his son have been threatened. The whole village is nowhere close to being safe!"

"I shall not go near Mr. Johnson or any nobles. I will talk to the women about Kate's soaps, just as innocent as can be." She finished knocking down a cobweb and stalked off down the back hall, avoiding the schoolroom.

"She'll go with or without our permission," Damien told the frustrated innkeeper. "And much as we might wish to do so, we cannot wrap ladies in cotton batting and store them in a vault for safekeeping. Sometimes I think they are better prepared to survive than we are."

Rafe rubbed his orange curls. "Verity has given me attacks of the heart confronting scoundrels. I had hoped to protect her but— my wife has survived situations on her own that raise my hair. I suppose what Brydie means to do is mild in comparison. It's just a lot of misguided fools out there, not dangerous ones."

"Except Zeb Johnson and his immediate cohorts," Damien warned. "Let me take these papers upstairs. Don't let her leave without me." He dashed up the stairs before Rafe could question his knowledge of Johnson.

He left the writing supplies with Evans. "I'm off to spy on Johnson, see how much he knows about our plans. See if you can make any sense of those papers we found, and I'll be back later to sort through the legalese. We may need to write the solicitors if there is no survey."

Having already started sorting yellowing documents, Evans nodded absently. "I'll put together some calculations based on what I'm finding here. Be a good chap and arrange for Johnson to fall in the river. The world will be a better place."

"Better idea than shooting, leastways. Fewer people get hurt." Damien went to his room, stuffed a pistol into his pocket, and a knife into his boot. Whatever he may have said about leaving Brydie to herself, he wouldn't let anyone harm her. She had been the brightest part of his childhood.

He dashed down the backstairs to the stable yard under an overcast sky. Brydie was already hooking up the ancient pony cart he'd seen her sister use. An equally ancient nag stood in the traces, but it appeared adequate for short distances.

"Do you need to go back to the farm for the soap?" he called, distracting her and gaining time to saddle up.

"Rafe lets us keep our stock in the shed. We sell some to the manor and hope to sell more to the inn once he opens." She patted the pony as she buckled it in. "The mercantile stocks it too. The ladies like the lavender one."

They used to give soap away as gifts. Damien wondered about the state of their finances if their father had died. Was Kate's husband not competent? He'd have to quit lying low and go to the tavern for the latest gossip.

He really didn't want to be involved in village affairs. He was leaving as soon as he sold off the place. He needed to talk to Weston about his plans. Damien preferred to have people working out there and not leave an empty lot—which is what he suspected the earl had in mind.

He managed to saddle his horse almost in time to follow her out. He shouldn't have hurried. The pony plodded, and he didn't want to be seen arriving with Brydie. He just didn't know where to find the campsite.

He remembered the place once they reached it. He'd delivered shoes to the old Irish gent and his wife, and they'd fed him tea thick enough to hold a spoon and bread stuffed with currants. The yard was no longer well tended but the stone farmhouse had weathered the hands of time.

A sheep field provided very little shelter. A few caravans had parked by a stream, where they'd tethered horses. The rest of the folk had sensibly set their tents further upstream. He stopped in the lane behind the hedgerow, while Brydie boldly steered her cart up the drive. She tied her pony to a tree, then carried a basket over the stile into the field near the tents.

A few of the curious turned to look. Damien studied their faces, watching for known troublemakers, but the bulk of the men were working further uphill, cutting firewood in a copse of half-dead trees. He located Tom Butler talking to Johnson down by the stream simply because they wore frockcoats and expensive knee boots. Even wearing Quaker-style hats, they didn't blend in.

Butler noticed Brydie first. A tall redhead was pretty recognizable, even if he hadn't seen her in years. Damien waited for him to greet her, but she was aiming for the women at the campfire and Butler vanished in the direction of the trees.

A thin woman, wrapped in shawls, her hair in a long silver plait, emerged from one of the caravans by the brook. Assuming the better equipment belonged to Johnson and Butler, Damien eased his mount in her direction. Although he'd watched Johnson and his crew over the years, he didn't think he'd ever seen their wives. Still, something about how this woman moved seemed oddly familiar. What he could see of her old-fashioned gown hung on her as if it had belonged to a larger woman.

Apparently noticing very noticeable Brydie, the woman startled and stared. Instead of crossing the field to join the other women, however, she limped over to Johnson, who was drinking from a tin cup and keeping an eye on the proceedings.

Damien tore his attention from the preacher and the mysteriously familiar woman to urge his horse a little closer to Brydie. She was having a fine time, as expected, chatting and handing around soap for the women to sniff. Curious, some of the men had finally started down the hill.

Brydie might actually make money with this gambit, as well as lure them into her lair. It was a pity women couldn't direct armies; they'd be dueling at needlepoint instead of blowing each other up.

Musing on that ridiculous theme, Damien almost didn't hear his name called. Once ascertaining it wasn't Brydie, he turned back to the woman standing beside Johnson. She waved excitedly —at *him*? He was barely visible behind the hedgerow.

Before he could decide whether to dismount, an ominous blast reverberated across the peaceful clearing.

To his horror, the woman screamed and crumpled to the ground.

EIGHT

BRYDIE

Accustomed to hunters, Brydie dropped down at the detonation of gunshot and scanned the field for the addlepated duck hunter shooting around so many people.

The scream turned her head. It took a moment for her to understand, and then, heart racing, she ran with the crowd toward the stream—where Damien was running as well.

Johnson stood between the caravans, bellowing about not being hit, ordering his men to find the bastard who'd shot at him, sending them scrambling back up the hill. Undaunted, the women crouched down by the fallen figure at Johnson's feet. Blood gushed from just above her left breast.

"Give me your scarf to staunch the wound," one of the older ladies ordered, gesturing at Brydie. "Someone fetch water and some of that gin."

Brydie handed over her birthday scarf and crouched down to help. It took her a moment to recognize the delicate cheekbone with the scar. She gasped, then glanced up at Damien, who'd just arrived on foot.

At seeing the victim, he turned pale with shock but dropped

down to hold her while a woman cut back bloody clothing and poured gin into the wound. Silence fell. The blast had torn through the victim's upper chest and was pouring blood.

"Take her to Meera Walker," Brydie whispered. "She's a physician. She should be at the manor at this hour." She knew nothing of battlefield injuries, but this had to be a mortal wound.

They couldn't leave Damien's mother to die on the ground.

The older woman set aside the flask to pad the wound with everything handed to her. Then she wrapped her patient in a faded quilt brought down from the caravan. She didn't protest as Damien lifted the frail form of the mother he hadn't seen in fifteen years.

"Search for that confounded madman before he kills me," Johnson bellowed from where he cowered inside his caravan. "If the local law won't stop him, we must!" He didn't send a single glance to the woman struck in his place.

"Put her in the cart," Brydie murmured, folding her cloak over the shivering form attempting to speak while Damien carried her. "Lay her on the bench. You'll have to stand to drive it."

He nodded and wordlessly ran with his burden.

This was not the tea party Brydie had anticipated. She ran after him, carrying her basket of soap. Without her cloak, the cold November wind tore at her wool gown, but Damien's mother. . . She could hardly swallow as she followed him over the stile.

NINE

DAMIEN

Damien lay his mother on the bench seat of the pony cart. He thought she murmured, "I'm sorry, so sorry, we never. . ." but he was too concerned with holding the scarf tightly to her gaping wound.

She'd *waved* at him, as if happy to see him. She'd *waved*. And before he could even wave back. . . He shoved aside the horror and concentrated on doing what was necessary.

"I'll fetch your horse and tie it to the back when you reach the lane." Brydie strode off. The cart would take eternity to travel to the far side of the village, but he had no alternative.

He got the patient settled as best as he could, but as Brydie predicted, he had no room to sit. He couldn't drive and hold the patient at the same time. He stood, holding the reins, cautiously steering the cart back to the road. It wasn't exactly a galloping chariot. He halted to let Brydie tie up his horse. Where would she fit in?

Apparently having done this before, she climbed in and knelt on the floorboards beside his boots. He caught a flash of. . . breeches?. . . as she tugged up her gown, and took charge of pressing the bandages to the wound.

"We had no choice. . . He would have killed us," his mother murmured frantically. "I love you. . . I wanted to see you. . ."

She coughed and Damien saw blood. He urged the old nag into a trot.

He desperately wanted to question but she'd choke on blood if she talked. He'd not been in the war, but he'd visited friends in the hospital who had come back with chest wounds.

None of them had lived long.

Rather than listen to all the screaming demons in his head or heed the moisture rimming his eyes, he focused on avoiding ruts and Brydie's comforting murmurs. She'd had experience with patients, he could tell. His mother calmed down and coughed less. Or she was dead.

The many towers of Wycliffe Manor loomed over the village from a wooded hill. Originally a monks' priory, the first manor block had been built in a medieval era requiring solid defenses— like the river and a rushing brook at the foot of a rocky, forested hill. The only access for horses was from a drive on the far end of town, near the chapel.

By the time the cart bumped up the rutted drive, the manor's staff had seen them coming. A contingent of helpers was in the yard and waiting when he halted the cart. A plump, exotically brown lady pushed past him to examine the patient, urging caution and calling for a stretcher. Stable lads ran up to take the pony and his horse.

Damien stepped down and out of the way as others eased his mother's still form onto a crude stretcher. Brydie joined him. It only seemed natural to hug her when she wept against his shoulder. He couldn't think, wouldn't think. The horror and unfairness overwhelmed him.

Eventually, they followed everyone through the kitchen garden, neatly mulched in brown leaves for the winter, and into the back service hall. Apparently, the manor had an infirmary and

53

a lady physician. Gravesyde had changed tremendously since the days of the imperious, impoverished, French viscountess.

Damien paced the hall. Brydie rubbed her gloved hands and looked frozen. He cast off his own cloak to wrap it around her.

The estate's African steward stepped out of the infirmary. "She's trying to speak. Meera says to hold her hand and listen so she calms down."

Damien didn't think he could move. He'd blocked all the old memories for so long that the woman in there was a stranger, but she was his *mother*, the one who had tried to defend him—however unsuccessfully—when he couldn't defend himself.

Brydie grasped his elbow and steered him into the sickroom. He couldn't watch what the physician was doing. He focused on his mother's lined, gray face. She was so much older than he remembered. . .

"She's been ill for a long time," the lady—Dr. Walker—said. "The shot wasn't close range, but it entered her chest and pierced a lung. I'm sorry. I don't think she has the strength to lose more blood."

The form on the bed restlessly attempted to speak, her breath rattling with gasps for air.

"Say your farewells," Brydie whispered when he froze.

The tears rolled then. Damien dropped to his knees beside the cot and took a cold, frail hand. "We missed you," he tried to tell her, lacking the loving words he'd never heard.

"Damien." She spoke barely above a whisper, but he heard love or affection, or told himself he did. At least her face eased as she stroked his hair. "I'm so sorry. Tom said—" She started coughing.

Tom? Damien let it flow over him. "I'm here. I won't leave." Like she had. Did he dare ask. . . ? No. She was gasping for air.

Whatever she strained to say died with her. As her thin form relaxed into stillness, he could almost see her soul rise and fly away, finally free from torment.

He was becoming fanciful in his old age. He bowed his head but didn't know any prayers.

"I'm sorry, Mr. Sutter." The physician pulled the sheet over the patient once Damien stood. "She was wasting away. She should have sought help earlier, although I suppose the best we could have done was make her comfortable. The bullet simply took her a few months sooner."

"She chose her life," he said gruffly, swiping at his face with his handkerchief in a pretense of blowing his nose. "Thank you for giving us this small chance."

Picking up her cloak and the thin quilt and folding them over her arm, Brydie led him away. A petite general introduced as Miss Peniston, the librarian, led them to a small drawing room and handed him brandy. Brydie shoved him into a chair.

His mother had been alive for *fifteen years* without letting anyone know. And died when he found her. Fitting, perhaps. He took a large swallow of brandy.

"Rafe has gone out to the campsite with a few men," the librarian murmured, reminding them that a crime had been committed. "I think he plans on confiscating weapons while interrogating witnesses."

Damien needed time to settle everything inside his head, but the whole situation. . . reeked. What he recalled was all wrong. He simply couldn't pin down why.

Various other members of the household wandered in as word spread. Brydie must have identified his mother for him. The women politely left him alone as he sipped his brandy.

Captain Huntley wasn't as reticent. A big man, younger than Damien, without a hint of gray in his thick dark hair, his host poured himself a brandy and began to pace with a slight limp. "I'll need a full report of everything you saw and heard. Shooting women. . . That is beyond the pale."

"Hunt, sit down. Mr. Sutter is still in shock. At least give him a few minutes to mourn," Mrs. Huntley scolded. A blond, slender woman almost half her husband's breadth, she tried to steer him toward a sofa. He resisted.

Damien took another swallow of his drink, then shook his head. "It's all right, ma'am. Your husband needs to act before the scoundrels escape. I won't be very helpful, but I'll do my best."

"Do you want to come into my study and speak privately?" the captain suggested.

"No, I think Miss Calhoun can help me keep it all straight. I was in too much shock at finding my mother after all these years. And then, to have—" He gestured helplessly. "I'm not thinking clearly, I apologize."

"You have nothing to apologize for, sir," Mrs. Huntley said. "And please, call me Clare. Everyone does."

"Mr. Sutter gets that from his mother," Brydie said, giving him more time to pull his thoughts together. "She was always apologizing for herself, for her sons, her husband. . . She was apologizing with her dying breath. I think I shall give up apologies. They are singularly useless."

The women protested. Damien almost managed a smile. Brydie was absolutely correct. His mother's apologies had not healed a lifetime of wounds. "She also said she had no choice, Brydie, and I think that's the crux of the matter. She was powerless. Apologizing was all she could do."

Everyone waited, but he didn't know how to go on.

Brydie stepped in again. "I wasn't in a position to see what happened, Captain. I was talking to the women by the fire, trying to stay warm, invite them to tea, and sell them soap. The fire was some distance from where they'd set up the two caravans. The men weren't about, although I noticed some up the hill, cutting wood. Oh, and I believe they were skinning a sheep. I hope no one is missing one of theirs and that they paid for it."

"I'll look into that," Hunt said. "Perhaps I can lock them all up for theft."

"You'd have to feed them," the librarian reminded him. "Elsa isn't likely to give them gruel."

"But they'll be where they can't cause more trouble," Clare suggested with a smile, presumably understanding her husband.

Incredibly, the silly argument relaxed Damien more than the brandy. Just hearing sensible voices instead of his mother's haunting apologies. . .

He turned his brandy glass about in his hands. "I was only there to see that Miss Calhoun was safe. I watched from behind the hedgerow, some distance away. I couldn't make out faces, but I recognized Zeb Johnson and Tom Butler from their attire. They weren't on the hill but near the caravans, until Butler saw Brydie and walked away. I worried and watched him until I was assured that he wasn't walking toward her."

"Tom Butler?" Brydie asked. "Didn't he used to work for your father? *He* was with your mother?"

She had a right to be surprised. He was too. Damien nodded and continued. "When Butler entered the copse, I turned back to watch Zeb, and a woman stepped out of the smaller caravan. I couldn't see her well enough to recognize her. I was watching Brydie when I thought I heard a woman call my name. I could tell it wasn't Brydie. I turned back to Johnson, and the woman at the caravan waved. I could swear she was calling my name and waving at me, although from that distance. . . It didn't seem reasonable after all these years. And then I heard the shot. . ."

Brydie reached over to rub his hand. He clasped hers. Even in gloves, her fingers felt icy cold. He warmed them by cupping them between his.

"Could you tell from which position the shot came?" Hunt asked.

"The hill and trees, where the men were," Brydie said firmly. "None of the women had weapons, and they were all crowded around me and the fire. I would have seen a shotgun. Mr. Johnson immediately shouted about being unharmed and ducked inside his caravan. There was no one in the open field between the tents and the brook. The men on the hill had the best view."

57

"It couldn't have come from the opposite side of the stream? I'm not familiar with the place." Hunt continued his pacing.

"It's Paul's grandfather's farm," Miss Peniston explained. "There's a high hedge along the lane. If Mr. Sutter was on his horse behind it, he had a good view of both fields and the lane, but the area is very large and open. It would be impossible to see everywhere at once."

"The shot could not have gone through the caravans," Damien explained. "I suppose you might ask Dr. Walker about entry wounds, to see if it came from inside. I'm not certain which way she or Johnson faced at that point."

"So, whoever is targeting Johnson is among his *followers*?" Clare asked in incredulity. "And a bad shot?"

And there was what was wrong with the picture, Damien realized. The shot came after Tom Butler had left Johnson alone with his mother.

"Talk to Butler," Damien demanded. "He was in the trees near the men on the hill. He had to have seen—or done the shooting."

TEN

RAFE

RAFE AGREED TO FOLLOW THE CURATE TO HIS GRANDFATHER'S HOUSE and speak to the old gent first, so as not to worry him. He did not hold out much hope for a feeble old farmer to act as witness.

A maid escorted them upstairs to a wide bedchamber at the front of the house. Remarkably, it had a view from two sides—one of them over the fields. No wonder the old gent was entertained by his new renters!

Probably never a tall man, Mr. Corcoran had collapsed in on himself with age. He nearly disappeared into the wing chair meant for much larger men. Under a thinning crown of white hair, his eyes were bright and alert.

Paul Upton introduced Rafe as the bailiff, and Corcoran nodded knowingly. "Come to interrogate me, have ye?"

"Just wondering what you might have seen or heard through yon window, sir. Did you hear the weapon go off?" Rafe twisted the brim of his hat in his hands. Verity had bought him the high-crowned hat to replace his old tricorne, but he was uncomfortable wearing it.

"Weren't no Old Bess," the old gent warned. "I'd recognize that sound. Lucky to hit a horse with them things."

"You saw the shooter?" Upton asked cautiously.

Rafe studied the field from the window. He could see the campsite, but the distance was too great to make out faces.

"Watched a scalawag carrying a rifle through the trees back along the drive, afraid he was after the sheep. I heard the report but didn't see him do the shooting, couldn't even see the sheep. There be a section by the copse that can't be seen from the window. Best start there." Mr. Corcoran seemed well pleased with his report.

"I see what you mean," Rafe said, watching small figures scurry about the camp. "You're not at the right angle. Thank you, sir, you have been extremely helpful."

"Got some life in the old man yet," he chortled. "You boys come back and tell me all about it. Maisie says a lady was hurt? Will she be all right? Don't know what the world is coming to that people would shoot at women."

"The lady died. She'd been ill. It's a tragedy, but we're assuming the shot was an accident. Let us know if you hear anything else?" Paul tucked a knitted blanket more firmly around his grandfather's shoulders.

"Maisie brings me all the news from them that come up to the yard. They don't think it's an accident," Corcoran warned. "They think the manor folk wants to kill Mr. Johnson."

"Or it could be one of his followers," Rafe said, heading for the door. "We may have to hope he knows which one."

"There's them that come around who don't stay out there," Corcoran called after them. "They sneak up at night, right along that tree line."

"Why would they do that?" Paul asked as they clattered down the stairs and back to their horses. "Do we have local people who support Johnson and don't want anyone else to know?"

"Don't know. I heard he's trying to start his own church. I can't see why that would cause trouble. Poaching another man's woman is more the usual thing, unless gilt is involved. A farthing is hard to come by around here." Rafe left his horse in front of the house and strode toward the copse he couldn't see from the window.

He found the trail the women had carved through the grass to reach the well and the privy. He assumed the old man allowed them to use his facilities, since he was obviously unable to reach them. Rafe traced the worn path back through the winter-bare trees lining the drive. A large evergreen that may have once marked a boundary obscured a tumbling stone wall. A shooter could easily conceal himself behind the wall.

Paul joined him as he searched among the fallen leaves and needles under the low-hanging evergreen. Rafe didn't know one tree from another, but this one had extended branches dangling long needles into the unmown weeds along the wall—more excellent concealment for a sharpshooter. How many of the men here had been in the military?

"Found it," Upton said in a low voice, exposing his find in a litter of pine needles and debris by lifting one of the low-hanging branches. "Do I leave it here?"

Damnation, a rifle, one of the newer styles carried by the cavalry. "I'm not sitting here all night waiting for a killer to come looking for it." He couldn't imagine any of Johnson's starving acolytes owning one. This was a nobleman's weapon. With heavy heart, Rafe carried it over his shoulder and climbed over fallen stones to enter the field.

A ragged, middle-aged guard bearing an ancient wheellock stepped from the copse of saplings and dead wood. "State your business."

"Removing illegal firearms." Rafe snatched the weapon from the would-be soldier's careless grip. "I'm Sgt. Russell, the bailiff. This land comes under Gravesyde Priory's jurisdiction and unauthorized weapons are not allowed."

"No one told us that," the guard complained angrily. "How are we supposed to hunt?"

"Obtain a permit." Rafe completely made that up on the spot. Firearms in the hands of untrained clodpolls could kill more than rabbits. "Who is the owner of this one?" He displayed the one they'd found.

The man shrugged. "Never seen the like. Can I have mine back if I get this permit? And where do I get one?"

"After the shooting earlier, no one is getting one until we find who's responsible. Did you see anything?" Rafe didn't hold much hope for this line of questioning.

The guard shook his head. "We were digging a pit to roast meat. Must have come from the other field."

Rafe didn't intend to argue with a lying fool. The men had to have seen what happened. "Where's Tom Butler?"

The guard shrugged. "Not my duty to know where everyone is."

"Right-o, good luck telling trespassers from those who belong, then." Rafe started down the hill, studying the scene below. It was pretty much as Sutter had described it.

"Let me talk to the women," Upton suggested. "I'll mention we keep a few supplies at the chapel, see how loyal they are to the cause."

"If I don't get answers, I'll have to come around to them," Rafe warned. "Women know all the gossip."

Upton looked harmless in his worn tweed, without his clerical collar. The women were already watching the young, handsome curate as he headed down the hill. He'd probably fare better than Rafe.

With his height and bulk, Rafe had no illusions about appearing anything other than intimidating. If it wasn't for his ridiculous hair, he'd probably be shot on sight. The firearms over his shoulder held their attention though as he approached the men surrounding a firepit containing tonight's mutton.

"You have a sales receipt for that ewe?" he asked as he came closer.

Noting a rough hand reaching for a torn coat pocket, Rafe

caught the man's arm and removed the pistol in a bare fist. He emptied the barrel and the pan and stuck it in his own pocket. "No firearms without a permit. You'll have to see me at the inn with your credentials—after we solve Mrs. Sutter's death."

"Credentials?" A man wearing tailored frockcoat, knee boots, and top hat approached. "What the devil are you talking about? This is a free country."

"Nope, it's not," Rafe said cheerfully. "We have laws to protect the innocent. You are in Gravesyde Priory's jurisdiction, under our laws, and we don't allow firearms unless we know you. We'd have half Birmingham down here poaching our game, elsewise. Can anyone at the manor vouch for you?"

The man practically spluttered in his fury. "This is ridiculous. We have permission to hunt this field. I'll file a complaint."

"You'll have to file it with the magistrate." Rafe maintained his cheery attitude. He enjoyed annoying people into talking. "I'm the appointed bailiff and all I'm doing is upholding the law. Sgt. Rafe Russell, and you?"

"Butler," he growled. "Is this about the incident earlier? You should be talking to the folk at the manor. They're the ones who want us gone."

Incident? He relegated a woman's tragic death to a mere *incident*? And was this the man Damien had claimed had once been a neighbor?

Rafe had difficulty maintaining his smile. "Nope, actually, the manor folk don't give a flying fig about you. They just object to unpermitted firearms. Everyone at the manor was accounted for when poor Mrs. Sutter was murdered, accidentally or not. Who else here has a weapon?"

Rafe thought he was getting good at this lying business. Verity was teaching him well. If the ends justified the means and no one came to harm. . .

"Mrs. Sutter?" one of the younger men inquired in puzzlement at the repetition of the name.

Butler talked over him. "Someone tried to kill Zeb Johnson

63

and you're blaming *us*?" he asked in incredulity. "This is harassment."

Rafe let the first man's question slide by. He'd pick up on it later. "Just doing my duty. Do you have a receipt for that sheep? If not, I'll have to ask where you got it. That's someone's winter provisions. They'll need compensation."

Rafe would ask what constituted harassment later, because he thought he might be good at that too.

"We *paid* for it," Butler said gruffly. "We're not thieves, like the lying nobles and their greedy church. Don't come sniffing around us because we're poor. You look to the duke. He wants us all gone."

"Actually, I doubt the duke knows of your existence," Rafe said with great pleasure, finally finding a use for his hat. He tipped it and walked off.

Bitter men like Tom Butler were a shilling for the dozen. What was more interesting was that he was claiming to be poor while wearing Hobie's best boots.

He stopped when he saw a lone woman hobbling down the hill from the privy. She seemed to be stumbling, reaching out to find familiar trees or shrubs. He stepped up and introduced himself, then placed her hand on his arm. "May I lead you back to the ladies?"

She studied him for a long while through cloudy eyes, then nodded. "They will be gossiping about which of the husbands shot at Zeb."

"He has a reputation as a ladies' man?" Rafe asked carefully. There was motive if he'd ever heard one.

"He's not married for a reason." She said no more.

Rafe couldn't wait to introduce himself to Zeb Johnson.

ELEVEN

BRYDIE

Declining offers to stay at the manor for dinner, Brydie and Damien took the pony cart back to the inn. The devastated gentleman at her side had once been closer than a brother, but he was a stranger now. She had no means of consoling him—didn't know if she ought to be consoling the dastard, but she wasn't heartless. Losing a mother hurt—losing her twice. . .

At the inn, Brydie watched Damien walk away, hugging his mother's worn quilt, then turned to her sister, waiting impatiently for the cart to take the children home. "If you wish to come inside while I explain to Verity, come along. Otherwise, I'll explain this evening."

Kate shivered in the wind and gestured at the children rushing out to pet their pony. "Later, then. I've too much to do at home."

Brydie hugged her and returned to the inn. If Rafe was out playing bailiff, then Verity was left preparing a meal—never a good thing.

The lady schoolteacher had a taste for nice clothes, a little too fine for a kitchen. Brydie found her wrapped in a bulky apron and staring helplessly at the vegetables Rafe had left on the table.

"I can cut them, I suppose." Verity studied the peeled potatoes soaking in water. "But how small? And when do I put them in the pot? And is that dough meant to be a loaf or rolls?"

And then she actually looked up at Brydie, exclaimed, "What happened?" and pushed Brydie into a chair before reaching for the tea kettle. Verity might not be a cook, but she had a good heart.

Brydie explained as best as she could while drinking her tea and warming up. "It just seems exceedingly strange for Mrs. Sutter to return at the same time as her son, after all these years," she finished.

Verity tentatively attempted sawing a potato in half while she thought about it. "I believe Mr. Sutter is here to sell the property he inherited?"

"So, I've gathered, although no one has said exactly. He and Mr. Evans have papers scattered all over the library, working on some plan for the shoe business." Brydie finished her tea and began slicing carrots. She had to moderate her force when one flew off the table. Whacking knives about wasn't the safest way to release anxiety.

"And it is fairly common knowledge that Mr. Sutter lost his older brother recently? Do I put these in the pot yet?" Verity gestured at her meager stack of crudely cut potatoes.

Brydie stirred the pot over the fire and checked the meat. "We can wait a bit. Not knowing when Rafe will return makes it difficult to time. You want stew, not mush. Both fill your stomach, so there is no harm done if overcooked. But men like something to bite into."

She checked the bread dough and punched it down for another rise before answering. "Captain Sutter's death was listed with all the other casualties, yes. Vultures that we are, everyone reads those lists. Mr. Oswald reads them to those who can't read."

Verity nodded and studied a turnip. "So, it is possible Mrs. Sutter read of her son's death and wished to return, for a memorial, perhaps?"

"Fine thing to return after he's dead." Grumpily, Brydie returned to hacking carrots. Mrs. Sutter had never been a particularly *friendly* person, but to disappear without letting her sons know where. . . Damien was mourning a woman who didn't deserve it. The shock had to be terrible. "You need to peel that turnip."

"Perhaps she hoped her younger son would return to the property and she might see him?" Verity studied the vegetable and the chopping knife.

Brydie pushed a paring knife in her direction. Rafe had purchased fine cutlery for his kitchen. Or, more likely, Lady Elsa had given him her old ones so she had an excuse to buy new. Lady Elsa was a generous woman when she could worm her way around her trustees. "I think it doubtful that Zeb Johnson would have brought his tribe here because one woman wanted to see her son. The duke and the earl are the draw somehow."

"Well, it was certainly not the *earl* shooting at Zeb Johnson. He wouldn't have missed. From all reports, Weston has provided the manor kitchen with enough ducks for a wedding feast." Verity tentatively scraped at the turnip. "This is harder than potatoes."

"Which is why I left it to you." Unrepentantly, Brydie set the carrots aside to chop thyme. "I wonder how good a shot Damien is. He was in a position to aim at Johnson. His shock at seeing his mother was very real, though. I see no motive."

"You think his mother ran off with *Johnson*?" Verity asked, scandalized.

"I have no notion why she was there. It was all quite horrid and does leave me wondering where his father is." Brydie caught a movement out the ancient glass of the window and stood up. "We have company. I may have invited the women of the camp to come by when they could. It's perishing cold out there and they have little food."

Knowing their plans, Verity jumped up without questioning to add more water to the kettle while Brydie stepped into the yard.

The older woman who had helped with Mrs. Sutter stood

there uncertainly, wrapped in an assortment of old crocheted shawls.

"Come in out of the cold. That wind says a storm's brewing." Brydie ushered the woman inside.

Verity was already setting a fresh cup on the table. "Welcome. How may we help you?"

The woman dithered at the door. Taking advantage of her height, Brydie took the visitor's shoulders and steered her toward a chair. "We are extremely grateful for your help today. I am a very bad nurse and had no idea what to do."

"The poor thing didn't survive, did she?" The woman reluctantly sat down. "She'd been ill. Perhaps it was a blessing." She stared at the cup Verity filled, then warmed her hands around it. She wore no gloves and her hands were gnarled and age-spotted. "She'd had a hard life, as most of us have, I suppose. But she didn't seem like she was brought up to it."

Rather than gossip about the deceased, Brydie changed the subject. "I'm Brydie Calhoun." She gestured at Verity. "This is Mrs. Russell. She and her husband run the inn."

"Pleased to meet you." Their guest twisted the cup nervously and didn't add the sugar Brydie pushed toward her. "I'm known as Mrs. Hatter. My man died long ago. Zeb's people took me in or I'd have died in a workhouse. I owe them."

"I'm sure you've earned your way," Brydie said reassuringly. "We'd love it if more of your ladies visited. The village has been empty for so long, it's good to meet new people."

Mrs. Hatter nodded. "I don't suppose. . ." She clutched her cup until her knuckles whitened. "I don't believe I can last another winter in the open. Zeb has big ideas about a church and community where we all take care of each other, but. . ."

"That's exactly what we're doing in Gravesyde," Verity said smoothly, a little too smoothly since she'd only been here a few months, but she'd been learning from Clare Huntley, who made dreams happen. The need for shelter and community was universal.

"We're a work in progress," Brydie warned. "But there are people here who share their hearths just for the company and mutual assistance. Am I wrong in thinking you have some experience with nursing?"

"Took care of my brother after he lost his leg. Took care of his house. Did the same when my husband got the gout. I can cook and clean. If you know anyone—" Mrs. Hatter dared to look up with anxious hope.

"We'll start you right here at the inn." Verity pushed the turnip and a paring knife at her. "I'm a schoolteacher, of sorts, and a very bad kitchen worker. My husband does the cooking. Brydie, here, can do almost anything."

"Except keep the accounts," Brydie reminded her. "I've no head for numbers. That's Verity's task. We all find our own places as needed."

Despite her gnarled fingers, Mrs. Hatter peeled the turnip with expertise. "For a decent roof over my head and a bit of soft under my back, I'll do what needs doing, if ye'll have me."

"I think we can do better than that. You might find a place you prefer later, after you meet new people. We—" Brydie halted her eager spiel as a thought occurred, belatedly, as usual. "We discuss who needs what after church on Sundays. We're Anglican. Will that be a problem for you?"

Mrs. Hatter kept paring, her jaw setting firmly. "God provides, miss. I don't reckon He cares what the church looks like or who's doing the preaching."

"That is a commendable attitude, Mrs. Hatter. The world will be a better place once we are all so reasonable." Verity reached for the bread bowl again.

Brydie tapped her employer's hands to prevent her removing the towel and moved the bowl closer to the dying fire. "How did you get here, Mrs. Hatter? It's a long walk back if you need to fetch your things."

"My belongings are out by the fence. I caught a ride with the deacon that nice young priest sent. Most of the others have men and won't leave the camp. But I ain't got no one and accepted his offer. I feared I'd have to sleep in the hedgerows tonight, but I had to try."

"And we're glad you did," Verity assured her. "We need all the help we can find. We don't have any live-in servants, so let's fetch your things, and see what we can put together. The rooms off the kitchen should be warmer than the attic this time of year."

Brydie waited until they were gone before washing her hands, drying them on her apron, and preparing a tea tray. She had nurtured a grievance against Damien Sutter for years. She was no longer certain of her attitude. He'd scarcely noticed Kate. He really had been shocked at his mother's death. He didn't seem the sort of callous man who would turn his back on family—if he knew about them. So, she'd do what she would for any mourner.

She carried the tray up to the library and knocked. Not waiting for permission to enter, she shouldered the door open. She'd never make a proper servant, had no intention of doing so.

The gentlemen had loosened their neckcloths and unfastened their coats. She saw no sign of the fancified valet who was supposed to be waiting on them. She set the tray down as they hastily rose to greet her as the lady she was not.

She gave Damien a quick glance to see how he was doing, but his expression revealed nothing. "We have hired one of Zeb's followers, the lady who helped us with your mother. If you wish to interrogate her, here is your chance."

"I'd rather have interrogated my mother," Damien said wearily. He gestured at the papers he'd presumably brought from the shoe shop. "My father had a fortune the solicitor knew nothing about—or certainly never mentioned to me. The accounts are here. They stop with his disappearance."

An interesting, if irrelevant development. "Wouldn't the bank know about them?" Brydie signaled for them to sit while she poured the tea.

"They're not those kind of accounts. These are investments in various companies and bond issues and so forth. A solicitor should certainly have known about them. The certificates ought to be in his vault." He sipped his tea without noticing if it contained milk or sugar.

"Perhaps your father used a different solicitor from your brother," Mr. Evans suggested.

"Or perhaps you should ask Tom Butler," Brydie added dryly. "He is, after all, a known thief. And your mother was with him."

Damien closed his eyes and set down his cup with a bang. "She should have run away a lot sooner than she did. She must have been glad to see the back of me that last summer."

Sensing his black mood, Evans cleared his throat and picked up a stack of papers. "I think I'll look these over. See you in the morning, Sutter."

He departed, but Brydie waited for explanation, unconcerned with being left unchaperoned with Damien.

"You wouldn't consider leaving me alone in my grief?" Damien asked rudely, not looking at her.

"You're not grieving. You are furious. You've bunched your fingers into fists and your boot is bobbing like a bad apple. Your mother was never the friendliest person I've met, but she loved you and your brother. I cannot imagine any mother being glad to see her sons gone."

"Given the volatility of our relationship with our father, she knew, sooner or later, once we were large enough, that we'd either have to kill him, or he would kill us. I need something stronger than tea." He rose abruptly and shoved past Brydie as if she weren't there. "Jacques, where the devil are you? Bring me my flask!"

WEDNESDAY

TWELVE

DAMIEN

Nursing an aching head, Damien met the curate at the chapel the next morning. Brydie sailed in while they discussed his mother's funeral.

He'd treated her rudely last night, but he'd feared he would have treated her worse had she stayed. She was still this brilliant sunflower in his dismal garden, and he didn't deserve her comfort.

In the light through the chapel's stained glass, with her glorious auburn hair and gold frock, she resembled an exotic bird floating toward them. He couldn't cage a bird any more than pluck a sunflower. But this morning, her cheery presence lightened his grim mood—until she spoke.

"You have a. . . visitor, Mr. Sutter."

Using his surname said she was still mad at him, but he remembered that grin of mischief too well.

"A visitor?" he asked warily. He supposed news of his mother's death had spread, so his anonymity was shot. But he didn't know anyone here anymore.

"A Mr. Zebediah Johnson is at the inn, wishing to see you."

She crossed her hands demurely over her apron and ducked her head to hide her smile of anticipation.

He wanted to murder Johnson and laugh at her at the same time.

"We can discuss the service later," Upton suggested. "Our facilities are rather simple, I fear."

Funerals could certainly wait. Damien had spent the better part of his life manipulating people and situations, usually to achieve mutually beneficial outcomes. This time, he had a grudge to pick. Opportunity beckoned. "Why don't you come with us, Mr. Upton? I understand Mr. Johnson is desiring a church of his own. His views might be. . . enlightening."

Not a stupid man, the curate eyed him with curiosity and followed him outside, escorting Brydie.

"Do I put poison in his tea?" she asked, easily keeping stride with them. "Meera has an entire yard of poison now that the manor has bought the herbalist's cottage."

"Mr. Johnson is simply an ambitious man," Upton said pacifyingly. "If he can shepherd people into his flock and teach them God's law, he is doing his duty."

"Fomenting unrest is his religious duty?" Damien asked cynically, holding the parsonage gate open for Brydie. She smelled of cinnamon and vanilla, but that wasn't what had him almost drooling. Her shawl drooped off her shoulders, leaving only the tantalizing gauze above her bodice covering her curvaceous beauty. She was no longer the gangly adolescent of his childhood.

"The Americans fought to keep religion out of government so they could worship freely. There are some here who want the same," Upton explained.

The children were at their desks in the pub when they arrived, sing-songing the alphabet. Wearing his best frockcoat and top hat, Zeb Johnson paced the empty lobby that Rafe had yet to furnish. The giant wolfhound sprawled in a corner, ears on alert.

A thin, older man in an unfashionable business coat and well-made trousers stood in the opposite corner, hat in hand, keeping a wary eye on the monster dog. Ignoring the stranger, Damien concentrated on the imposing presence of the troublemaker. Johnson was most likely in his forties, physically fit, with a full head of dark hair graying at the temples.

"Johnson, is it?" Damien didn't tip his hat. "What can I do for you?"

"Bury your sainted mother on the land she loved, the land she has been denied these past years." Fierce dark pupils ringed by an enormous expanse of white flared beneath heavy eyebrows.

Unintimidated by theatrics, Damien turned to Upton. "I wish my mother to be interred in holy ground. She was no saint, but she was a good woman. Is the Priory cemetery consecrated?"

"It is. The community has used it since the monks built their church. She has been a member of our small congregation since birth. I have checked her baptismal records."

Brydie bobbed a curtsy to forestall argument. "Would you gentlemen prefer to use the library? We do not like to disturb the children."

Damien had left his father's papers under lock and key in the library. Reminded of his mother's lessons, he lost his appetite for dealing with sanctimonious bastards. He swept his hat in the direction of the front door. "We can talk outside. Mr. Upton and I have business to conduct."

Seemingly relieved to escape the lobby and the watchful dog, the gray, skinny businessman hurried to join them. "Pardon me, sir, we have not been introduced. I am Harlan Terwilliger, fiduciary for Mr. Johnson and his church. We have a proposition for you."

Damien continued into the yard. "You heard the curate. My mother will be buried where her parents are interred. I cannot think what else I can do for you."

Brydie stayed inside, but he heard the window creak open behind them, even as Upton closed the inn's front door and joined them in the yard.

"You own property you do not intend to use," Johnson

declared in his sonorous speaker's voice. "We wish to lease it from you. I will consecrate a new cemetery for my followers, and we will build a memorial to your sainted mother."

The unctuous tone grated on memories Damien preferred buried. "I repeat, my mother was no saint. There is a very good chance she killed my father, and I hope she did. I already have several offers to *buy* the land and no desire to lease it. Now, if you will excuse me. . ."

So much for his hard-earned negotiating skills. His anger had got the better of him.

Leaving his audience stunned at that revelation, Damien strode off. He considered walking until he reached the Outer Hebrides. He had never wanted responsibility. He'd been happy traveling about, meeting important men, steering the future one piece at a time.

Brydie singing a taunting rhyme about black birds flying away pierced that illusion.

In his youth, he'd been happy to escape the shouting arguments of his home to explore the countryside with her at his side. When they were older, and his father wasn't around, he'd been happy puttering in the shop, showing her how to work leather, listening to her laugh and sing. Her cheerful presence had showed him a less grim and brutal world where violence didn't have to be an answer. She'd given him hope and the strength to escape. He hadn't wanted to harm her happiness with his reality.

And now he was living in a cage he'd built for himself.

Upton, apparently after placating the other men, caught up with him. "What do you think their real purpose is in wanting your land?"

Excellent question, far better than asking about his grim declaration about his parents. "The fields aren't large or particularly arable. The manor and shop are the most valuable part of the property. I assume having an actual facility for a church would provide some legitimacy for his preaching. The Methodists began in a similar manner, I believe. My mother and Butler will have told him about the property. She had a life estate and could have returned anytime." Odd that they'd waited until now to make her claim—right after she'd died. "Guilt, perhaps, that the bullet hit her and not him?"

What Brydie had said about Butler being a thief had nagged at him the whole time he'd been drinking last night. Where had his father kept the certificates of his investments? How easy would it be to forge his signature? Someone had ransacked that office.

"So, Johnson cannot benefit from your mother's death." Upton seemed satisfied.

Damien wasn't so sure. Where did the funds come from to keep Zeb's flock fed? How did he mean to pay for a lease? Why would he need a *fiduciary*?

Not wanting to darken the curate's impending nuptials, Damien didn't express his concern but arranged a quiet interment once Upton finished the casket. Very clever of a man of the cloth to be a carpenter who could provide more practical elements than the funeral service.

He ought to be mourning. Instead, once his business with the curate was concluded, Damien took his anger in search of Rafe.

Drat her clever, interfering mind, Brydie had anticipated him. In the lobby, already wearing a cloak and donning a bonnet, she nodded in the direction of the kitchen. "Rafe is taking bread out of the oven. We thought you might like to retrieve your mother's belongings since Mr. Johnson was so unkind as not to deliver them."

He didn't remember the village as being so helpful when he'd lived here, but then, Brydie hadn't been in charge back then. Should the village ever become a real town, they ought to elect her mayor.

"There is no need for you to come," he said curtly, as Jacques ran down the stairs, carrying Damien's greatcoat, probably on Brydie's orders. A woman who could order about his temperamental valet. . . "It's a cold ride and you're not dressed for it."

Which caused him to remember the glimpse of men's breeches

under her gown yesterday and wonder if she wore them today—and if she planned to ride astride. He didn't need prurient thoughts clouding his already confused mind.

"I find the pony cart is more useful for hauling trunks than saddles," she retorted, jolting him out of his misery and back to the practical. "And I am hoping we can persuade more of those poor women to come in from the cold. I don't think it will snow, but the rain has already started."

Before Damien could argue, Rafe stomped in from the back hall, donning a multi-caped greatcoat. He slapped his tall hat on to complete the look of burly coachman. "I had the lads saddle up the horses. Don't know about you, but I'm not fond of rickety carts."

"Manipulating witch," Damien whispered in Brydie's ear as he held the door open for her.

"Remember the fable of the grasshopper and ant. Planning ahead averts disaster." She sailed past him, undeterred by his insult.

Of course, he'd called her worse than witch when they were children. She'd never cried. She'd simply borrowed an ancient volume of Shakespeare from his mother and memorized retaliations. *Veriest varlet* had been the least of them. He almost grinned. He supposed he was the feckless grasshopper. She wasn't too far wrong. He'd certainly not saved for a bad winter.

Rafe whistled at his hound and pointed. "Stay. Guard." The dog actually appeared to nod as he settled by the lobby door.

While Brydie traveled behind in the cart, Damien rode beside Rafe. "Did you discover anything in your interrogations?"

"The sheep was reportedly dying from a broken leg and they did not pay for it. I'm to collect payment, if I can. Otherwise, Mr. Johnson is a smarmy, grasping blowhard no worse than any other politician or preacher I've met. And Butler is a dangerous man. Oh, and your mother was his wife."

Damien wasn't as shocked as he ought to be. "Which means —" He grasped for consequences.

"They evidently have a source of information in the village. They married after your brother had your father declared dead."

As her husband, Butler controlled anything his wife had possessed. They could have moved back to the house at any time —until she died. At that point, the land reverted to his father's heirs.

"She had no funds of her own," Damien said, to reassure himself, if nothing else. "If she had, she would have left my father much sooner."

Rafe grunted. "One of the reasons for the law preventing wives from owning property, I suppose. Keeps them from walking out on brutes any time they like. She had no family?"

Very perceptive of the innkeeper, or he was simply speaking in generalities. "No family that I'm aware of. It was my father who had dozens of relations." She'd probably thought it would be wonderful to have a large family and wealth. Any woman would.

What did Brydie want? He had a notion she wasn't looking for someone to take care of her.

Distracting himself with restless thoughts, Damien didn't attempt questioning the bailiff further. Rafe wasn't a gossip. He simply stated facts he'd learned pertinent to the case and expressed his observations, leaving Damien to make his own surmises. So far, he wasn't learning anything useful.

Once they reached the lane in front of the Corcoran farm, they waited for Brydie to catch up. Instead of continuing up Mr. Corcoran's drive, she stopped the cart near a half-buried stile in the hedgerow. She climbed out to show them a gate through the brambles, one the horses could use to enter the field on the far side of the brook from the encampment. Rafe inspected the gate, determined it had been used recently, then led his horse through the field, keeping Brydie company since she was on foot.

Damien had seen his mother's wound. The shot had come from in front, not from this field, but it was good to know escape routes—and that they'd been used.

He rode ahead, determined to have the confrontation with

Butler over. His horse took the stream without a qualm. The rain was icy but not a deluge, yet.

To his surprise, women had gathered at the smaller caravan by the time he arrived.

"We've packed her things," one woman as faded as her home-spun said. "There's a chest inside that's hers, and she made the quilts, so we put those on top. We want to come to the service, if we might."

Brydie had left the cart in the lane and crossed downstream over a log bridge, but she was in hearing of this declaration. "Of course, you're welcome. She should have her friends around her. Is there someone here who would like to help with her laying out?"

Damien waited for Butler to appear and object. As her husband, he had every right to take charge of his wife's funeral. But he played least in sight. Interesting. So much for a memorial. Had he not been in favor of it?

A younger woman pushed one of her elders forward. "Take Mrs. Mayfield. Can you put her up for the night? She shouldn't be out in this weather with that cough of hers."

"Run, fetch your things," Brydie said, taking charge. "If someone else wants to come, I can fit two of you into the cart."

Brydie stayed outside, listening to the women, until Damien and Rafe hauled the quilt-covered trunk from the caravan. Damien wanted to get the hell out before anyone else started shooting, but even as he stepped out, Brydie led a contingent of women inside the caravan.

The rain poured. Crossing the brook would be difficult shortly, but Damien couldn't abandon the fool female. He was becoming aware of the tension of the men building shelters and tightening tents against the wind—while they kept an eye on him and the women.

Brydie emerged, carrying a linen bundle of someone's belongings. Another woman followed, also carrying a bundle. An older woman with still another bundle rushed from the camp to join them. As the three marched toward the bridge, farewells were called. Exchanging glances with Rafe, Damien followed behind, lugging half the trunk, feeling as if he wore a target on his back.

Once out of sight and hearing of the camp, Brydie halted to murmur, "Tom Butler's sister. She's nearly blind, but she hears everything."

THIRTEEN

BRYDIE

Brydie settled Elizabeth Butler and Martha Mayfield into rooms next to Mrs. Hatter. The arthritic older woman had blessedly left a cold luncheon in the kitchen and was apparently banging around in the upper rooms, sweeping, earning her keep and more.

With Verity still in the schoolroom, they all shook off their wet garments, then tucked into luncheon. The nosy kitten claimed her scritches and cheese nibbles, producing coos of admiration and alleviating any awkwardness. Once relaxed and fed, the newcomers fell into preparing supper, accustomed to working together.

Miss Butler listened well and had enough eyesight to find her teacup and pare vegetables. Approximately of the same age as Miss Butler, and younger than Mrs. Hatter, Mrs. Mayfield took over watching the stew and transforming dough into loaves.

As the rain poured, the new servants spoke little but appeared content to be out of the weather. Brydie grabbed the last sandwich and left them for her next task. The kitten padded ahead, eager to explore.

While Damien and his business associate worked out their plans, Brydie followed Damien's request to sort through his mother's belongings and find something suitable for her laying out.

They'd taken the trunk to one of the unfurnished bedchambers upstairs. The gray light from the window barely created shadows on the wood floor, so it took a second before Brydie realized someone was already digging through the trunk.

Opening her lantern, she startled Damien's valet. He hastily stood and scowled at her. "What are you doing here?"

"I could ask the same. Did you think you could find something to wear in there?" Brydie cast a light over the contents. He didn't seem to have disturbed them much, so he was digging about surreptitiously.

"Mr. Sutter is a gentleman. He has no notion of what to do with women's clothing," Jacques said stiffly. "I only sought to help."

Brydie sniffed in disbelief, set down the lantern, and began lifting out stacks of clothing. "Curiosity kills the cat." As if to prove the aphorism, the inappropriately named Marmie got up on his hind legs to peer in and nearly tumbled.

"This is how one *sorts*." She separated linens from gowns, shaking each out to determine their level of usefulness. "Pull out the ribbons on these. The fabric is too thin for more than dust rags, unless one knows how to make paper with them, I suppose."

"I don't. . ."

Brydie fixed her gaze on him. "If you are not here to help, then leave. These are personal, private possessions and not matters of curiosity."

"I am not being *curious*." Grumpily, he sat on the bare floor and began plucking ribbons, much to the kitten's delight. "I wish to make shoes. I thought, since she'd been a shoemaker's wife. . ."

"She'd have fifteen-year-old shoes? Unlikely." Brydie rummaged until she found a pair of black cloth slippers. "These

85

will do better for her laying out than the old boots she was wearing. We should find a decent gown as well."

Mrs. Butler had been kept in better style than the other camp women, but the dresses were devoid of frivolities or fashion. Brydie remembered her wearing silk and lace, but there was none of that here. She chose a new-looking navy wool and a black shawl and set them aside with the slippers.

Lynly ran upstairs, her thin voice piping Brydie's name as she sprinted down the hall. Finding them, she almost bounced in the doorway. "Mama says we can't leave until the rain stops. Can I help, please? Is that a pirate chest?"

"Pull ribbons," Jacques said resentfully, handing over the linens.

Like the footman and the cat, the child was more intrigued by the trunk's contents. She peered in and happily rummaged. "This hat is crushed!"

"But Lavender can use the trim on another. Be careful, take out only one thing at a time until you know what to do with it." Brydie set aside stockings needing darning. The village was filled with poor women who could use anything.

"Pirates hide treasure," Lynly declared with the certainty of an eight-year-old. Instead of pulling out garments, she began poking at the trunk's lid.

Jacques happily joined her while the kitten prowled.

With a sigh, Brydie gave in to curiosity, too, and removed the wooden box buried under the remaining garments. She didn't expect treasure and didn't find it—not in the monetary sense.

Damien walked in as Brydie removed a stack of letters from the box and Lynly cried in excitement, "I knew it! It's a treasure map!"

Jacques had neatly severed some large stitching in the fabric of the lid and removed a slender, folded document. With no other choice, he handed it, unopened, to his employer.

His morning garments unchanged and drying in wrinkles,

Damien sat down cross-legged beside them to read the document in the light of the lantern. He studied it longer than Brydie thought necessary. She opened one of the letters in the box, found it addressed "to my sons," and closed it again.

Damien shook his head in evident puzzlement. "I do not understand why she had this. It's a list of companies and addresses. I'm fairly certain they're not shoemakers and I cannot see how they might be creditors. But this is in her hand."

Brydie handed him the wooden box. "Perhaps she explains in these. I have a notion that a day did not go by that your mother wasn't thinking of you and your brother."

"She was a hard woman." Damien took the box. "Life made her so. She seldom expressed affection, but. . . She defended us." He glanced at Lynly and Jacques and stood. "I'll take these to my room. Thank you."

Forsaking the trunk, the kitten followed him out.

Brydie set her helpers to picking ribbons and hat trim. Emptying the trunk revealed nothing else, although she allowed her eager pair to take off the bottom liner in pursuit of more treasure. A thin gold chain that had worked its way through a worn seam was all they discovered.

"Have you told Mr. Sutter that you would like to make shoes?" Brydie asked as she dusted herself off. The quilts were too old and thin to be useful but she and Lynly might make something of the patches later. She folded them and returned them to the trunk.

Jacques shrugged. "It takes gilt to open a shop and buy equipment. I have none."

"You have experience?" Brydie wished she'd brought baskets for carrying loads. She gave Lynly the stockings to tote while she filled her arms with the garments to go to the women who would do the laying out.

"My father, he worked for the English shoemakers after we escaped the sans culottes. I helped. I could make beautiful boots. . ." He shook his head and reluctantly carried a stack intended for Lavender's sewing circle. "I will fetch the tea tray."

That explained how Damien had picked up a useless French valet. He must have known Jacques' father.

Dying of curiosity, Brydie was not so bold as to ask Damien to share his mother's papers. Instead, she led her troops into the kitchen, where her sister, Kate, was telling the newcomers about the sewing shop at the manor. Blind Miss Butler wasn't interested in becoming a seamstress, but the coughing Mrs. Mayfield seemed to be.

Perhaps Gravesyde could seduce away all Zeb's followers, and he'd crawl back under the rock where he belonged.

She shouldn't be so negative. But a man who had been shot at twice since his arrival—evidently stirred baser emotions.

Brydie liberally distributed Rafe's excellent scones to Damien's tea tray and the company in the kitchen, including the children.

Once Jacques trudged off, she turned to her sister. "I know you need to go home to see to the chickens and dinner. Why don't you leave Lynly with me? I'll find a room for us so neither of has to get soaked."

Scarfing down the scones, Arthur and Rob didn't mind leaving their useless baby sister behind.

Kate looked torn, but an icy rain like this one could be worse by morning, and Lynly's health was frail. She nodded reluctantly. "If the road is passable in the morning, I'll bring fresh clothing for you both. Are you sure Rafe won't mind?"

Coming in from cleaning up the schoolroom, Verity caught this last. "Rafe never minds anything except evil. What are we plotting?"

"Not revolution," Brydie said firmly. "Although we may need to plot how to repay him for all the food, since hiring workers when he has no income could be a problem."

Verity poured herself tea and admired the work of her new kitchen staff. "I am no longer poor. I can invest a little in my husband's establishment. The sooner we have the inn up and running, the sooner he can start earning a profit. Having staff is a large step toward that end."

Brydie knew Verity and Rafe had married soon after meeting, a mutually beneficial arrangement. But she'd seen them together. They adored each other.

Relieved that she hadn't overstepped too drastically, Brydie waved off her sister and nephews while Lynly regaled the company with tales of pirate treasure.

Rafe tramped in a while later, dripping from all his capes and shaking out his new hat. His eyes widened at the bustling kitchen. "Are you putting me out of work, then?"

"We are." His wife stood on her toes to kiss his stubbled cheek.

Brydie left Verity to introduce their new kitchen help while she took Lynly upstairs to find a room. Brydie despised the cold but usually didn't mind traipsing home in any weather because she knew Kate needed her help. But it might be fun to pretend she was an independent woman of means who could afford a room at an inn, even though she carried a basket for her many tasks.

Raised voices emanated from the library, so Brydie turned in a different direction. Built and added onto over centuries, the inn rambled unevenly up and down stairs and halls. Brydie knew Rafe was furnishing the rooms closest to the main stairs first, so guests and servants needn't have far to walk. The newly thatched roof didn't leak, but many of the window panes were still cracked or broken. She found a room in back, directly above the kitchen, with whole panes, two narrow cots, and a grate. They needed warmth more than pretty draperies. The bare shutters Mr. Upton and his carpentry crew had installed kept out the wind.

"I'll find more covers and bring up coal and we'll be just as snug as can be," Brydie promised.

Lynly peered at the shadows in the unlit room with wariness. "No ghosts?"

"You think Rafe would allow ghosts? He'd arrest them! Let's gather more of Mrs. Sutter's clothes to go to the sewing ladies."

She couldn't think of the woman she'd known since childhood as Mrs. Butler, wife of a convict.

While they were filling their arms and baskets, Mr. Evans stormed out of the library, shouting, and slammed the door on his room. Knowing perfectly well it was none of her business, Brydie peered into the library.

Damien tapped a pencil up and down on the table and appeared more angry than sad. At her appearance, he muttered, "It appears I can manage other people's futures far better than my own."

Not knowing enough to comment since she had no future whatsoever, Brydie wickedly offered, "The pub is open. Rafe has a kitchen staff now and a barrel of ale he keeps for himself."

Damien glared, started to speak, then glanced down at a wide-eyed Lynly. He bit back whatever he'd intended to say. "Thank you." Then recognizing the loads they were bearing, he rose and took the baskets. "My mother's?"

"Unless you have another use for them, I thought we'd donate the better bits to Lavender's sewing ladies. They refit and refurbish for any who need them. The worn pieces will go for cleaning rags. We throw out nothing."

"She had a lot of ragged bits," he said sorrowfully, glancing at the contents. "There was no reason for her to live like that."

"You've read her letters?" Brydie led the way down the stairs.

"I have skimmed through," he said curtly. "They are not helping my decision making."

Brydie nobly refrained from questioning further. She had him leave the basket in the lobby where Kate would find them in the morning, then ordered him to start a fire in the pub hearth. "I'll have Rafe join you. The kitchen is inundated with women and there's scarcely room for him."

"You've grown into a bossy woman, Brighid Calhoun."

"That's what Calhouns do best," Lynly piped up, mocking her late father's words.

Chuckling, Brydie followed him into the enormous drafty pub, just as Rafe joined them, yanking on his still damp frockcoat and carrying his hat.

"Weston is missing," he said, as Verity rushed in with a dry cloak. "We need to join the search."

Brydie gazed out the window at the bleak, wet afternoon. If anything happened to the duke's eldest son—

It did not bear consideration.

FOURTEEN

DAMIEN

Alarmed, Damien sent Jacques running for his hat, overcoat, and to notify Evans. "Where was Weston last seen?"

"Fishing," Rafe answered curtly. "I'll fetch the horses but damned if I know how we'll search that steep hill by the river."

Brydie threw Damien a speaking glance that jarred horrifying memories. "*The river,*" he recalled before Rafe could depart. "If he fell in the river. . ."

"In this deluge, he's dead," Rafe finished flatly. "Yonder brook is barely passable. The river will be out of its banks."

"The river flows south." Unable to contain herself, Brydie interrupted. "There is one place. . ."

Damien knew of what she spoke. The manor grounds were north of the village. The river flowed south.

He shoved his arms into the coat Jacques held for him. Since Evans hadn't arrived. . . "Brydie, can you go up to the manor and warn the others where we're headed? We'll need help."

Weston might be beyond help, but if there was even a glimmer of hope. . .

Intrepid Brydie raced for her cloak. Ordering his wolfhound to stay, Rafe loped after Damien into the downpour.

Evans didn't put in an appearance. Damien couldn't blame him. He had no interest in Gravesyde other than the property he wished to purchase for his manufactory—the sale of which Damien was having second thoughts about. The older man didn't know the earl.

Damien did. He found it highly improbable that Weston would get lost much less fall into a river he'd been fishing since he was a toddler. They saddled up and raced from the inn yard.

"What the devil do you have in mind, Sutter?" Rafe called over the pounding of rain and hooves. The bailiff hadn't lived here more than a few months.

"You'll see. It happens every time the river floods. He may be up the hill with a broken leg, for all we know. Hunt's hired hands will find him, if so. But if he was at the river, we have only one chance." Damien wasn't a praying man, but he sent words into the heavens. Weston was one of the truly noble nobles. Unselfish men were few and far between.

With rain running in torrents off their cloaks, they galloped in the direction of the highway. On the far side of the village, around a wide bend, past the last cottage, the muddy country lane cut across the normally sleepy river to the macadam toll road, by way of a low bridge. The water was already tumbling over the stones, making it impassable.

Damien drew up his horse, jumped down, and opened his lantern. Debris gathered like a dam under the low arch of the medieval bridge, forcing the racing water to flow to either side as well as over. In the deepening twilight and downpour, they could barely make out the muddy current reaching the lane.

Leaving his lantern on high ground, muttering profanities, Rafe joined him in wading into the overflow. On the dam of old wood and trash, barely discernible in the meager light from their lanterns, lay a sprawling figure in sodden brown and muddy leather.

93

They stumbled through the rushing shallows. A bit of the dam broke, letting a surge of water pass. Damien almost lost his balance. Steadying himself, plunging in to his knees, he dug his gloved fingers into a sodden tweed coat.

Taller and broader than Damien, Rafe splashed through the current, swearing, to grab leather-clad legs. "Weighs twice as much wet," Rafe grumbled as they lifted the earl's limp form.

Weston didn't move.

"Garden Cottage," Rafe ordered as they clambered out of the flood. "Closer. Now that they have a babe, the Walkers are setting up their own household. Meera will likely be there at this hour."

Damien had a vague memory of the herbalist's cottage and gardens not far from the river, at the base of the manor's rocky hill. He helped Rafe heave the earl over his saddle. Weston was not a small man. At the rough treatment, the unconscious man disgorged the contents of his stomach. Or lungs. That must mean he lived, but inured to death, Damien didn't allow relief.

While the burly bailiff galloped ahead to find help, Damien trudged alongside his solid gelding, patting its neck reassuringly. The cottage, with its extensive garden, was on the opposite end of the village from the manor drive. It saved half a mile of walking. By the time he reached the garden gate, a lantern already swung at the entrance, and shadows ran out to retrieve the earl's limp body. He breathed a sigh of relief that Rafe had guessed rightly and the Walkers were in their new home.

The plump physician waited inside, lips pursed anxiously. Rafe and Walker, the manor's steward, laid the earl out in the front room on a cot by the fire.

Rafe stepped back to where Damien was shedding his coat. "Meera's setting up an infirmary for the village here. It's a work in progress like everything else."

"Kettle is boiling." Walker, Meera's husband, pulled off the earl's ruined boots. "There's tea. I've sent a lad up to the manor to call off the search."

Rafe squished off to prepare tea. Having almost caught his

breath, Damien helped remove Weston's sodden attire. "He's alive?"

"For now," the physician acknowledged. "He's frozen through. Walker, add more coal, please? Do we have blankets?"

"You hunt blankets. Let me and Mr. Sutter finish pulling off these wet clothes. My nightshirt isn't big enough, but it will have to suffice."

"Add nightshirts in all sizes to our supply list," the lady muttered, hurrying off.

By the time they had the shivering earl stripped of his wet garments and in dry linen beneath stacks of blankets, he was stirring.

Damien breathed a small sigh of relief but knew the patient still wasn't out of the woods yet, so to speak.

"Pushed," Weston muttered, tossing his head feverishly. "*Pushed*," followed by a string of incomprehensible syllables that were probably profanities.

Having thrown back his tea as if it were water, Rafe cursed under his breath, then practically growled, "I have never wanted this job, but I'd like to keep my head. Can we lock everyone inside the manor until it's time for the guests to leave?"

A halloo from outside warned of the improbability of that. Damien let in Henri, The Monk's owner he'd met his first night here.

"I have my covered cart. Miss Calhoun thinks it might be needed?"

"She has the Sight," Rafe muttered. "Scary."

"No, we had to rescue a young boy here one spring," Damien explained. "Times like that stick in one's mind. Is Weston well enough to move from the cottage to the manor?"

"No broken bones. Contusions, but his pupils are normal, so he's unconscious from the cold. He must be kept warm," Mrs. Walker warned.

"Bricks heating in the oven," Rafe headed toward the kitchen.

"They're life savers in a mountain winter. Never thought to need them here."

Pushed. Damien pondered the possibility on his ride back to the manor, watching the dark streets for signs of stealth, guarding the cart against attackers. *Pushed.* Anger roiled.

Meera and her infant traveled with the patient, through the village and up the hill inside Henri's covered peddler's cart. At the manor, she directed the transfer of the earl to her infirmary in the service hall. Another time, Damien might have been amused watching a short, brown, foreign lady, wielding a wailing bundle, direct towering British gentlemen, but his thoughts were too frazzled to attain the necessary distance for amusement. He handed his mount to a stable lad and followed the others.

It seemed he only called on the towering manor as a visitor in a hospital.

Inside, he left his sodden outer garments to a footman and took a seat to pry off his ruined boots. If he was fortunate enough to escape Gravesyde alive, he'd need a new wardrobe.

Brydie appeared like a ghost haunting the halls. The gray gown she wore might have something to do with the illusion. She usually wore bright colors. Someone must have given her dry garments.

"Come in by the fire," she ordered. "The captain's valet is looking for dry shoes and stockings. You're easier to fit than Rafe."

Definitely not a ghost. "Whose gown?" he asked irrelevantly, because his thoughts did not want to settle yet.

"Patience's." She tugged uncomfortably at the sagging bodice. "She's my height but. . ."

Henri's wife was more generously endowed. The muslin fichu did not succeed in hiding Brydie's perfect cleavage. "You were always skinny." He had to keep his distance. Sparring had always served.

"Thin skin, as well," she retorted, leading him to a less-than-elegant room with a roaring fire, inhabited by several of the

96

manor's ladies. "Meera says I must wear gloves and keep my feet up near the fire to prevent chilblains. Feet up, can you imagine?"

Knowing Brydie, she was on her feet even when she slept. Grateful that she did not force him to tell their tale just yet, he bowed to the ladies, then grounded himself by studying the drawing room.

The walls were painted instead of papered. Lamps did not clearly illuminate the plaster designs on the tall ceiling, but they appeared original to an earl's manor. As was the case in many old homes, the carpet was worn, but large and blended well with the scattering of sofas and chairs, some worn, some new. Delicate blues and silvers predominated, despite the confusion of styles. A trio of magnificent landscapes depicting the Priory's orchards in different seasons adorned the wall above a sturdy buffet, where Captain Huntley was filling a brandy snifter.

Best of all, a vacant wing chair waited by the fire, across from Rafe, who had placed his wet stockings on the fender.

"Your thin skin is translucent," Damien whispered to his escort before sinking gratefully into the empty seat to which she led him. He was chilled to the bone and not just by the weather.

He left Brydie blushing as he accepted the brandy from his host. He should make her blush more often instead of teasing her. The pink looked good on her high cheekbones.

"The duke sends his utmost gratitude. He's with Weston now." Huntley offered Rafe a refill, but the bailiff shook his shaggy orange curls.

A moment later, Brydie appeared with a steaming mug of what smelled like coffee. "I added a touch of whisky," she warned as she handed it to Rafe. "My grandmother recommended it to stave off the ague." She returned to converse with the ladies on the far side of the room.

When Damien realized he was only watching Brydie in her plain garb and wild stack of sunset locks, instead of all the other elegantly garbed and coiffed ladies in the room, he finished off his brandy. He was about to suggest that he ride back to the inn when the Duke of Castlefield entered.

Not a particularly tall or imposing man, his dark hair only slightly threaded with silver, His Grace wore a crumpled suit with an expensive gold watch and tie pin. Ignoring the rest of the company, he crossed the room to the fire. "He should be fine," he said gruffly, removing a pipe from his pocket. He reached for his pouch, then remembering the ladies, he merely placed the bit between his teeth. "I owe you everything. The country owes you. My son is destined to make his mark on the world."

Weston was a good man, admittedly, one who could make a difference, although Damien might argue the usefulness of lords. He stood and bowed. "I am most relieved to hear he is well."

"Is he awake?" In his stockinged feet, Rafe didn't bother removing himself from his comfortable chair. Obsequious, he was not.

The duke's brow drew down in a scowl. "He is saying he was pushed. We need to drive Johnson and his renegades out of town or no one will be safe."

Rafe instantly straightened to attention. "He knows who pushed him?"

"No, he does not." The duke tapped his pipe impatiently against his trouser leg. "But it stands to reason. The scoundrel and his father used to work one of my tenant farms, until they started complaining about rents and bleating about worker rights and other stuff and nonsense. Had to end their lease and heave them out. Johnson has hated us ever since."

"Enlightening." Damien gestured for the duke to take his chair and pulled over a smaller one. Their host, Captain Huntley, politely declined to join them, wisely so. As an American, he most likely took exception to His Grace's attitude. "But times are changing. As we open more and more manufactories, men have more choices. We can no longer count on controlling the population in medieval fiefdoms."

The duke lowered himself into the chair with the weariness of age. "I imagine I know a little more about how to run this country than louts like Johnson."

"I can't arrest Johnson or evict his followers without evidence of wrong-doing." Rafe looked ready to escape. Mere sergeants did not converse with dukes.

But this was Gravesyde, Damien realized, a microcosm of independence, where the sons of dukes fished for their dinner. Perhaps the American's influence? "Zebediah can't be arrested for wanting change. If I understand rightly, everyone in the manor is here because they wanted to find a different sort of future."

The duke sucked on his empty pipe and watched invisible smoke rising. "Won't do, you know," he finally said. "Folk in the manor are educated gentry, brought up proper. Don't hold with women running things, mind you. Their minds are weakened by irrational emotion. Sewing and the like are their purview. In the real world—we need educated, civilized gentlemen like yourself, Sutter, not puling fools like Johnson."

"What about like me and Fletch, Your Grace?" Rafe asked politely. "We're buying the inn but we ain't gentlemen. Or Mr. Oswald who runs the mercantile or Deacon Jones who pretty much runs everything else. There are hardworking folk every-where who never had a chance to better themselves because they ain't lords." He dragged himself from his chair. "I better get back to work."

The duke frowned as Rafe walked off. "If your bailiff sides with that rapscallion. . ."

"It's not about taking sides, Your Grace." Damien rose as well. "Men are declaring their independence from the yokes of the wealthy. Weston understands. Have a chat with him when he's ready."

Brydie hurried up as he followed Rafe. "They've offered a carriage to take us back. I need to return to Lynly. Will you go with me?"

A dark carriage and Brydie by his side while he was at his weakest—what could possibly happen?

FIFTEEN

BRYDIE

ALREADY SOAKED TO THE BONE, BRYDIE ONLY AGREED TO THE carriage ride to prevent an embarrassing argument with Damien over walking or riding pillion. And because he looked completely done in.

Ever aware of his moods—as well as his disturbingly physical presence—she distracted him the instant he climbed in. "There's none to hear now. What was in your mother's box to put you in this humor?"

"No ecstatic congratulations on my heroism in saving an earl and the nation?" he asked sardonically.

"We know that is who you are and what you do, because you're a gentleman and not a puling fool," she retorted, mocking the duke. "His Grace deserved your speech and more."

"You listened? Of course you did. Rafe thinks you have the Sight, y'know." He leaned wearily against the cushions.

"Put me in London, and I'd be lost. We only have a few more minutes. Tell me what's wrong." She reached for his hand to warm her own. Her gloves hadn't dried yet, and she'd left them off.

"Your hands are icy." His big hand swallowed hers as he rubbed her fingers with his thumb, heating her in ways they shouldn't.

"Her letters are naught more than excuses, explanations," he continued. "She feared someone would read the letters, so they're written with mostly gushing declarations of love and missing us and how good Butler was to take her away. He sold our carriage to buy the caravan they lived in."

"She's been traveling for years." Brydie knew there was more, things he wouldn't tell her, things that festered and had kept him away all these years. She didn't know how to lance his wounds.

"Not always. They stayed with supporters upon occasion, some rather wealthy industrialists back their cause. She mentioned them in her ramblings. I have to study the letters more closely to divine what is said between the lines. Taken at face value, they are meaningless. Only someone who knows her would realize she'd never normally chat and gush."

"Ah, understood." The carriage rattled into the inn yard and the driver jumped down to open the door.

They tugged their outerwear closed and dashed for the lobby, where someone had set out a lamp to welcome them.

"I am famished. Shall we see if our new help have prepared a feast?" Brydie hung her cloak on a hook.

Damien seemed hesitant. As much as she would like to draw him into the kitchen camaraderie, she understood. He'd lost his mother, his brother, and his rudder and was washing out to sea as surely as Weston might have if they hadn't found him. "Or send Jacques down to fetch a tray. You know he wants to be a shoe-maker, don't you?"

A ghost of a smile crossed lips chiseled by maturity. In the lamplight, Damien was heartbreakingly handsome. "He only reminds me once a day. He's polite like that. I'll send him down, thank you."

She wanted to affectionately kiss his stubbled cheek as she felt certain no one had ever done, but she wasn't his mother.

101

And her feelings for him weren't maternal. Despite her belief that Damien had fathered her sister's child, he was the only man who had ever stirred her like this, which annoyed her immensely. So, she abandoned him to find his way in the dark. Add lamps and candlesticks to the inn's needs if they were to begin taking guests. Restoring a town to life was costly.

She found Lynly in the pub, sitting on a high stool at the bar, cutting biscuits of raw dough, while the marmalade kitten explored, hoping for tidbits. Her niece grinned at Brydie's entrance. "I'm to make faces with currants and sprinkle them with cinnamon for freckles, like mine."

Brydie laughed. "And mine. It is a great pity currants do not come in gray to match our eyes. Have you eaten yet?"

She nodded vigorously. "I had roast chicken and potatoes and carrots. But I am to let Sgt. Russell have peace and quiet to enjoy his meal. Do you want peace and quiet too?"

"Me? What would I do with it? Let me prepare a tray for Mr. Sutter and I will bring my plate here to join you."

The new kitchen staff had melted away while Rafe and Verity talked in what had once been their private kitchen.

"You need your own parlor," Brydie told them, checking the warming oven for her dinner.

Rafe had his boots off and his stocking feet on the hearth while balancing a plate on his lap. Verity had apparently eaten with their new staff and was in the process of filling a tray for their guests, while Jaques waited to carry it off.

"There are rooms off the lower hall." Rafe waved a chicken leg in the direction across from the kitchen. "I was thinking they'd be private parlors for traveling ladies, not that I expect any soon since we have no coaches coming through."

"There are better rooms for parlors down the other wing. We can make this wing ours, have Henri find a table and chairs next time he goes to the city. Although I'd rather like to choose them myself," Verity said wistfully, after Jacques departed.

The teacher had lost all her family's fancy possessions in a fire.

Knowing people's stories helped to understand them. Brydie added flatware to her plate. "There is no reason why you should not, now that you have help. I don't believe the two of you have had a day off since you wed. I wonder if we could persuade a furniture maker to live here if the manor offered a shop?"

"Not in time for our suppers," Verity said in amusement.

Brydie shrugged. "The manor is running out of castoffs. I'm to join Lynly for dinner. Thank you for minding her."

Making mental lists of all the tasks she must accomplish on the morrow, including returning Patience's lovely gown, Brydie enjoyed Lynly's chatter, ate her dinner, returned the currant-faced biscuit dough to the kitchen for baking, and took her niece upstairs to put her to bed. She noticed a light in both the library and Damien's room, which was a bit odd. He couldn't be in two places at once. And she thought she'd heard Jacques grumbling as he cleaned Damien's boots in the cloak room.

Lynly fell instantly to sleep. Brydie covered her in blankets, added a few more coals on the grate, and returned to the corridor. She was accustomed to working well into the evening at home. Despite her icy journey, she was too restless to sleep.

It wasn't in her nature to resist curiosity. She stopped at the tiny library and peered in. Damien sat hunched over the square table, papers spread around him, his mother's letter box on one side.

"Can I help?" she dared ask, because that had always been their relationship. She'd learned to make shoes by helping. She'd never had enough practice to be good at it, but like sewing— which she didn't do well either—it was a chore that could be learned.

The remains of his dinner lay cold and only half-eaten on his tray, along with an empty mug of Rafe's ale. Damien sat back and rubbed his brow.

"I don't know why I'm obsessed with these nonsensical letters. I should bury them with her on the morrow."

"Would you like me to look through them with a woman's eye

before you do?" she suggested. She really should just carry away his tray, but this was Damien, the lad who hadn't minded when she'd climbed trees and beat him at battledores, despite the difference in their ages. There hadn't been any others to play with besides their older siblings, who seldom joined in.

He gestured at the empty chair across the table. "If you have naught else to waste time on."

"I'm usually at home, doing mending at this hour." She set the tray on an empty bookshelf and settled in. When they were very young, they'd studied together—because Brydie had insisted and he'd generously tolerated the company. His books had been more interesting than hers. She wanted to pretend this was no different, but Damien was a grown man in his thirties now, not a gangly schoolboy. And she was a full-grown woman and no giggly child. This had probably been a mistake.

He'd be a good husband for Kate, if she could ever forgive him for abandoning her. Brydie would simply have to move out if that ever happened.

"I have no notion why I believe she's leaving us a message." Damien drank the dregs of his mug. "Wishful thinking, I suppose, wanting to hear a message from beyond."

Brydie squeezed his hand in sympathy, then scanned the papers quickly, noting the gushing style. No one would want to read this fustian—it was very definitely not Mrs. Sutter's usual terse commentary. Still, the handwriting mirrored that on the invoices for the Sutters' shop, the notes his mother had once sent to Brydie's mother, the lists she had given them when they'd gone into town. It was a distinctive, elegant hand. Most people in Gravesyde—and probably in Johnson's camp—couldn't write.

"She almost prints the names of the people in the places where they stay, as if she wants to remember them, so makes them distinctive. Do the names mean anything to you? Should they?" She jotted down a few of the towns and families who had apparently welcomed his mother and Zeb's followers even before she became Mrs. Butler. Fifteen years of writing to her sons but never mailing the letters. . . "She even gives dates. These are a diary of sorts. She's keeping track, as if they're your father's ledgers."

He frowned and dragged her notes into the light of the lamp. "So, the first year after they left, they traveled to Birmingham and met. . ." He looked at the list, then reached across the table for the letters Brydie had already studied.

"They first met up with Zeb Johnson there. She gushes about him too," Brydie said absently.

"I know some of these names," Damien said cautiously. "As a lawyer, I was often called in to write up or go over contracts. It's how I met the people I work with now. These are, by and large, industrialists, men establishing factories, transportation, investing in steam engines. . . They are not wealthy lords. They quite often live in debt, desperately seeking wealthy men willing to invest in the future."

"As Zeb Johnson is attempting to do for his church?" Brydie said impatiently, writing faster. "Johnson has no use for aristocrats or parliament. These may be the men who support his revolutionary ideas?"

Damien pulled over the thin, folded paper they'd found in the trunk lid. "The men in the letters. . . own the companies listed on this paper."

Brydie scanned the list of names she'd been compiling from the unsent letters and compared it with his mother's more precise list. "There are several names and companies on mine that are not on that list." She marked them.

Damien studied the result and whistled. "I've never heard of the companies you've checked, but the owners she lists—are not known for their honesty or their financial ability. This one," he tapped one name, "has gone bankrupt."

Brydie shook her head, not understanding.

Across the table, Damien grinned in delight. "My mother was tracking companies to invest in!"

Brydie widened her eyes. "The preacher invested in industrialists? Couldn't he have built his church instead?"

Damien shook his head. "My *mother* invested." He reached for the stack of papers he'd brought from his father's office and waved them. "I've been wondering where these certificates had gone."

"She sold them and bought more? How?" To Brydie, he may as well have said his mother had flown to the moon. "Women can't own property, can they?"

"Wives can't, but there are ways to circumvent the law, depending on how they're invested." Unaware of the ominous implications of his explanation, Damien continued. "We need to find her stockbroker." He shoved back his chair and tugged Brydie out of hers. "You are brilliant, Brighid Calhoun."

And he kissed her.

THURSDAY

SIXTEEN

DAMIEN

Brydie's kiss was the solid reality Damien needed to return him to earth, to Gravesyde, to everything he'd been ignoring in his anger and grief. She kissed like heaven, if lust were allowed behind the pearly gates. She was warm and pliable with just the right curves to fit into him. . . Brydie was no coy miss but a sensible woman who kissed him as a woman does.

A knock at the door ended that wicked thought. Damien's valet stood scowling in the doorway, holding a steaming mug of what smelled like whiskey. "I caught Mr. Evans going through your papers when I brought you this."

Brydie hastily escaped Damien's arms and picked up her shawl. "I saw a lamp lit in there earlier. I thought it might be Jacques."

"I've been doing laundry and scrubbing mud from boots downstairs," Jacques said peevishly. "I am not *sécurité.*"

"What did Evans do when you caught him?" Damien hastily gathered his documents.

"Shoved papers in his pocket and pushed past me. I believe he ran down the stairs. I can hope he broke his neck in the dark on those treacherous steps." Jacques gave up on handing over the mug and set it on the table instead.

"Shall I call Rafe?" Brydie asked worriedly. "After the earl's fall—"

Damien shook his head. "Evans doesn't know Weston. And the only documents he could steal were related to my father's deeds. He's probably taking them to a banker in hopes of obtaining a loan. He'll need my signature, and I'm inclined not to give it. His resources are more limited than he originally led me to believe. I told him so earlier. I assume that is why he's taking matters into his own hands. If the bank will risk a loan. . ." He shrugged, not worried.

If it hadn't been for that kiss, Damien would have called it a night and departed in the morning. But he'd suddenly developed a reluctance to abandon this town he'd once been so determined to escape.

"Go to bed, both of you," he ordered, reluctantly sending Brydie out of temptation's way. "I need to store these papers in a safe place. In the morning, I hope to have a plan."

"In the morning, Rafe will be hunting down every man in town to determine who had the opportunity to push an earl into the river. Let us hope it was not your friend Mr. Evans, if he just bolted into the night." Brydie brushed past Jacques.

Evans had no reason to push an earl—did he?

"There are only so many banks who will hear him out. He'll turn up again." Damien called after her. Evans must have been drunk to behave so rashly—another reason not to work with the man. He refused to invest in drunkards—which left him with a land and shop he couldn't easily sell unless he offered them to Weston to lie fallow.

Thursday morning dawned clear and bright. Damien had spent the rest of his evening creating a copy of his mother's list of companies and then made his own inventory of all the investments he'd found in his father's papers. These lists, he kept on his person. He had concealed everything else in various hiding places it would take a search party to locate. If he dropped dead tomorrow, he wondered what would happen to all that stock, if it truly existed. He had no heirs. He should write a will.

After dining on the excellent breakfast Jacques carried up—and very definitely had not cooked—Damien strode down to the lobby just as Rafe entered with his pony of a wolfhound on his heels. The students were already singing in their unusual classroom.

"Weston is feverish," Rafe said without preamble. "I hope he's not taken leave of his mind. He claims he was fishing with Gavin Smith, that city investor his father brought along to talk with Hunt. Smith got bored and wet and took both their catches back to the kitchen. The staff verify that. Our noble earl stayed, wishing to feed the multitudes." Rafe reached for the steaming mug Brydie handed him.

She had emerged from the back corridor looking glorious with the morning sun highlighting the rich red in her thick hair. Damien wanted to see that wayward mass out of its pins. He had dreamed of nothing else all night. He was most likely hallucinating too. She didn't even look at him as she rushed back to the kitchen.

"Weston isn't fond of company." Damien returned to matters at hand. The tasks ahead were countless and possibly dangerous. He couldn't involve Brydie. "One assumes he must have lured Smith away to talk business out of hearing of others, then stayed to catch whatever he deemed necessary for dinner. Is there any way of knowing who else might have been on that hill?"

"After all that rain, Wolfie hasn't found any trace. Hunt usually has men and hounds patrolling, but they took cover in the downpour, not expecting anyone to be climbing around a muddy hillside. It's rough terrain in good weather. Your noble lordship was mad to be out there."

"He's a sportsman, would have made a good soldier if he hadn't a duke for father."

Rafe grunted what might have been agreement. "I'll start

poking about, see who may have been out on a right nasty day. But *why* would anyone want him dead? His father has the power and wealth. From what I understand, Weston is more likely to favor Johnson's radical ideas than *His Grace*." The bailiff wrinkled his nose and wielded the title sardonically. "Why must dukes be called like bishops?"

Assuming the last question was rhetorical, Damien pounced on the more logical one. "I'd like to speak with the duke's investor, Gavin Smith, is it? He was the one with Weston? If we discuss money, I might persuade him to tell me more than he might you."

Rafe looked grateful. "I'd rather not rattle about at the manor, stirring things up. Never having had any, I know nothing of money. Talk to Weston, while you're there. He owes you. If you'll do that, I'll owe you. I'll start on people who might have been out and about, see if anyone noticed anything."

Leaving Rafe and his intrepid hound to badger his way through the locals, Damien donned his best frockcoat, pinned his neckcloth with a gold pin larger than the duke's, and put on his newly cleaned top hat. Despite his querulous complaining, Jacques really was an excellent valet.

Striding up the drive to the manor in the autumn sunshine, he drove out thoughts of Brydie by contemplating Rafe's question— who would want to kill *Weston*? The earl was a sportsman who rarely graced Town. He handled the estates his father didn't wish to visit but Damien doubted the earl had much wealth of his own —and no heirs to leave it to. The younger brothers weren't much better. Like their father, they had interests outside society's usual entertainments. He couldn't imagine one suddenly craving his brother's courtesy title—and the responsibility that came with it.

Handing his hat and greatcoat to the manor's massive butler, Damien made discreet inquiries about who else might have gone out in yesterday's downpour. The servants knew whose boots had to be cleaned.

Learning even the curate had stayed at the manor all day,

working on the coffin in the stable, and that only the horse-mad Lt. de Sackville had ventured out to check on his livestock, Damien went in search of Gavin Smith. Weston and de Sackville hunted together. No motive there, although the former lieutenant might be questioned about whom he saw while riding back lanes.

Damien found the investor with Captain Huntley and Walker in the west wing study. They looked up from their ledgers in relief at his interruption.

"You know anything about investing?" Hunt asked. "I've left the maintenance trust to my aunt's stepson, but the marquess is a busy man. I need to learn how it's done before we fritter away the funds we're suddenly earning."

Damien bowed to Smith and shook hands with Hunt and Walker in the informal American way, then took a seat. "I've some knowledge of companies and the men running them, yes. I haven't played the markets myself, although I'm still exploring my recent inheritance." He glanced at Smith. "Do you have any idea if this Harlan Terwilliger has dealt with Zeb Johnson for any length of time? I've not heard of him."

"Mushroom," Smith acknowledged. "Started out in the slave trade, still may do some shipping there. Deals with men like Johnson. Doesn't ask where the money comes from, but he's shrewd and works with a decent brokerage. Some of his clients are doing well."

Damien's distaste for Terwilliger grew at mention of the slave trade, but a great many men had made their fortunes that way. "Since he's inquired about my land, I assume he deals in more than stock?" He knew Hunt listened, but the captain kept his thoughts to himself.

"Terwilliger has been known to buy up companies in bankruptcy, divide them up, and sell off the different lots for three times what he paid. As I said, he's no gentleman, but the sort willing to do what's necessary. Wishes to buy your land, does he? Do you have bits that can be sold separately?"

"If Johnson wants to turn the house into a church, then he

could sell off the small fields adjacent, not that local farmers have the means to purchase. There's a shoemaking shop. I'd thought to sell it to a manufacturer, except Evans wants to lease only the shop, which rather leaves the rest of the place worthless, and I've declined."

"The earl was inquiring about that parcel," Smith said cautiously. "Has he approached you?"

Damien nodded. "I daresay he merely wants to keep it out of the hands of Johnson and his like. I'd rather see it helping the community. Was that what you were discussing yesterday in the pouring rain?" He smiled, as if finding it amusing.

"Muttonheads, both of them," Hunt muttered. "But Lady Elsa was overjoyed to have the catch. Feeding a large household for a week is straining even her inventiveness."

"We did discuss Johnson," Smith said tentatively, as if searching his memory. "I gather the earl would prefer to keep him away from places his father frequents, which is where Johnson always shows up. He's blocked him from other areas, as well. Don't let the duke know that," he added hastily.

"Any chance that one of Johnson's followers might have been lurking and overheard you?" Out of the corner of his eye, Damien saw Hunt straighten and go on alert.

"They'd have to be barking mad to be out in that storm. And as I understand it, they'd have to trespass across the manor's grounds to do so, unless they were bobbing about in a boat, asking to drown. I can't see how it was done," Smith admitted, understanding the direction of the question.

"Well, some might say some of Johnson's followers are barking mad, but I take your point. Now what companies did you wish to ask about? And might I impose upon you to create a list of stock-brokers who might handle the purchase and sale of stock for a woman?"

Smith snorted. "Start with Terwilliger. He'll deal with anything and anyone. But I'll see what I can do. Now there's this manufacturer in Birmingham. . ."

Damien indulged in business talk for as long as the captain had the patience.

The whole time, he spent plotting means of getting at Terwilliger. How much money could an itinerant preacher possibly have that required a financier to linger in his company?

SEVENTEEN

BRYDIE

"I seem to have just missed Mr. Sutter at the manor." Paul Upton, the curate, removed his hat and bowed when Brydie ran out to the lobby to see who had entered.

She'd rather hoped it would be Damien. Shame on her. That kiss had unsettled her nerves. The man was a callous womanizer and she ought to run in the other direction.

"He left for the manor earlier, but I believe he and Rafe are working together. If he's not there now, perhaps they've gone out to your grandfather's farm to visit the camp?" Possibly a dangerous enterprise for either of them, but something had to be done if the earl truly had been pushed into the river.

It seemed quite odd that someone was shooting at the demagogue and someone else was trying to kill an earl. Had an entire raft of criminals moved in? And who else might be caught in between warring factions besides poor Mrs. Sutter?

"I'll just leave word with you, if I may?" At Brydie's nod, Upton continued, "His mother's casket is finished. We may hold the service at his convenience, although I think it would be polite to give notice to the people in the camp so they might attend."

"Some have indicated they'd like to be there, even with the chapel being Anglican and all. I'll tell him, thank you. Is the parsonage ready for your bride?"

The curate beamed. "Our wedding gifts have been immensely practical. Everyone has been generous. We have new linen, a shiny new tub and washbasin, and new pots for the kitchen. And I've finally finished work on the table and cabinets so Minerva has a place to put her grandmother's dinner set. I didn't think we'd possibly make the place habitable so quickly."

"It's lovely having the chapel active again. We missed it all those years that it was empty. I suspect you will be showered with more gifts on Sunday. Everyone is looking forward to some festivity before the winter truly sets in."

Grinning like the besotted fiancé he was, Upton lifted his hat and hurried away on his many errands.

Brydie returned to the kitchen. It was time to start questioning their new staff.

Mrs. Mayfield was currently coughing her way about upstairs, dusting and sweeping. Unable to clearly see dust, Miss Butler sat at the kitchen table rolling out dough for Rafe's meat pies. Arthritic Mrs. Hatter scrubbed pots and kept an eye on the younger woman. These two would suffice to start, Brydie decided.

She studied the pantry for lunch makings. "They're arranging Mrs. Sutter's, or is that Mrs. Butler? Anyway, the casket is ready. As soon as the funeral service is set, we should start the laying out. Do you think your friends from the camp will attend?"

"She was Meg Butler, all right." Elizabeth Butler spoke up. "I witnessed the ceremony."

"In a Church of England church, so it was all registered right and proper?" Everyone knew the law required marriage in the church, unless one had a special license, and that still required an Anglican minister.

"We don't recognize the church of the oppressors," Miss Butler said stiffly. "Mr. Johnson registered the marriage and issued a certificate and all."

"Oh, then he's an Anglican minister and they had a special license." Brydie could tell that she'd hit on another difficulty, one Tom's sister struggled to deny but couldn't without relegating Mrs. Butler back to Mrs. Sutter again. "Do you think Mr. Butler will wish to put up a headstone?"

"They want their own cemetery," Miss Butler finally said, skipping over the special license, which would have cost a great deal and still been worthless unless Johnson was ordained. "I don't know that Tom will wish to attend anything held here. I don't understand a great deal of the difference, though."

"Men rant and rave and want their own way," Mrs. Hatter said with a sniff. "It's all stuff and nonsense. You go to that service. She was good to you. The service is about Meg, not what Johnson or Butler want."

"That's what I was thinking," Miss Butler said, a trifle defiantly. "My brother has a hard life and he's bitter about being imprisoned for theft when he was innocent, but I do not have to obey him if I'm capable of supporting myself."

A bitter man who believed he was wrongfully accused and incarcerated. . . Brydie knew she needed to learn more, but she'd ask someone besides the sister.

"What do Mr. Johnson and Mr. Butler want?" Brydie asked. "I hear so many things but understand none of them."

Miss Butler wrinkled her brow in thought. "They argue many topics, but I believe what they want most is the vote. They think if the working man could vote, we'd remove all the wealthy scoundrels who control our government. And the way to encourage working men to demand the vote is from the pulpit."

That almost sounded rational, except. . . "I don't suppose they include women voting as well? We must certainly represent half the country."

"Wives can't own property," Mrs. Hatter explained. "The vote goes to those who work for a living and have earned enough to buy property. Women only stay home and mind the house and babes."

Speaking as an unmarried woman and sister of a widow who managed a large property, Brydie decided their policies lacked insight. She didn't bother arguing goose and gander but nodded sagely and took another path. "And the church? Admittedly, our little chapel isn't a grand cathedral, but I've always thought it was the people who attended that mattered most."

"The Church of England is owned by the oppressors," Miss Butler said, a little more certainly. "That is why Parliament gives the Anglicans privileges they deny the rest of us. Wealthy bishops will never allow the working man from under their thumbs."

How very tedious, as if lords and women didn't work and that *working men* were the only ones who had a job? Someone was spouting slogans without thinking, although Brydie supposed it was a message people understood.

"Well, we must have laws, I suppose. We can't go back to the days when men called themselves minister and married anyone who gave them enough coin. There would be no legitimate records and a man could have three wives and never claim a single child. But I suppose they are being unfair to the Catholics," Brydie acknowledged. "My grandparents had to give up their church if they wanted to marry or vote. What will Mr. Johnson do if he builds his own church? Set up his own laws? Build his own city?"

"Tom and Zeb argue a lot," Miss Butler acknowledged. "I believe Meg wanted them to emigrate to the Americas, where she said they could set up their own church anywhere they liked. But Zeb. . . is not reasonable on the matter."

"Most of us wouldn't emigrate," Mrs. Hatter claimed. "I wouldn't want to go far from all I know, never see my grandbabies again. We have people here."

"People who won't help us build the church or community. Meg said the cost is lower in Gravesyde than elsewhere, and we could all have our own little cottages," Miss Butler said excitedly.

"And we can all be one big family and help each other, even if our real families won't."

Brydie thought they might be better off joining the Methodists, but it seemed Mr. Johnson and Mr. Butler wished to be in charge —like lords—and they'd have to start at the bottom in any other church. That rather sounded like they were thinking of themselves more than their followers—which men generally did, she feared. Hence the reason for the women defecting to the inn to escape the weather.

But understanding what the people at the camp were thinking gave some insight that Brydie hoped would lead to whoever tried to shoot Mr. Johnson and push the earl into the river. The person wasn't very competent and his agenda was murky, at best. It was rather like small boys getting even with each other for perceived wrongs and grudges. Could there be two killers?

Damien burst in not long after, looking even more haunted than usual. "Do I need to provide food for mourners? I wish to do this right, if I can."

He'd evidently heard that the curate was ready to hold the funeral.

Brydie tried to maintain a distance and treat him as the inn's guest, but even though she had reason to despise him, her heart went out to him in his dilemma. He'd never had a chance to properly grieve his brother or his parents. "If you still lived on the farm and were part of the church, we might bring you dishes and stay to mourn with you. But in this instance, I think just the service will be sufficient. We can remember her in our own ways. Unless you think there will be a very large crowd?" She turned to the ladies who'd known Damien's mother these last years.

Miss Butler looked uncertain. "I doubt Tom will attend. He is the one who should be making arrangements, but he has refused."

Brydie didn't believe their marriage was at all legal, but she had no reason to disturb Miss Butler. She'd have to find a way to tell Damien later, in case it might matter.

"There will be a few of us," Mrs. Hatter said. "Most will obey their husbands, and if Tom and Zeb talk against the service, they'll not come."

"Why don't we put out some bread and cheese in the pub, along with some cider, so those who have traveled a way can refresh themselves?" Brydie suggested. "Hold the service after school lets out? I think Kate would like to come."

"Let me pay for whatever you do," Damien said in relief. "I want to respect the people who looked after her all these years. It's rather late today. Tomorrow, perhaps?"

"If you have a carriage or cart to carry people back and forth, it can be done today," Mrs. Hatter said. "The camp may up and move on the morrow. Or it might rain. Best have it done with, sir."

Mrs. Hatter was turning out to be a rather bossy soul. Brydie hid her grin.

Damien nodded agreement. "I can ask for a carriage at the manor." Then he realized what he'd said and corrected. "Or perhaps your friends won't want to travel in anything from the manor? I don't know if I can summon a farm cart. . ."

"They'll love the carriage," Mrs. Hatter said dryly. "But they'll accept whatever you find. They'll want to dress up a little, and Tom won't be taking anyone in the caravans."

And so, Rafe returned at lunch to learn Brydie was increasing his business to include catering funerals. As she assumed—eager to make his new establishment work— he put aside his bailiff duties to do far more than set out bread and cheese.

Brydie thought that by the time he was done, all the ladies from the camp would be volunteering to work at the inn just to be fed.

EIGHTEEN

DAMIEN

After consulting with the curate, Damien took a bench to one side of the chapel, in an alcove almost out of sight of the congregation as it filtered in for his mother's service. Rafe, good bailiff that he was, had abandoned his frenzied baking to stand in back. Damien didn't know what was going through Rafe's head, but in his own, he hoped to spot guilt on the face of whoever had killed an innocent woman.

He didn't recognize most of the people, except Brydie and her sister. Kate had brought her children. Since school was out, she had nowhere else to leave them. They weren't old enough to have known his mother. She'd left shortly after Damien had, and Kate hadn't even been married then.

He supposed any of these women may have shot at Johnson for any number of reasons, especially if he was a rake, but would they have pushed Weston into the river? Should he assume both assailants were the same person? Or go with Rafe's theory that a jealous husband had shot at Johnson and missed? Henri had passed on gossip from the tavern, confirming that the preacher had an entire flock of obedient ewes to choose from. He was an easy man to hate.

Damien focused on the only man in the chapel from the camp. Terwilliger occupied a back bench. As predicted, Butler and Johnson didn't show their faces inside an Anglican chapel.

If, as Damien surmised, his mother used Terwilliger to sell stocks, the financier had lost a lucrative source of business— unless he had the ability to access his mother's holdings. Selling them, given Terwilliger's reputation, might be feasible. *Butler* not knowing about the investments. . . seemed unlikely. Damien wanted to pin everything on Butler simply because he disliked the man and his relationship with his mother.

Not seeing any expressions of guilt, Damien listened to the service. Upton had done an excellent job of collecting anecdotes and reminding people of his mother's value, letting the congregation mourn. Damien had mourned fifteen years ago when she'd vanished. At the time, he'd feared his father had finally killed her, then run away. Now, he didn't know what to think.

After the service, Brydie walked out with him. Kate and her children were just ahead.

"Thank you for all you've done." Damien didn't know how to express his gratitude that she'd come to his aid without question after all these years. He wanted to hug and kiss her, but given their heated kiss the other night, that probably wasn't gratitude.

"I do what I can, when I can." Brydie shrugged off his appreciation and indicated her family ahead. "I wish I could do more for my own family. Arthur is fourteen now. He needs better schooling than we can provide. Kate's been struggling since her husband died."

She sounded oddly stiff, unlike her usual bubbling enthusiasm. Damien cast her a sideways glance. Her auburn hair caught the weak rays of sun like a fiery sunset, but she directed her flashing eyes ahead and not at him. He hastily returned to watching the crowd milling about the inn yard. "I am sorry to hear about her loss. He left her nothing for his son's education?"

"Her husband worked the farm. He never had money. My father chose him because Morgan was a good, kind man and adored Kate. Morgan was Welsh, built small and dark. He was a sickly, poor man. He made Kate happy, which is what matters, but he left nothing. But look at Arthur—tall, more blond than you, big-boned, nothing like either of them."

Why was she telling him this? There was a message in there, Damien was sure of it. And watching auburn-haired Kate and her children continue into the inn yard, it slowly dawned on him. . . His brother, like Damien and their father, had been tall and dark blond and big-boned.

"You think Harry. . ." Damien shook his head, appalled at her suggestion. "That's impossible. Harry went to the Continent that summer."

Brydie finally glanced at him. She was nearly as tall as he and could look him in the eye. Another man would quiver at her glare. Damien just glared back.

And then the shock hit him. No wonder she'd hit him. "You think *I*. . ." He shook his head in vehement denial. "And your sister? *Absolutely not*. She barely knows I exist. Harry admired her, so I stayed out of his way. Besides. . ." Angered that she could possibly think such a thing, he said what he might never have said before. "I never looked at anyone but you."

That startled her. Her clear gray eyes studied him briefly, before her long lashes lowered, and she turned back to watching her sister.

"Arthur was born six months after she married Morgan," she said softly. "She denies any father but Morgan. But I know Kate. She would never have dallied with a laborer without a ring on her finger. She spent most of that summer in your father's workshop, with *you* and your father, because she wanted to learn to make pretty shoes for us."

A cold chill seeped into Damien's bones as they stopped at the inn gate. He needed to go with the men up to the manor and cemetery. But what she was telling him brought back memories he'd erased for fifteen years. "She wanted sturdy but pretty. I hated the shop, probably because my father was in it. I avoided it that summer. He showed her far more patience than he ever showed us."

She turned a worried gaze to him, letting the others enter the pub without her. "You hated your father?"

He clenched his teeth against the secrets he'd kept all his life. His father had been a respected member of the community, the shoemaker for the village. Only Damien and his family knew. . .

What did it matter now? "My father was a brutal drunk." Those words had never crossed his lips before but he had no difficulty saying them now that they could hurt no one. "I spent that summer standing between him and my mother, as my brother had done before me. To be fair, my mother was not an easy woman. She raged and stormed at him, as if she wanted us to see the brute he was. I couldn't get away fast enough. I hadn't realized how much Harry had protected me. I asked her to leave with me. I'd just taken a position in Birmingham and could have put her up. She refused."

He'd been devastated when she'd refused. In his youthful self-importance, he'd wanted to rescue her.

There was no relief in revealing the past. There could be no taking back his lost childhood.

They both glanced toward Kate and the children. They'd gone inside the pub.

Images from the past rose, unbidden, and Damien shuddered, recalling his father's rages. Had he taken them out on other women besides his mother? Women who might not fight back?

An adult now, with an adult's knowledge, he followed that thought to the next level. He'd never considered what happened behind the closed doors of his parents' bedchamber. If his mother refused the brute. . . ? The horror rocked him. Kate? Sweet, defenseless Kate? She couldn't have been more than eighteen that summer.

Tears ran down Brydie's cheeks. She must have followed his

thoughts. There could only be one conclusion. "I never knew. I was so young and utterly dense."

"You weren't even fifteen. You were the light of my life, of everyone's life. No one would want to visit ugliness on you, not even your sister." Damien brushed a kiss against her bonnet, put a hand at her back, and pushed her toward the inn. "Go, do what you do so naturally. I must see to the burial."

Mind spinning in revulsion as events of that summer built in his mind's eye, Damien walked up the hill to the cemetery with the curate and Rafe. Terwilliger had apparently disappeared with the women. He had to bury his mother. . . who had to have known everything about Kate, sooner or later.

Had she stayed, when he'd asked her to leave, to protect the girls? Of course she had. Part of his burden lifted. His mother had been fierce in her protection of her sons. She'd be equally fierce in defending the girls she'd treated like daughters.

How soon after Kate married had his parents run away? He'd never known the exact date. If his mother had known. . . She must have forced the old bastard to leave so he couldn't ever hurt Kate again. . . or touch Brydie.

Thoughts spinning, Damien followed the curate around the circular drive of the enormous stone manor to the stairs in the bell tower. Apparently, the medieval priory had a crypt that the conquering earls had used for storing prisoners and bodies. The underground tomb mow was little more than dirt and stone and a coal furnace for the manor's gas lamps.

In the light of his new realization, Damien touched his mother's forehead in the casket, fought back a tear that he'd never really understood her, then helped the others nail the lid.

That final action left him hollow. The conversation with Brydie had emptied Pandora's box, exposed the darkness he'd held inside for so long. The horror was out in the light of day. He had to face it. May she rest now in peace.

While he lived in the hell of grief and anger her death had returned.

Captain Huntley and his large cousins helped Damien and Rafe haul the coffin out of the crypt. To Damien's surprise, Tom Butler waited at the top of the stairs and joined them in carrying the coffin to the waiting cart. They nodded at each other but didn't speak.

Upton kept the graveside service simple, acknowledging Butler as the deceased's loving spouse and gesturing for him to throw the first dirt. Damien didn't mind. He hoped his mother had been happy in her last years or at least happier than in her earlier marriage.

He wanted to ask what had become of his father, but Damien really didn't care as long as he was harming no one else. Perhaps they'd arranged to have him locked up for assault. His mother had threatened it often enough, but there had been no law to call on.

Before he could even form a question, Butler walked off after the service, leaving Damien to pay the gravediggers and the curate. He'd have to go into town soon to replenish his cash. He had never intended to stay this long. . . or to bury anyone. Perhaps someone at the manor would take his bank notes. He couldn't expect the poor innkeeper to have coins.

The curate stopped at the manor to visit with his betrothed and family. The wedding was on Sunday, only a few days away. Damien hoped nothing else happened to put a damper on this happy time. He returned to the inn in Rafe's company. The funeral banquet was another bill he needed to pay. Perhaps Rafe would accept a bank note, if it was a generous one.

Damien accepted the wary condolences of women he did not know but who had known his mother these last years. Kate kissed his cheek and took the children out to her pony cart, their hands full of goodies from the table Rafe had laid out. Damien watched Arthur and saw himself and his brother in the boy's stride, the lift of his chin. His gut churned.

With apologies, excuses, and a promise to return quickly, Damien dashed upstairs to remove his outer garments and rein in a tempest of fury and grief. He flung open his bedchamber door, expecting Jacques to be there.

Instead, the room had been ransacked, the mattress turned over, his clothes cast to the floor. His gaze traveled up to the areas where he'd concealed a few of his father's documents. Thieves seldom looked up. The books were undisturbed. He checked to verify the copies, along with his keys and purse, were still in his pockets.

The library should be locked. Tossing his top hat and overcoat on the bed, Damien rushed out to check the library.

A hard object crashed into the back of his skull and the lights went dark.

NINETEEN

BRYDIE

LISTENING TO STRANGERS SPEAK OF A WOMAN SHE THOUGHT SHE'D known—a respectable lady who had once dressed in the finest fashion a small village could provide—Brydie felt adrift. Damien's story had yanked her anchor out of still water and set her sailing on a turbulent tide.

All these years. . . She didn't think she could even look at Kate. Brydie had resented Damien for so long. . . It was as if the puzzle picture she'd put together had been ripped apart, shaken up, and was now missing pieces of a completely different image.

So, she didn't notice at first that Damien didn't return. He'd provided a feast for the mourners. Presumably, he meant to talk to these women who had known his mother in her last years. So where was he?

And then, realizing the people in this room could very well know who had killed his mother, might even be the one who'd pulled the trigger, her insides knotted, and she went in search of Rafe. He'd retreated to the kitchen.

"Damien went upstairs and never returned." She tried to say

this calmly, but her next question bordered on the hysterical. "Could you check on him?"

Without questioning, Rafe slammed down his kitchen knife and left for the backstairs. Stirring a pot over the fire, Verity stared at Brydie as if she'd lost her head, which perhaps, she had. Damien was a grown man who could take care of himself, not one of the students who must be monitored constantly.

Brydie gestured toward the pub. "All those people in there are from the camp where Mrs. Sutter was killed."

The schoolteacher wrinkled her brow. "Until I moved here, I never thought about such things. I just thought people died, accidents happened. To live believing people one knows can deliberately harm you. . . takes some adjustment." She sent an anxious glance to where Rafe had departed.

Verity had been as protected as Brydie from the world's cruelty. But Brydie's days of innocence were over. Instead of rejoining the mourners, she followed Rafe up the stairs. "Rafe?" she called, traveling the meandering halls.

"Fetch Meera," he hollered. "Better, find one of the boys to fetch her and Hunt and anyone else willing to—"

Brydie arrived in the upstairs hall before he finished. Terror turned her insides to ice as she saw him outside Damien's room.

The look of fear on her face apparently caused Rafe to rein in his angry shouts. "He must have walked in on a thief. He'll be all right, but I have to find out who was up here."

She wanted to run down the hall, see that Damien truly was fine, but she had no right. Instead, she sprinted down the front stairs to the lobby, found one of the stable lads sneaking food from the pub, and sent him racing up the hill to the manor for the physician and help.

Then, picturing Damien beaten and in pain, she set her jaw, and returned to the mourners. *Someone had to be held accountable.* She counted heads first, but most of these women had no way to return to their tents without the carriage and cart that had brought them here. They were all present.

The men were the ones with horses—and none of them were present.

She stopped in the kitchen to warn Verity to keep an eye on anyone taking the back stairs. She wished Kate hadn't already left. She needed more eyes. While Rafe guarded Damien, Brydie roved through the pub, murmuring pleasantries, talking about the food, asking after husbands and others who had known the deceased, taking mental notes of replies. She even watched to see how often people left for the privy.

"I saw Mr. Terwilliger in the church." Trusting the older lady to some extent, Brydie spoke to Mrs. Hatter as she passed around trays in the pub. "Did he return to the inn with you? I was delayed and didn't have a chance to speak with him."

"He and Tom were about." Mrs. Hatter wrinkled her already wrinkled brow. "Saw them talking with Zeb before services. I reckon only Mr. Terwilliger dared show his face in chapel though. Zeb preached against it, but Terwilliger isn't one of us. He and Meg. . . They'd have words. He didn't much like being told what to do, but he listened."

So, the men had been in town. Any one of them could have sneaked into the inn while everyone attended the service. "I don't suppose they stayed? Do we need to take them a little of our repast?"

Mrs. Hatter snorted. "Not much of it left now. Irene is carrying half of it in her apron. She and a few of the others will see them fed. Meg's son is a good man for providing. It should have been the other way around. Where is he anyway? They're waiting to thank him."

"He is ill, I fear. We've sent for a physician. I know he wished to speak with the people who knew his mother these last years. I know!" A thought overtook her and she didn't hesitate. Setting down her tray, Brydie climbed onto one of the benches to attract attention.

The talk gradually died and everyone waited expectantly.

"Mr. Sutter has been taken ill." Still in a state of panic, Brydie fumbled for just the right words. "He wished so much to speak with you and offer his gratitude for looking after his mother. Would it be possible if each of you shared a memory or two I could write down?"

"A memory book," Mrs. Hatter said, catching on quickly. "You could stand at the counter in the lobby. Sgt. Russell keeps paper and ink there. Each of us can go to you when we think of summat to say."

And Brydie could watch the front stairs, the front door, and the pub entrance all at the same time. Excellent.

From her position on the bench, Brydie gestured toward the lobby. "Come along, then, Mrs. Hatter. Let's have your memories." She jumped down and led the way to the lobby, hoping and praying they would listen. They owed Damien this much, and maybe, just maybe, she could learn something valuable.

While the women paraded through, hesitantly offering up remembrances of gifts and encouragement, nursing illnesses and injuries, a few laughing reminders of how Meg Sutter Butler had stood up to the men, Brydie wrote as fast as she could, while still keeping an eye on the doors.

Meera must have gone up the backstairs. She could hear her voice floating down. Men gathered out front. Horses rode in and out. Hard to start a search party without knowing who one was searching for. Perhaps Damien had told them.

With the food gone in the pub, the women carried the party into the lobby, where they laughed as they recalled moments from these past years. This was as it should be, Brydie decided, like an Irish wake without the whiskey. She wished Damien were here to hear it, but he'd be a trifle overwhelmed by all the women, and they'd be intimidated by his presence.

Unfortunately, nothing they told her indicated why anyone might have shot at Zeb or pushed the earl into a river—or why anyone would harm Damien. They gossiped about the times Meg —not Johnson or Butler—had separated warring men, as she once had fought her own husband? She'd always been a forceful woman.

Brydie had the odd notion that it was Johnson or Butler creating the feuds, while establishing their authority. No one mentioned Terwilliger. Mrs. Hatter had said the financial man wasn't part of the camp.

When the carriage and cart rolled into the yard, the mourners finally filtered out. A few hugged the women who had elected to stay behind. Apparently, some of the men had followed the vehicles, and they lingered to eat the leftovers the women carried. Zeb's followers were not well fed.

"The meat pasties went over well," sour-faced Miss Butler said from behind Brydie. "It was generous of Mr. Sutter to provide such a feast."

"I think Rafe may have gone a little overboard." Brydie gathered the papers she had scribbled. "He is eager to open the inn and pub. It would be lovely if your camp could find a place here. There is more than enough opportunity for everyone now that the manor is open again."

"But that's the way of it, isn't it?" she said bitterly. "We must have the lords and ladies to pay our way. Zeb and Tom are trying to change that."

Worried about Damien, terrified of lurking evil, Brydie lost her patience. "You do understand that they are preaching a different form of bigotry? All lords and ladies aren't alike any more than all the people in your camp are alike. Are there no selfish, mean people in your group?"

A lean woman of pale complexion and straw-like hair, Butler's half-blind sister was of indeterminate age but older than Brydie. She startled at the accusation. "There are mean people everywhere. What does that have to do with lords and ladies hoarding wealth, spending on fripperies, while the rest of us starve?"

"Mrs. Sutter wore nice clothes and lived in a caravan while the rest of you wear rags and live in tents. Did that make her evil?"

"Of course not. She was one of us. She had money when she

133

came to us and she gave freely to the cause. She did not live in a castle and wear silks and eat pheasant." Miss Butler seemed more puzzled than angry.

Tired now, Brydie shook her head. "Wycliffe Manor was a cobweb-ridden, haunted shell when Captain Huntley, half blind and badly injured, sailed from America and settled here. His wife was an impoverished spinster trying to raise her nephew after losing all her family. They might be the descendants of earls, but they have done nothing but work day and night to bring the manor—and Gravesyde—to life. They didn't complain and blame others for their misfortunes. Yes, they were handed a roof over their heads. That is not the same as silk and lace and pheasant. Gravesyde is full of roofs to be had, should one wish to work and earn them. And everyone at the manor will be happy to help you, as they are helping Sgt. Russell and his wife."

She left Miss Butler to work that out for herself. She couldn't tolerate doing nothing. She had to see how Damien fared. She ran up with her sheaf of written memories.

Instead of finding an invalid with physicians hovering, she found the dratted man in the library, looking hale and hearty, presiding over a council of war. Or an army. Looking only slightly pale, with that tell-tale tick of fury over his angular cheekbone, Damien glanced up with narrowed eyes at her entrance.

In fury, she flung the papers on top of all the others scattered across the table. "You could have at least come down and waved everyone off."

She stomped out, fuming. She would never marry. She would take over the empty shoemaker's shop and. . .

She would make shoes for Lynly while she could.

Gathering up her cloak, waving farewell to Verity, she marched home, seething.

TWENTY

DAMIEN

AFTER BRYDIE'S FURIOUS DEPARTURE, DAMIEN LET HIS POUNDING head drop onto his folded arms.

"You should be in bed," Rafe said.

"What set her off?" Unsympathetically, Hunt reached for the papers she'd flung and popped in his monocle to sort them.

Damien didn't even try to lift his spinning head until the nausea settled. He'd just buried his long-lost mother and learned Arthur might be his half-brother. Someone hated him enough to nearly kill him, trash his room, and empty his pockets in search of. . . what? He owned nothing but the land. He had good reason to turn his back on Gravesyde and never, ever return.

No one answered Hunt's question.

Rafe studied a few of the papers Hunt handed him. "Testimonials. Brydie collected memories from your mother's friends."

Damien heard the papers rustle and assumed Rafe was passing them around. Miniature evil blacksmiths used his skull for an anvil and writing blurred before his eyes. The apothecary's medicine wasn't working. Nothing would. Cyclones whirled his thoughts like autumn leaves. Hell, no, entire trees slammed around.

"Looks like all isn't milk and honey in the Land of Zeb," Walker, Hunt's steward, commented, perusing one of the pages.

"Are the women trying to tell us something?" Hunt shoved one of the reminiscences under Damien's nose.

He tried to look at it cross-eyed from his resting position. Unable to manage actual thought, he simply asked, "Why was Brydie angry?"

"Disappointed you weren't dead?" Rafe asked facetiously. "She about tore my face off trying to see you when we thought you'd booked it. Then she summons Meera and half the manor, rounds up all the mourners and interrogates them, probably hunting your thief. She's a one-woman army."

Hunt laughed in understanding. "And then she finds you with us instead of lying on your deathbed. After all that, Clare would have thrown more than papers at me."

"There's still some folk down there waiting for a ride." Fletcher, former soldier and Rafe's silent partner in the inn, spoke up. "They might talk to you, not us."

"I've got three of their malcontents in my kitchen." Rafe dropped his tankard on the table with a loud thud. "If we have questions, they can answer. I just don't know the questions. Who would rob a man who just lost his mother?"

Damien moaned at the clank, then propped his head on one hand to eye the papers full of Brydie's scribbled writing. "We need to know if any of the women are strong enough to knock me out. Who else was here?"

"Who would want your documents?" Hunt countered. "Can you tell what was stolen?"

Damien searched his coat pockets, just in case he'd missed anything the first time he'd looked. They were still empty. "I had a few coins and coded lists I believe to be my mother's investments. Not useful to anyone but me. Evans already stole the deeds. Are my mother's letters still behind Shakespeare?" He couldn't move his head to nod toward the shelf.

The only black man in all Gravesyde, and probably more educated than any of them, Walker located the volumes and produced the stack of ribboned letters. "Do we need to take everything back to the manor?"

"Probably best. If I'm fortunate, there are documents inside a stack of books on the top of the wardrobe as well." Damien wasn't certain he could stand to reach them. Just *thinking* about it hurt. "What does the thief believe I have that would be of any use to anyone besides me?"

Not answering, Walker left to fetch the investment documents Damien had hidden.

"Unless you're carrying gold, I have to suggest your land," Hunt said. "There aren't too many parcels the bank doesn't own, especially this close to Birmingham."

Damien frowned blurrily at the stack of documents on the table. He simply couldn't think straight. The thief had taken his keys. . . "I've only had Evans, Weston, and Johnson express interest in my property. It's just a shop and a few acres, not a gold mine."

"I'll talk to Weston, when he's able." Hunt stood, ready to set off. "But he certainly didn't crawl down here to attack you in his current fevered state. I think he's still hacking up fish."

"He could have hired someone," Fletcher suggested. "Nobles do that sort of thing."

Damien winced. He didn't like it, but the cynic was right. "Weston has no reason to do so. We've known each other for decades. I'll take another look around my father's shop in the morning. How long will the duke be here? Do we know if Johnson plans on staying?"

"I don't expect His Grace to linger much past the wedding. Let us gather all your important papers, lock them up, and meet again in the morning," Hunt suggested.

"We probably ought to haul Sutter back to the manor as well,"

Fletch added. "What if the thief returns? He's in no shape to fight."

Damien groaned and returned his head to the table. "I'm not going anywhere tonight. My head would roll off."

"Where's your servant?" Rafe asked. "Fletch and Jacques can take turns guarding your door."

Damien couldn't shake his head at the fallacy of thinking his valet would do more than polish boots. "Jacques wants to be a bootmaker, like Hoby. He could be conspiring with Evans for all I know. I'll bar the door. I'll be fine."

After the others left with all Damien's documents, Rafe lingered. "I've had men questioning everyone in the vicinity, but those back stairs are hidden and few were in a position to watch them. With all the camp followers and villagers gathering in the pub, I doubt anyone noticed a thief coming or going."

Damien rubbed the lump on the back of his head. "Were there any men in the crowd? I don't think a woman could have hit me that hard, unless she was built like Brydie. She might want to crown me, but that's not her way."

"Mostly women, but some of the men lingered about." Rafe grunted as he stood up. "Can't tell what they used as weapon. Meera thinks it might have been a hammer. Curate carries one, but not when holding services."

Damien offered a ghost of a smile. "My father had a selection in his shop. Maybe he's hiding here." Although he rather thought it would be as a ghost, if so. Or perhaps he'd been dumped on a ship for the Americas.

"Let me go with you to your shop in the morning," Rafe suggested. "Two sets of eyes are better than one."

"I'd take the whole bedeviled village if I thought it would help. But Brydie and her sister are the ones who know the place best. Talk them into joining us. I'll cover any lost wages." He ought to be furious with Brydie for believing he'd fathered Kate's son, but she'd only been an innocent, motherless fifteen at the time and probably knew nothing of babies. Her father might have put the notion in her head. He didn't want to be angry with Brydie. In his current state, he couldn't summon anger at anyone. He just wanted to sleep.

Dr. Walker had told him not to sleep.

"Stay in bed in the morning. I'll go up and talk to Weston first. If the only connection between his would-be killer and your thief is the land, I need to know more." Rafe headed out the door.

"Weston is protecting his father," Damien called after him. "He'd buy up half the shire if it kept Johnson out."

Rafe waved acknowledgment, leaving Damien to find his own way back to bed.

Neither Johnson nor Weston actually wanted the shoe shop. Evans was the only one who could put it to use—and he'd already stolen from Damien once.

Just exactly how desperate was the man?

TWENTY-ONE

BRYDIE

BRYDIE COULD WALK HOME FROM THE VILLAGE IN THE DARK, blindfolded, backwards. She wasn't one to sit by the hearth, knitting. She'd spent these last years, while Kate was having children and keeping house, earning her way in any manner available. Besides being nursemaid and cook for her family, she'd run their errands, sold jams at the mercantile, exchanged harvests with neighbors, while collecting blackberries and apples from abandoned farms along the way. Walking the countryside was what she did.

The manor offering employment to Kate after her husband died had been a true godsend, but there were only so many hours in the day she and Kate could work.

Arthur would have to give up any hope of further education and learn to farm. He was smart. He'd do better than his father, well, George Morgan, had. *His father*. . . Brydie winced. She wished Kate would tell her what had happened. Or. . . maybe not. Kate had kept her secret all these years. She wouldn't speak of it now. She wouldn't even admit that Arthur was anything but George's.

Kate wanted her son to be a gentleman, to escape the toil of worrying about weather, tending sheep, and raising grain—and support her in her old age. Dreams didn't live long out here, as they both knew.

And still, Brydie cut from the walking path to the lane when she approached the Sutter property. Once upon a time, she'd hoped to catch a glimpse of Damien, speak to him for even a few minutes. Those days were long gone, but childhood memories lingered.

Instead, she needed to concentrate on Lynly's new shoes. She should pick up the pattern at the house and take it over to the shop while she had the chance.

She hesitated at a flicker of light from the direction of the shop. She'd left Damien in a conference with other gentlemen. He wouldn't have raced out after her. Perhaps Kate had decided to work on the shoes? Her sister knew how, but she refused to go over there anymore. Brydie had always thought she was being proper, but she shuddered, realizing now there might be more to the story.

The movement of the light seemed furtive. One didn't cobble shoes while walking around.

She wasn't fool enough to go in alone, unarmed. She ran the last length of lane to the farm and up the drive. Kate and Arthur were in the kitchen. They glanced up, startled, at her abrupt entrance.

"There is someone in Sutter's shop," she announced. "Where is the shotgun?"

"Don't be a goose, Bree. You couldn't hit a cow if you tried." Kate hesitated, thinking. "They could mean to burn it down, force Damien to lower his price. Arthur, take the pony and ride to the inn. Rafe should be around. See what he says."

Eager to be considered a grown man, the boy grabbed his hat and waited for Brydie to move from in front of the door. She didn't want to. He was still a boy. But Kate was right. "Put on a cloak. We'll have frost by morning. I'll hide in the hedgerow to see what I can."

Kate protested, but Brydie wasn't a frail miss. After her mother's warnings, and Brydie's own experience as a child, she was cautious about chilblains, but nothing more. She found warmer gloves, pulled on one of Arthur's knit hats, and helped him corral the pony. The boy rode off eagerly. Brydie wasn't quite so quick. She located a lantern and a short-handled mallet and hugged the hedgerow as she returned to the lane.

Tom Butler was a thief and used to work in the shop. Was he hunting for things he left behind? Tools the camp might use? Or was the person who had hit Damien in there now? She'd like to wallop him over the head, if so.

Mr. Terwilliger from the camp had wanted to lease the house for Zeb's church. She could find no reason for him to creep around.

Zeb Johnson had wanted to bury Mrs. Sutter Butler here, create a memorial. She'd been a decent woman, Brydie supposed, but the world was full of decent women. Why a memorial? Or was that just his way of claiming the land for his church? Still no reason to sneak around.

And hadn't she heard Damien say that the Earl of Weston had offered for the land? Why? He could have sent an army to prowl around if he wanted, but again, why?

More likely, it was a common thief who'd heard about the funeral and hunted for what he could find—but had this thief hit Damien first? To steal his keys? That made the best sense—and also pointed fingers at Butler again.

She really needed to learn to shoot, but their old shotgun was the problem, not her aim. She didn't think she could hit an intruder with a hammer, so all she could do was wait out here and see if she recognized anyone leaving.

The light disappeared behind the shop.

TWENTY-TWO

DAMIEN

Damien had been sitting in his dark, locked room, fighting sleep, when he heard the commotion outside the inn's thin window. He glanced out to see Kate's eldest riding up on a pony, shouting about thieves. The second dose of the apothecary's medicine had reduced the number of demon blacksmiths pounding in his skull, or perhaps just not thinking had helped. The cry of "thieves" had him dragging on his boots. He'd sent Jacques off to his bed for the night.

Perhaps Johnson had brought an entire band of murderous ruffians to the village. Whatever was happening, he couldn't let Brydie's family be harmed. And if that was actually his half-brother. . . He didn't have enough family left that he could afford to lose another.

He'd rather not think about the boy's origins. Action was what he needed now.

He ran into Rafe's partner, Fletch, racing into the lobby.

"Rafe's up at the manor, left me in charge," the former soldier explained.

Together, they rushed out to meet the boy, who scrambled a tale of lights in a shop that ought to be locked.

"Do ye have your keys?" Fletch demanded, sending Damien a concerned glance.

He must look worse than he felt. With his brains addled, he'd forgotten about his missing keys. "I know how to get in without them. It's probably a beggar after what he can find. There's not much worth stealing. I'll ride out with Arthur, have a look around."

He hadn't grabbed his sword or pistol either. Stupid. He wasn't in any condition for thinking, much less riding, but he wasn't leaving Brydie to deal with the problem, as she surely would. And he was in no shape to run back up those stairs.

Fletch appeared dubious, but the man was still in his shirt-sleeves, and with Rafe away, he had to watch the inn. "I'll fetch your mount. Will my sword suit you?"

Damien bowed his head once to indicate gratitude.

"Might I have one too?" the boy asked eagerly. "Brydie won't let me use my grandad's."

Fletch glanced to Damien for an answer. At his gesture of acceptance, he trotted off. A soldier was likely to have weapons to spare.

"Did you see anyone when you rode here?" Damien asked while they waited. What time was it? He fumbled for his pocket watch. Had the thief taken it? No, he remembered taking it off with his waistcoat. If he hadn't hurt too much to undress further, he may have run out in his nightshirt. At least he'd had the sense to pull on his greatcoat. He took the time to tie his neckcloth against the chill wind.

The tavern down the road was still going strong from the sounds of it, and a woman's singing rose above the chatter, so it was early enough for the curate's sister to be present.

"No one in the lane, sir. I didn't see the light across the way either, but Aunt Bree says as it went behind the shop. She feared mayhap it was the person who hit you." The boy had calmed down enough to be nervous.

"If nothing else, we need to keep your aunt from attacking the intruder," Damien said with what he hoped passed for humor. "There's not much anyone could steal."

The boy nodded uncertainly.

Fletch returned with Damien's gelding, a long sword, and a short sword for Arthur. The boy perked up—until he realized he had no way of carrying it. The pony didn't even have a saddle. The lad's legs were far too long for riding a pony only tall enough for child-size stirrups.

"I'll put it in my saddle," Damien offered, having planned that much. The demons in his skull had shut up briefly enough to plan weaponry, although they complained at his mounting and setting out down the lane. His head spun even at the pony's leisurely gait.

The boy appeared too nervous to speak. Damien made his living by talking. Although the demons preferred silence, the cool, dark night seemed to help. He wanted to know more of this lad who looked too much like himself and Harry to be denied. "What are you studying in school?"

Arthur sent him a surprised glance, then stared at his pony's head. "Nothing. I don't need schooling to tend sheep. My da taught me all I need."

That nearly shocked Damien off his horse. Kate and Brydie had been raised properly, with all the schooling the village offered and more at their mother's knee, but they were girls. Boys needed a proper education, especially if they were to inherit a large property. His grandfather had been the village squire in his day.

Damien hadn't given it much thought, but two women weren't likely to earn much on their own. They hadn't given him any indication that their fortunes had changed, but with their father gone and apparently the husband recently deceased. . . He winced at his obliviousness. Kate and Brydie weren't working because they were bored.

"Taught you how to buy and sell crops and sheep and how to bank the funds and all that, did he?" he asked casually.

Arthur shrugged. "Taught me how to shear and feed and plow."

"That's a good start, but if you learn to invest your profits, you can hire men to do that, as your grandfather did. Do you like mathematics?" Damien was finding it easier to deal with the demons if he talked and distracted himself.

"I can count shillings well enough," the boy said with a shrug, losing some of his nervousness. "We don't have enough to need more."

Damnation. Damien didn't know what to say to that. He'd abdicated all interest in his past when he rode away and never returned. Studying law, building a career, meeting people, seeing new places, had been all he wanted—not the people he'd left behind. Brydie was right to call him a grasshopper.

He could justify not thinking about his parents because they had been miserable excuses of parenthood—and then they'd vanished. But Kate and Brydie—had been as close to him as sisters. More, in Brydie's case, but given his temper and upbringing, he wasn't the marrying sort, so he'd left her to find someone who would treat her right.

In Gravesyde, where everyone lived with one foot in the grave. Stupid.

The demons pounded anew, with a vengeance. He was barely maintaining his seat by the time they reached the lane dividing his property and the Calhouns.

Brydie was waiting for them, of course. "I think he's in the house now. Shall I go in the back, make a lot of noise, and drive him into your welcoming arms?"

That was actually a decent plan, except this was Brydie, and he wasn't endangering her by letting her anywhere near a possibly murderous thief.

"Do you have a rope?" Damien slid off his mount and resisted resting his aching head against its neck while he plotted.

"I'll fetch it," Arthur offered, running toward the barn.

"You think he's fool enough to gallop a horse in the dark if you chase him from the back?" Brydie asked, understanding instantly.

"Does he have a horse?" He diverted the question until he'd worked out all the dimensions. His plan lacked substance but the demons wouldn't let him think beyond keeping Brydie safe.

"I thought I heard a nicker, but unless I see fire, I'm not fool enough to go over there alone." She sounded defiant.

"Thank you. I don't think I can take one more death or injury right now. The whole place may burn down for all I care, but no more people, please. I'll take care of the horse." Damien nodded approval when Arthur returned with a sturdy rope. "Do you know how to tie a knot that will tighten if tugged?"

"A'course. But them gate posts are falling in," the lad warned.

"That's all right. We'll slow him down enough for you to wallop him over the head with the flat of your sword." He handed the weapon over, and the boy beamed as if he'd been crowned king. "Now, is there an old plow I can pull across the lane in case he takes another route? Just tell me where to find it while you tie the posts."

"I'll tie the rope," Brydie offered. "The plow will need both of you. If you'll tie the pony and horse to the posts on either side of the lane, they'll block it in the other direction."

Overgrown hedgerows hiding old fences and walls made effective barriers—unless the intruder knew his way through the fields. Butler would. Damien was counting on few others having knowledge of his father's property.

Carrying the rusted old plow without a mule almost completed Damien's demise at the hands of the skull demons. Well, the apothecary/physician had told him not to sleep.

He checked Brydie's knots on the gate post, then removed his sword from the scabbard. "Whatever the two of you have planned should the fool run this way, don't," he warned. "He's not worth anyone getting hurt."

147

Brydie snorted. Wide-eyed, Arthur held his small sword and blended in with the hedgerows in the same manner as his cloaked aunt. She'd pulled up her hood to conceal her fiery hair.

Damien hated involving them at all, but he didn't want to fight them and the intruder as well. Whoever was in there had time enough to clean the place out, but, as he crept up the drive, there was no sign of a wagon. He undid the knot holding the man's horse to the hitching post, hit its rump, and sent it toward Brydie.

Damien recognized the mare.

He'd spent a lifetime controlling the temper that had been his only inheritance, but now, the demons exploded in fury. Rage unleashed, he strode straight up the walk, flung open the unlocked door, and shouted, "Evans, you filching cove, I know it's you. Get your ugly phiz out here before I bash it in!"

The nodcock actually dared rush him—or stumble into him. He stank to the heavens of gin. Well past gentlemanly decorum, Damien swung his sword with the force of his wrath, smacking his former business associate across the chest with the broad side of the blade, sending the older man sprawling across the parlor floor. He deserved that much for giving him this splitting headache.

Then he bunched his fingers into fists and stood over the mongrel. "I ought to tell Brydie you're the one who scuttled my nob earlier. She'll shred you into mincemeat."

Brydie didn't tolerate mills of any ilk—and apparently, Damien had scared her. That's why she'd stormed off. *Fighting* scared her, one of the many reasons he'd had to leave her behind. It had taken him years to unlearn his upbringing, to keep his fists and his temper to himself, and here he was, not back a week and behaving like an animal again.

He stomped his boot heel into Evans' gut, just in case he had some fool notion of getting up to try again. The wretch spewed up a day's worth of drink.

"Arthur," he shouted through the open door. "Bring that rope!"

"I can explain." Evans groaned as he struggled to raise himself. "You just caught me by surprise. You were supposed to be talking up the old biddies."

Damien unrepentantly dug his heel into the culprit's ribs. "What the devil did you hit me with? Let me try it on you so you know how it feels." He heard *two* sets of feet running toward the house—of course.

"Didn't mean to." He groaned and propped himself up on one elbow. "The damned banks wouldn't give me a loan. I *need* this place. So, I got to thinking."

"And drinking," Damien added with scorn. "Because the two go so well together."

"I can make this work," he begged, struggling to sit upright. "You saw those papers. The shop used to be flush with the ready. I just needed to see how. I need my family back, Sutter. You can't throw me out now."

"I didn't take you for a sapskull, Evans. You prove yourself with *numbers*. You boil down your own experience and fit those numbers into a smaller setting. . ." Damien watched in relief as Arthur trampled through the door bearing a rope, followed closely by Brydie bearing. . . a mallet? And Arthur's short sword. Damn, but he didn't know whether to laugh, shout, or fall into her arms and ask her to hold his pounding head.

He was exhausted. The temper had drained out of him. Evans was a drunken, desperate fool. He should have recognized that the businessman he'd once known had become a sot.

His own desperation to be rid of the despised farm and be done with Gravesyde had addled his wits.

Brydie took in the situation, nodded at her nephew to tie up the rogue, then indicated the door. "Kate will find you a bed and a whiskey. You'll think better once that knot on your head goes down."

"Hogtie him and put him in with the swine," Damien

suggested wearily, not wanting to move another inch. "I've got beds here, if you'll take the horses."

"You won't find the whiskey or a fire. And someone needs to wake you up every few hours to make sure you aren't dead yet. I've dealt with enough broken noggins to know what's needed."

Damien meant to refuse her offer, until he helped Arthur haul their prisoner to the Calhoun's barn and bedded down the horses. By the time they'd finished their tasks, Kate had the fire built, hot toddies waiting, and a cot made up in the kitchen.

Damien passed out before he had his boots off.

FRIDAY

TWENTY-THREE

RAFE

Rafe set out for the manor early Friday morning, wearing his best coat and hat to interrogate an earl—again. The apothecary hadn't let him near Weston last night.

He had never wanted to be a bailiff, but if the village wasn't to earn a reputation for lawlessness, someone had to do it, and he had the incentive. He meant to make his inn into one that welcomed gentry and nobles who paid goodly sums for his food. They wouldn't come near a place filled with thieves and killers.

Big lout like him had a *wife* now, a beautiful, useful lady accustomed to silk and lace. He wanted Verity to have nice things. The inn had to succeed, thus, villains had to go.

At the manor, he asked for the earl. He got Captain Huntley, the earl, and His Grace. Deuced good thing he didn't consider any of them suspects. Yet.

"I need to know what happened," Rafe said bluntly, ignoring the *my lord* that he should have used when addressing Weston. If he wanted truth, he had to establish some form of equality to justify his authority. "Who you saw the day you were pushed, any conversations that might have been overheard, everything."

Weston seemed paler than usual but dapper as ever. He rested in one of the windowless old study's leather wing chairs, wearing a silk banyan over his shirt and what appeared to be a hot towel around his throat. Hunt had a roaring fire in the grate but the earl still coughed.

"It was a miserable day. No one wanted to leave their creature comforts." Weston gestured at the cozy, book-lined room. "But I wanted to talk to Smith privately." He glared at his father. "Without interference."

An older man, not tall or distinguished in any way, his dark hair threaded with silver, His Grace—obviously interfering—glared back at his son. "I am not ready to cock up my toes yet. You fret too much."

"You are not to cock up your toes until one of us has married and produced heirs. My brothers expect me to keep you alive." The earl glared back, two peas in a pod. "And Zeb Johnson interferes with our comfort."

Rafe refrained from rolling his eyes. Hunt wasn't as polite, but the blunt American hid his expression behind his morning coffee.

"You were talking about Johnson with your financial advisor?" Rafe pried the topic back on track. "While fishing in the rain?"

The duke drank his coffee and shut up.

The earl shrugged. "I think better outdoors, with no one to interrupt. I've been fishing this river since childhood. The fish bite better in rain."

"And you wanted to irritate Smith," His Grace added. "Not everyone enjoys outdoor activities."

"This is not to be discussed beyond these walls. He was arguing with me about buying Sutter's property, and I thought maybe he'd listen better if he was in a hurry to return to the house. He stayed longer than I expected. The fish were biting. I think he finally began enjoying himself, until the downpour started." Weston sipped something that didn't smell like coffee, but it calmed his cough.

"And you noticed no one out there?" Since he hadn't been

invited to sit, Rafe remained standing. He preferred looming intimidatingly while steering his noble victim's memory.

Weston shrugged. "It was a filthy downpour, and we were on the riverbank, surrounded by trees and weeds and brush. It's not as if anyone has maintained that rocky stretch of land. That was the whole point—to be alone. If someone followed us. . . I would not have noticed."

"Focuses on his objective," His Grace muttered. "Doesn't see the nose on his face."

"So, Mr. Smith left you in the downpour. Then what happened? Did you not hear or see anything?" Rafe persisted.

"I may have heard what I thought was an animal in the brush. I was battling a ten-pounder at the time and paid no heed. Next thing I knew, something shoved me between the shoulder blades, and I was in the water. The rocks were slippery." Weston grimaced at the memory. "I cannot express my gratitude enough for being pulled out. I'm a good swimmer but there was no fighting that current. I think a branch may have hit my head at some point."

Rafe grimaced. "I regret that you had to suffer while visiting Gravesyde. I will do my best to see that it does not happen again. Might I have a word with Mr. Smith?"

Smith had nothing further to add. Respecting his client's privacy, the financier merely agreed to what the earl had said.

Rafe had made a list in his head last night of what needed to be done while he was here. He verified with the butler and the housekeeper that the only muddy boots that day were the earl's and Smith's. Everyone else had the sense to stay out of the storm. . . although Rafe supposed some of the lads in the stable might have been out and about. If someone had been *hired* to harm the earl, Rafe could spend the rest of his life hunting them. For now, all he could do was wait to see if anyone suddenly had extra coins. Villages had advantages over towns; there weren't too many places to spend ill-gotten gains. He'd have a word at the mercantile and tavern.

By the time he returned to the inn, Brydie had arrived with the children and his vanishing guests. Fletch had told him about last night's incident and Rafe had thought Brydie's place would be his next stop. He was grateful that he needn't make another expedition, and that Damien appeared better than yesterday.

In the back of the pony cart, bound and trussed, definitely worse for wear and stinking to high heavens, was the inn's other missing guest, Evans. Damnation, there went the inn's reputation.

"We caught Evans searching my house. He admits to hitting me over the head and stealing my keys. I suspect we'll find my missing deeds wherever he's been hiding. What would you like me to do with him?" Damien wasn't wearing a hat, and his linen was well beyond wrinkled, but there was no mistaking him for anything less than a gentleman.

Rafe grimaced. There went one paying guest. "If I may borrow the pony cart, I'll take him up to the captain. I'm not in a mood to feed him, but I'll fix the rest of you a good feast when I return. How's the head? Do I need to take you to Meera?"

Evans cried a muffled protest. No one paid heed.

"We've been fed, but I'm not adverse to coffee, if you have it." Damien dismounted and helped Brydie down, while the youngest two scrambled out on their own.

Brydie, at least, looked as proper as she ever did. The eldest boy stayed on the cart.

"I'll drive you up, sir," Arthur offered. "Mr. Sutter says I may stand as witness."

"Mister Sutter is a *lawyer*." Brydie brushed Damien's hand aside and sounded offended. "He knows what's best. I'll take the children inside and start your rashers." She stalked away, shepherding the two wide-eyed youngest ahead of her.

Damien just rubbed his head and held onto his horse.

Rafe hid his amusement at the crackling energy between the pair. Instead, he addressed the young lad eager to prove himself. "I'll crush your cart if I sit in it and can probably walk as fast as the pony. I'll follow you up."

He nodded at Damien's horse. "Fletch is in the stable this morning. He can brush him down. You need to take yourself inside and rest. I'll be back for the whole story."

"Beat the name of any accomplice out of the sot. Someone promised him something." Damien left his no-longer elegant associate whimpering protests through his gag.

Rafe smacked the pony and started the second trudge back up the hill, grateful for the overgrown trees breaking the brisk wind. He'd earn his breakfast this morning with all this tramping about.

TWENTY-FOUR

BRYDIE

BUSTLING ABOUT THE INN'S KITCHEN, BRYDIE DIDN'T KNOW WHY SHE was so agitated. Damien had been all that was proper last night and this morning, after spending the night with them. More than proper. Over breakfast at their kitchen table, he'd discussed schools and education with Arthur—as she had long dreamed of him doing. He hadn't made any promises, which was fine. He was just. . .

So bang up to the mark, so excessively citified, so. . . not the boy she'd known.

His family had always been a step above hers, with an income far beyond anything known in Gravesyde. Damien seemed to have done well enough for himself that he didn't even bother practicing law anymore. He could fix up his inheritance, call it Sutter Hall, and mix with the descendants of the earl at the manor.

And she was wearing a patchwork of cast-offs she'd sewed together to fit her great lumping size and boots she'd made herself —from stolen leather while working as little better than a char-woman. A *sturdy* lass, she'd been called, never an elegant lady.

Letting the kitten into the inn yard to do its business, she slapped a huge handful of rashers into the skillet over the fire while Verity greeted the children in the makeshift schoolroom. Verity was a Town lady, but she often wore frocks the sewing ladies had made-over and never put on airs. Still, her accent was far more citified than Brydie's would ever be. And her hands weren't callused and brown.

Brydie whacked an entire loaf of yesterday's bread into slices.

It didn't matter who or what Damien Sutter was, she reminded herself. He just needed to take Arthur under his wing.

At a shout from the lobby—Rafe really needed to install a bell —Brydie raised the skillet higher over the fire, wiped her hands on her apron, and hurried down the back corridor to greet their visitor. She almost stumbled over her boots when she recognized him. *Zebediah Johnson!*

"Mr. Johnson," she greeted him with a polite nod, congratulating herself for not kicking his shins, if only for his selfishness in ignoring poor Mrs. Sutter in her dying moments. "Sgt. Russell is at the manor. He should return shortly."

Keeping warm by the grate, as always, Rafe's wolfhound watched attentively. Rafe had taught all of them the dog's commands, so it was as if they had a silent sentry.

"I want to see Sutter." A tall man, with fierce dark eyes under thick brows, the provocateur wore a long, dark, old-fashioned frockcoat and breeches, resembling an undertaker more than a gentleman. He hadn't removed his top hat at her arrival.

She wasn't really a servant, but the three new ones Rafe had hired weren't precisely light on their feet. She'd left half-blind Miss Butler dicing onions, arthritic Mrs. Hatter ironing sheets, and Mrs. Mayfield clomping around, dusting, upstairs. Rafe needed a younger, more fleet of foot servant for running errands. Looked like today, that was her.

Rather than immediately obey, she smiled and bobbed a curtsy. "Let me fetch a chair. Mr. Sutter just came in and isn't prepared for visitors yet."

Before Johnson could argue, she dashed into the pub and snatched an unoccupied chair. The children preferred squirming on benches, and the wobbly, castoff chairs weren't exactly comfortable.

In the middle of reading a story and showing the illustrations, Verity didn't glance up. Rapt, neither did the children.

Brydie set the chair down by the lobby grate and busied herself feeding kindling onto the fire. "Shall I fetch some hot tea while you wait?"

She hoped Rafe would return before she had to disturb Damien. Without waiting for a reply, she left Johnson glaring at the ancient, rickety chair. With those coal-dark eyes, was he capable of more than glares?

"Zeb Johnson is in the lobby asking for Mr. Sutter." She informed Miss Butler of the visitor while pouring hot water over tea leaves. "Is there any chance he truly has the ability to lease or buy a shoe shop and manor?" Because the person Damien had counted on to start manufacturing shoes was currently locked in the Priory's cellar.

The village really needed more business. Zeb Johnson didn't appear to be the sort to start one.

"Meg said she had a life estate in the property. She tried to persuade Mr. Johnson to settle some of us there. Tom said it would not be financially feasible." The sharp-faced spinster looked up with her clouded eyes. "I assume with her death, that the property has passed on to her late husband's heirs, so no, I can't think he'd be interested in buying."

"Well, then, perhaps it is something to do with her death. He ought to express some regret to her son for the bullet that missed him and killed her." Brydie slammed a sugar bowl onto the tray she was preparing.

Elizabeth Butler stopped chopping and cleared her throat. Frustrated, Brydie almost didn't notice. Only, as she slid a cream pitcher onto the tray, the cessation of chopping caught her attention. She sent a questioning glance to Tom Butler's sister.

160

"Is everyone quite certain Mr. Johnson was the intended victim?" Elizabeth returned to slicing and dicing after dropping that firecracker.

If not Mr. Johnson. . . Brydie hefted the tray, her mind trying to hunt down and trap what Miss Butler hinted at. *Damien's mother* may have been the target? Possibly murdered and not an accident victim? That made utterly no logical sense whatsoever—unless Damien killed her to acquire the land free and clear. Which made no sense either, not to her. But to someone like *Evans* who wished to acquire the property without a woman attached to it for a lifetime. . . *Oh my word.*

Mind unsettled, she placed the tray on the lobby's reception counter and prepared a cup of tea while Johnson paced rather than take the chair she'd provided. "Will you be going south next? If the winter is as bad as last year, you'll freeze in tents."

The zealot took the cup and ignored her question. Wolfie's head turned to follow his pacing but the hound was too polite to growl.

Agitated, Brydie developed an aversion to being ignored. She poured her own cup of tea and waited. She wasn't a servant, after all. She merely offered her labor in return for the children's education. She might only be a farmer's daughter, but her father had *owned* his land. She'd been raised with a notion of how ladies dealt with callers. Of course, ladies had servants. . .

"Is anyone fetching Sutter?" Johnson finally demanded.

"It's improper for ladies to call on a gentleman," she said demurely, hiding her pleasure at his irritation. After Miss Butler's question, she did not want Mr. Johnson alone with Damien. "We are waiting for Sgt. Russell to return. Would you care to ask after Miss Butler and her friends? They are doing well."

Slapping his cup on the counter, Johnson started for the stairs. So much for being concerned about the *people*.

Thankfully, Rafe stomped in from the back hall at the same time. He startled at the other man's presence. "What can I do for you?" he asked gruffly, apparently not in the best of humors. He scratched the hound's head when Wolfie loped over to greet him.

"Mr. Johnson wishes to see Mr. Sutter," Brydie explained, starting to enjoy the preacher's discomfort. "I had no one to send up to find him. If you will fetch a table from the pub, I will bring in more tea and scones."

"I do not need tea and scones," Johnson roared, increasingly discomfited. "I simply wish to speak with Sutter. In private."

Finally, heavy steps clattered on the stairs—not Jacques. She'd seen the valet cleaning boots out back. Damien must have realized that Brydie would not be delivering his coffee. Mission accomplished, she slipped away for another tray.

Zeb Johnson had been in the best position to shoot Mrs. Sutter. Odd how everything changed from a new point of view.

Could Meera have discerned whether Mrs. Sutter had died from a pistol at close range rather than a rifle or shotgun from a distance? How could she ask?

When Brydie returned to the lobby with a laden tray, the argument had not gone in the direction she'd anticipated. Mr. Johnson was taking Rafe to task for stealing weapons when they were needed for hunting. Damien sat next to them, saying nothing.

"Take the matter of weaponry up with Captain Huntley," Rafe was saying, not in the least ruffled. Approximately the same height as Johnson, he was twice as broad and far more muscled. He wouldn't fear many people. "Your men may collect their weapons when you're ready to leave town."

"That's the point," Johnson shouted.

Brydie had to wonder if he normally communicated by shouting. With his mellifluous voice, he was quite good at it, far more so than the curate. But Mr. Upton seldom had to raise his voice to make his point.

"We don't wish to leave and we need our weapons to feed ourselves!" Johnson continued roaring. "You have no right to steal a man's property."

"Confiscate," Rafe said calmly, leaning against the counter and sipping the coffee she poured for him, while Wolfie lay at his feet, guarding him from noisy strangers. "Until the murderer is found, we have to confiscate all shot-firing weapons."

"You're not moving on?" Damien asked, ending the pointless argument and preparing his own cup.

Brydie took the cooling cup of tea she'd poured for herself and slipped into the back corridor, lingering near the doorway to listen and keep an eye on things. She hoped Miss Butler could smell if the bacon burned. She was rather enjoying being in town and on top of things instead of feeding chickens.

"That's what I'm here to talk with you about," Johnson thundered. "If only we could do so in private."

Freshly dressed in starched linen and a fashionable, tailored frockcoat, Damien sipped his coffee and shrugged. "My mother died in your presence. I'm not certain I wish to become another target. Rafe, if you will, stay."

Brydie beamed at his perspicacity. And he hadn't even heard Miss Butler's question.

Rafe fed a bit of scone to his dog and obeyed his paying guest.

Johnson stormed up and down the worn plank floor. "It's more likely one of your manor folk shooting at me. His Grace wishes me dead."

"You give yourself airs to believe His Grace knows you exist," Damien countered. "He is an extremely busy man and merely a guest of the bridal couple for the week. He will be gone shortly. Important men have enemies, so he's not likely to be out shooting so much as a rabbit without an entourage. You'd see him coming."

"Bah." Johnson threw up his long arm in dismissal. "I understand you have lost the buyer for your property. I'd like to see if it is suitable for my congregation."

My, word traveled quickly. Even for Gravesyde, that was lightning-fast gossip. Had someone been spying on them last night?

Did Evans have an accomplice? Brydie wanted to warn Damien, but he'd narrowed his eyes in suspicion already. He knew the village as well as she did, even if he hadn't been here in ages. Rafe was new, but he cocked his head, listening closely.

"Unless you are interested in making shoes, I doubt my property will be of benefit. The land is limited and the cottage is old and neglected."

"Anything is better than a tent," Johnson reminded him. "We have elders who need shelter for the winter. If the property is empty, you shouldn't mind us occupying it. We'll see to repairs and upkeep."

"Occupying? The property is for sale, not open for squatters. The shop needs a shoemaker. The village needs labor. The bank seeks renters for their empty housing. Can you provide any of that?" Damien gazed out the hazy mullioned window as if studying an interesting sight in the muddy yard. The clouds were lowering for another storm.

"We are willing to work, but we need a chapel for worship. I wish to see the property to see if it will suffice." Johnson lowered his voice and sounded firm.

Damien swung around to stare him down. "I would like to see the color of your money to see if it will suffice. I have other offers, from more reliable sources."

"Weston would steal it from us!" Johnson returned to shouting. "I won't have him deny me again!" He stormed out.

Damien turned his gaze in Brydie's direction, even though he couldn't possibly see her. "Which man would you prefer for neighbor, Miss Calhoun?"

She stepped into the lobby and, chin lifted, met his gaze. "One who opens a shoemaker's shop and hires locals. I suggest you search the grounds again before you make any sales. Evans may be working with Johnson. There is evidently something out there that they want, and it has been suggested to me that Johnson may not have been the target of your mother's killer."

That dropped a dead silence on the room.

TWENTY-FIVE

DAMIEN

His mother may have been *DELIBERATELY*, not accidentally, killed?

Damien's fury percolated as he pondered the possibility over his second breakfast. It seemed inconceivable—but Johnson was rumored to be a womanizer. Would Butler kill her if he discovered she'd been unfaithful?

His own father had come close to murdering her often enough, not for philandering as far as he knew. She had simply not been an easy woman to have around, but then, his father had been worse. She'd always fought back and held her own—but she'd been ill when she died, a danger to no one.

His thoughts circled, but the one fact kept returning—Tom Butler had walked away from her right before she was shot. And a weapon had been found in the direction he'd taken. If he'd been carrying the rifle, surely someone had noticed? But if he'd left it hidden in the trees. . .

Paul Upton, the about-to-be married young curate ambled in, apparently drawn by the aroma of baking bread and frying bacon. Rafe gestured for him to take a seat at the kitchen table. The innkeeper had driven off the women so the men could eat and talk while he prepared a roast. Rafe was a man of many talents, as an innkeeper must be, Damien conceded.

Upton accepted a plate. "I've just been to see the prisoner. He swears he is able to make a legitimate business deal. He simply needs to make his case with his financiers."

"I'm no longer interested." Damien dismissed his former associate. "I still have a knot where he hit me. I hadn't realized he'd become a toper. He used to be flush with cash when I knew him. He must have drowned his sorrows in what was left after his business went bankrupt. Drunks lack good sense."

He should have investigated deeper, but he'd been eager to offload the property and be done with Gravesyde. Desperate men lacked judgment as much as drunks. He rubbed his temple.

"We don't need his sort taking up residence." Rafe brushed aside the notion as if he had a vote. "I'm trying to return law to the district, not add to the problem."

"It's a shame." Upton sipped his tea. "He could have hired and trained young men, brought fresh business to the village. It's a grave disappointment. What will become of the property now?"

"I am talking to Weston. He knows nothing of shoemaking but may be amenable to my finding a suitable tenant, as long as he keeps Johnson out." Damien knew he ought to be more interested in the discussion, but he couldn't ignore Brydie's warning. "I want to search the place more thoroughly."

Rafe shot him a glance. "Why? Did Evans say something?"

"No, Brydie did. And Evans was out there for a reason. If he's working with Johnson. . . I fear my head is too scrambled to puzzle it all out."

"I'm at loose ends while everyone is making wedding preparations," Upton admitted. "Shall I help you search?"

Damien breathed easier at that offer. "You'll drive off the ghosts, thank you. I probably won't find more than mouse-eaten rubbish. You might poke around, see if there is anything you or others might use. The earl certainly won't want the furnishings."

"You should take Arthur and his pony cart," Rafe suggested. "Verity says there's naught she can teach him and he spends the morning reading from her father's library."

"Even better. Let me change into rougher clothes. Do we need to speak to Brydie about springing Arthur from confinement?" Damien pushed back his chair. He hoped to know Arthur better but needed to keep a safe distance from the boy's sister. As sorry a place as Gravesyde might be, Brydie was better off here with her family than wandering from city to city with a wretch who couldn't hold his temper. Last night had reminded him of his family predilection for violence. He'd kicked and punched a *drunk*.

Half an hour later, Damien, Upton, and Arthur were on their way back to the scene of last night's crime, if it could be called such. Evans had done no harm to anyone but himself, as far as Damien had ascertained.

"Do we have any notion of what we're looking for?" Upton asked, reasonably enough, as they rode.

"Evans claims the deeds he stole are with his solicitor in Stratford and that all he sought was proof that the business was once profitable." Damien rode beside the pony cart containing Upton, Arthur, and a substantial luncheon. The heavy cloud had begun to drizzle. It looked like a miserable day for the search. "That's fustian, of course. Fifteen-year-old accounts are worthless."

"But he was hunting papers of some sort," Upton suggested. "Most of our recent criminal cases have oddly involved books. Would that be the case here?"

"My mother kept our small library, but most of the books are old and probably insect-ridden by now. Arthur, you can start there, see if there are any worth saving for the school, look for anything hidden."

The boy nodded. "Aunt Brydie wished she had a key so she could rescue the books. I'd like to see what you have."

The lad definitely needed to be educated. Damien was uncertain how to broach the subject with Kate. She was likely to have

167

his guts for garters if he even hinted that George Morgan wasn't Arthur's father.

They tied the animals in the stable, out of the rain. Arthur ran across the lane to fetch grain from his family's stores, while Damien and Upton brushed the stock down and settled them in non-leaking stalls. Damien unlocked the back door while Arthur fed the animals.

"Shall I search the house while you take the shop?" the curate asked. "You'll know more of business matters."

"And you can sort through the rubble for anything useful. The inn could use some of that furniture. Throw rubbish on the fire to keep warm. No idea what shape the chimneys are in. If the place burns down, it will probably be a blessing." He entered the kitchen to inspect the grate but he wasn't sticking his head up the chimney.

"I'm grateful for the opportunity to keep busy," Upton admitted. "It's been a long time since I've been with a woman, and I'm suffering a bad case of wedding nerves."

"Not just nerves," Damien said in amusement as Arthur entered, shaking out his damp cap. "Months without a woman, and I'm ready to punch my fist through any man who looks at me crooked. We both need a rousing game of cricket." Or a whore, but he didn't say that in front of the boy.

At a sensitive age, Arthur caught on quickly and reddened while he started searching kitchen cabinets. A little more cautious, Upton tilted his head in the boy's direction and didn't respond.

If Arthur was his half-brother. . . "A boy needs a father to explain these things." Damien studied cleaner squares on the dirty walls where his mother had apparently removed some of her handiwork. "Did Mr. Morgan tell you how to treat women?"

"Not much," Arthur admitted, burying his head under the sink. "Just said to treat them careful and be polite."

"Good advice, as far as it goes." Damien's father had never explained a word, but his mother had smacked them at any sign of disrespect. He'd learned his carnal knowledge in a barn with an older milkmaid eager for a tumble. His mother had caught his father with the same maid a week later, and that had been his first lesson learned.

So, instead of searching the shop, Damien and Upton explained the facts of life while turning the first floor upside-down in search of rainbows or rats, whichever appeared first.

The rain poured on the tile roof when they moved to search the upstairs. Damien noticed no leaks, so it was solid. They lugged down good oak beds, but mattresses and linens were rotted and moldy. Burning them in the kitchen fireplace produced clouds of smoke. They couldn't fix tea that way.

The pump worked, but they needed a fire to heat the water.

"I saw a woodpile behind the shop," Arthur said as he doused the smoking linen. "It's in a shed. Might be dry."

"I'll wash off some of these plates," Upton offered, emptying the china shelf. "Could be some people can use them. They're rather fine for our sandwiches, though."

Pulling on his cloak and hood, Damien followed the boy around to the protected area he remembered from boyhood. Not all memories were unpleasant. He and his brother had spent many an hour chopping dead wood from old apple trees while nattering out here. Older brothers might be bullies on occasion, but other times, they were all each other had.

"Someone's been in it." Arthur picked up kindling knocked from the once neat stack. "They've left these too close to the door. With this wind, they're wet." He dropped them into a dry corner.

Damien assumed the scattered wood was Evans's work. Had he expected to find hidden gold? "You or your mother or aunt never came over here? The pile is going to waste."

"Mother won't set foot over here, and Father refused to take anything not his. We always had plenty of coal." Arthur loaded his arms with dryer pieces.

"And your Aunt Brydie would have helped herself if needed," Damien finished in amusement. "She's practical." He pushed at

169

rotten bits near the bottom of the stack with his boot—and uncovered loose dirt. Odd.

Arthur peered around him. "'Could be a badger." But he frowned. Badgers didn't move wood around in sheds.

"Pirate treasure. Isn't that what your baby sister seeks?" Damien tried to keep it light. Animals dug holes—but usually didn't cover them with a heavy woodpile. "Carry those inside. I want to look for a shovel."

"I'll be right back, if you can find two shovels." Arthur dashed into the rain with his stack of fuel. The boy was strong and carried a load even Damien might have found difficult. He was growing old.

He located a rusty spade and pitchfork in the stable. Any treasure boxes under the woodpile would be corroded after years of mud and rain. This wouldn't be pretty.

By the time Arthur returned and they'd dug out the first layer of mud, Damien realized it definitely wasn't pretty. Or treasure.

His stomach wrenched, and he stopped the horrified boy. "Fetch Rafe, and maybe the magistrate."

Arthur dashed off while Damien stared in revulsion at a graying bone very much resembling a human arm.

He may have just discovered where his father had gone.

TWENTY-SIX

BRYDIE

By noon on Friday, parents had returned to fetch their children from the school, fearing the floods of another storm. Even Kate ran down from the manor to take the children home. Discovering Arthur and the pony cart gone, she accepted Brydie's offer that Rob and Lynly stay at the inn, while Kate returned to work to earn a few more coins for their dwindling coal pile. In three connected buildings of ancient, rambling corridors, Rafe wouldn't notice their presence, and the children wouldn't mind.

Just as everyone, including Rob and Lynly, were settling down in the kitchen to their noon meal, a few more sodden, shivering strays from the campground arrived at the back door. Miss Butler helped them with their drenched cloaks, while the rest of their new staff prepared more hot tea and sandwiches and exclaimed over the state of the roads and the rising creek at the campground. Rafe ran outside to handle their carriage horse.

Brydie wondered where they'd found a carriage—until she carried a tea tray to the lobby where the driver waited. The stick figure that was Terwilliger rose at her entrance. Having driven the new arrivals to the village, he was apparently too lofty to enter through the kitchen as the women had.

Leaving the tray with the financier, Brydie sent Rob out to find Rafe to deal with their new guest, and Lynly to the now-empty schoolroom to eat her luncheon.

With order established, she joined her niece in front of the pub's warm grate to eat her sandwich. Intelligently not following Rafe or Rob into the rain, Wolfie lay on the hearth, with the marmalade kitten snuggling on top of him.

Before Brydie could enjoy her tea, Verity slipped into the pub, frowning. "Mr. Terwilliger has decided the weather is too inclement to continue on to Stratford. Rafe wants us to make up a bed for him."

Unwilling to leave Lynly alone, Brydie assigned the task to Mrs. Mayfield, who enlisted the aid of one of the newcomers. The inn might actually have a staff now, although not exactly an energetic or healthy one. Still, the older women knew what they were doing and worked well together.

Now that she had company, Lynly dragged out the sewing basket containing the makings of Kate's Christmas gift that they'd hidden behind the bar. Rather enjoying the quiet warmth away from the hustle and bustle, Brydie sorted the pieces Lynly had already worked, then shook out the quarter-finished cover she needed to finish piecing. "This might take me until next Christmas to finish."

Sewing the batting between two patches cut from one of her old dresses, Lynly eyed the finished rows. "We should have kept one of those old gowns from the trunk. They were prettier."

"Silk and satin with our cotton?" Brydie examined the rows. "A shiny star in the middle? Her quilts were made up of old gowns. I asked Damien what he wished to do with them, but he just said burn them. I thought they had some nice fabric, but she embroidered the squares tightly. It will take time to snip all those tiny stitches."

"Her patches are old and crackly." Lynly turned up her pert nose. "Ours are better."

"Our quilt is definitely better. Mrs. Sutter used hers to make her walls prettier and just stuffed them with old newspapers. Their beds had lovely soft wool and down comforters."

They hadn't made much progress on their project when the lobby door slammed open. The kitten leapt in fright and jumped into Lynly's lap. Alarmed, Brydie glanced out the rain-streaked window. Arthur's pony was out there—without the cart. She set aside her work, ordered Wolfie to stay with Lynly, and tried not to hurry and alarm her niece. What had brought the boy back so soon? They had provided enough food for them to stay late if the rain turned bad.

Rafe reached the lobby at the same time as Brydie.

Pale and a trifle shaky, Arthur spoke hurriedly. "Mr. Sutter says as he needs you and maybe a magistrate, sir." He looked almost green around the gills. "There's a bone, sir. In the mud. Under the woodpile."

Uttering a foul curse under his breath, Rafe strode off again. Brydie steered her nephew into the pub to warm up by the fire. For the first time in her life, she was at a loss for words. *A bone. In the woodpile.*

If nothing else, fall back on mothering. . . "Let me fix you some hot soup. You're wet to the skin."

Arthur shook his head. "No, I gotta go back. Mr. Sutter needs help. He thinks it may be his dad." He whispered the last, so Lynly couldn't hear.

Brydie almost sank to her knees in horror, but for the children, she had to be strong. With Kate working, she was their substitute mother. Kate wouldn't want her son out there. . .

Kate, who wouldn't return to the shoe shop after the last time they'd seen the Sutters.

Brydie's imagination ignited. She had to douse the flames and *think.* "You'll need my gloves, and a muffler around your neck.

This will turn to sleet before nightfall. Get some hot soup in you while I fetch them."

Always hungry, Arthur didn't argue again. While he scarfed down hot bread and soup, Brydie collected her warm garments. He wasn't as tall as she was yet, but he was close. The gloves would fit, for now. She wasn't going anywhere this evening and wouldn't need them. By morning, all would be clear again. Or the weather would. The mounting mysteries though. . . She had to talk to Kate.

But Kate was at the manor, relying on Brydie to watch her children. Tonight. They'd have to talk tonight. She couldn't leave the delicate subject to men.

The women in the kitchen continued working. All agog, they watched the coming and going and whispered among themselves. Rafe sent for Fletch to mind the inn, while he saddled his horse and rode off toward the manor to fetch whoever would witness and help dig. The curate was already at the scene to say prayers. . .

Mr. Upton's poor bride must be worrying herself sick. A bridegroom with another funeral to hold, probably on their wedding day. . . The price of marrying a man of the church. Brydie hoped the lady didn't change her mind. But then, with a duke and an earl and a houseful of noble guests, any woman would be afraid to back out.

Proud of her nephew, but terrified for him, Brydie watched Arthur on his pony following Rafe and Captain Huntley into the downpour. The boy was almost a man and needed a horse of his own. There was no way in this century that they could afford one.

Lynly frowned worriedly as Brydie settled beside her again and took up the quilt. "Is something wrong? What did Arthur want?"

"Mr. Sutter is trying to catch a thief. Perhaps they found him. Arthur just came to fetch Rafe. He's fine. We're all safe and warm. It's nice of Sgt. Russell to allow us to stay so we don't have to go out in this weather, isn't it?"

Satisfied, Lynly returned to stitching her squares. They were a long way from finishing the cover. They should do as Mrs. Sutter had done—cut great big rectangles that didn't take so much sewing. Had she even quilted hers?

Brydie sighed as the lobby door slammed open once more. Fletch hadn't had time to arrive from the other side of the village, where he trained horses. Verity was still dealing with the new staff, finding them beds and linen. If the inn was actually to open to paying guests, someone needed to greet them.

She set down the quilt and gestured for Lynly to stay. She had Wolfie follow her into the lobby, where they found a dripping stranger about to take the stairs without anyone's direction. At Brydie's gesture, Wolfie quietly intercepted.

"May I help you?" She thought the unshaven man seemed familiar beneath the gray, thinning hair, but she couldn't quite place him. Someone from the camp, possibly? She'd only been out there once and hadn't really noticed the men.

"Terwilliger here?" he asked gruffly, even his voice reminding her of someone.

"I don't know which room. If you will wait, Mr. Fletcher will be here and can fetch him. May I take your cloak or bring you tea?" She hated that he was dripping all over the floor, even if the worn wood had probably seen centuries of mud.

He scowled but divested himself of cloak and felt hat, hanging them on hooks by the door while Brydie ran off for a tray, praying Mr. Fletcher had arrived. The familiarity nagged at her.

"There's a stranger to see Mr. Terwilliger," she whispered to Verity as she reached for the teapot. "I left Wolfie guarding the stairs. Has Mr. Fletcher arrived?"

"Not yet. I imagine they're battening down the stable. Rafe wasn't expecting anyone to be out in this weather. He didn't give his name?" Verity worriedly added biscuits to the tray with the cream and sugar.

"No, but he looks familiar. I can't place him, though."

Miss Butler glanced up from the dough she was pummeling.

"Why don't I take out the tray? If he's here to see Terwilliger, he's probably from the camp, and I can take him up. I don't mind." She nodded toward the back stairs. "Besides, Lynly just ran up in search of more quilt pieces. You might want to go after her."

"Oh, botheration!" Brydie glanced at the stairs and to Verity. Rafe's new wife knew nothing of innkeeping or staff, but she was the authority here.

"I don't see where it would hurt," the teacher agreed reluctantly. "You really aren't a servant, Brydie, and the child shouldn't be up there alone."

She might not be a servant, but she owed Rafe and Verity a great deal. Still, she took the stairs without hesitation. Lynly might be small and weak, but she was as headstrong as any Calhoun.

She found Lynly as expected, in the box room with Mrs. Sutter's quilts spread around her. Surprisingly, Damien's valet was with her, helping her to snip the threads on the patches she designated. At Brydie's entrance, they both glanced up in the wintery light from the one narrow window.

"The silk ones are huge," Lynly said in excitement. "We can make a lot of stars out of them. The dark blue ones are really pretty."

"Who stuffs quilts with paper?" Jacques asked in disdain, carefully snipping an entire patch from the center of the old cover.

"Waste not, want not." Not eager to return to the unsettling visitor in the lobby, refusing to consider what the men were uncovering at Damien's home, Brydie watched as they snipped the pieces apart. "Paper keeps out drafts."

Lynly happily clipped seams while Jacques peeled open the piece he'd chosen. With experienced fingers, he removed threads while studying the paper he'd exposed. "Fancy writing for a newspaper. Looks important." He handed the thick sheet up to Brydie and began clipping the next patch.

"Can't be very important if she used it for a wall covering." Brydie frowned at the thick, ornately printed paper.

Voices echoed down the uncarpeted corridor. Miss Butler must have taken the stranger upstairs. The newer rooms were on the far end of the inn from this bare closet. The certificate in her hand held Brydie's fascination, but the light in here was bad. "You need a lamp. Let me run down and find one and see if Verity knows what this is."

She left the pair contentedly destroying the ragged old quilt while rain pounded distantly on the attic roof.

Verity had retreated to the small sitting room in the back hall where she sat in front of a brazier, copying receipts into a ledger. She glanced up at Brydie's arrival. "Is Lynly uncovering pirate treasure? I fear that's all the children are talking about since I started reading *Robinson Crusoe*."

"That's the fault of their parents believing there is pirate treasure buried at the manor," Brydie corrected. "The first Wycliffe earl was a pirate, and Captain Huntley's cousin found doubloons in the tower not too long ago." She handed over the certificate. "I couldn't see this properly upstairs. What do you make of it?"

Verity's eyebrows rose to her hairline. "It's a stock certificate, dated fairly recently. Possible treasure, indeed. Where was this?"

Recent? Odd. "Sewn into Mrs. Sutter's old quilt. She always stuffed them with paper. . ." Brydie put her hand to her mouth as she realized what she'd said. "All those big patches. . . ?"

Verity grabbed her lamp and followed Brydie into the hall, where sound carried better. Angry shouting and Wolfie's barking carried from the lobby.

Uncaring what happened to grown men, Brydie ran for the back stairs and Lynly, who might be sitting on Damien's inheritance. . .

Which was gone by the time Brydie reached the box room, along with Lynly and the trunk. Jacques lay unconscious on the floor, flat on his back, as if he'd been punched. Heart pounding in terror, she glanced out the narrow window and saw a carriage racing out of the yard.

The only carriage at the inn was Terwilliger's. If he had

Lynly. . . Why would he have Lynly? Because she saw him steal the certificates? Or because he'd hit her hard and killed her?

Even while she watched, the stranger bolted for his horse and galloped in the opposite direction. Something was very, very wrong.

She had no cloak, no gloves, and hadn't been on a horse in years.

It didn't matter. Shouting Lynly's name, just in case she was hiding, Brydie picked up her skirts, and took steps down to the kitchen two at a time to set the staff to searching the inn. But while they did that, she ran for the horses the guests at the manor had left in the stable.

She didn't have time to saddle up and adjust cinches. She found one still bridled, led him to a hay bale, and climbed on.

Her fingers and toes might fall off, but she wouldn't lose Lynly if she had a breath left in her.

TWENTY-SEVEN

DAMIEN

The mood was grim as Rafe, Captain Huntley, and Damien took turns shoveling beneath the woodpile. The curate had Arthur inside, sorting through pots and dishes and blankets for charity. The boy had never known his neighbors, so he was taking his grisly discovery in stride. Damien wished he could be so complacent. He may have despised his father, but. . . He couldn't fix his memories to a corpse.

"Leather breeches, gold buttons," the captain reported, leaning on his shovel and stepping away so Damien could look.

The buttons had mostly fallen off, but they were distinctive. The breeches were pulled past the hip bones.

His gorge rose, but he shoved it down. "My father cut and sewed his own leather. The buttons probably belonged to my grandfather. They both liked wearing a fortune. . ." He shut up and moved away, fighting the churning in his gut. Children did not think of the carnal lives of their parents, but his father had flaunted the gold over his. . . codpiece.

"Any other way we can identify him?" Rafe asked.

179

Damien shrugged and tried to recall, but even though he had imagined many a cruel fate for his father, the reality was vile. "Teeth," he finally concluded. "My mother knocked out one on the side." He pointed at his own eye tooth to indicate. "Does that help?"

He couldn't watch as they dug carefully around the skull.

"Yep, missing tooth," Rafe reported. "Looks like the back of his head connected with a small, hard object."

"This small, hard object?" Huntley asked.

Damien turned to see him holding a mud-encrusted, tacking hammer. He winced. "Not large but easily wielded with limited strength."

"A furious swing?" Huntley examined the small surface and then the skull. "We'll show it to Meera but I assume that point of the skull was a bad one to hit."

Or they'd buried him while unconscious. Damien had nothing else to add. He preferred to block out the scene that would rise too clearly in his mind if he thought about it. He'd known the old man was a letch who had castigated his sons for not swiving half the district. The nose-punching argument that had sent Damien riding off, never to return, had involved a shouting, drunken argument about Damien and his brother being man milliners for never having taken advantage of the two ripe girls across the lane. Brydie had been *fifteen*, Kate only a few years older. That he'd had nightly lascivious thoughts of Brydie had not aided his temper.

But Arthur's existence. . . Damien had never known his father to use innocents, but he should have realized. . . And if his mother had caught him. . . Damien shoved aside that thought as a horse galloped down the front lane.

On a miserable day like this, that couldn't be good.

Abandoning the woodshed grave, he hurried around the house to where Rafe's partner, Fletcher, had halted uncertainly at the broken gate. At seeing Damien, he steered his mount up the drive. The man had a hard, chiseled face, cold eyes from having seen too much battle, and he appeared as if he were fighting demons.

"Terwilliger and Butler apparently kidnapped a little girl and made off with your mother's trunk. I'm here to gather a posse. Brydie stole a horse and is on his heels."

In the downpour. Did she even know how to saddle a horse? How the devil did she think to stop a kidnapper?

"What little girl? How do you know who it was?" And then Damien realized there would only be one little girl at the inn. Brydie would ride a demon, if necessary, for her niece.

She'd never been able to handle the cold. She'd almost lost fingers one winter. She'd kill herself in this weather! He didn't care who the hell had taken the child, they were going to hang.

His misery and simmering anger rising to the level of raging terror, he cracked the rotted handle of the hammer in his fist.

"Lynly, Kate's youngest. Miss Butler and Brydie said Tom Butler and Terwilliger were the only ones at the inn when the girl disappeared." Fletcher held his prancing mare tight. "The bastards took the trunk and the child, as best as I can make out. The women are hysterical, said the carriage headed for Stratford."

"They left in a *carriage*?" Of course they had, if they had a trunk and a child. Out of the gloom, Damien saw a beacon of hope. "How good are you at cross-country riding? We can triangulate and cut them off if we're quick."

Leaving Fletch to do as he would, Damien dashed for the stable and his gelding. He shouted at his mud-covered companions while untying his horse, thankful he'd left it saddled. He hoped the others would work out his incoherent call and follow.

His mother's trunk. Why? They'd emptied it.

Terwilliger. Lynly and Brydie. Did his family do nothing but deliver disaster?

That was stopping now. . . Unless he killed Terwilliger. With the red rage boiling, that was always a possibility. He'd left Gravesyde to keep from killing his father—and apparently left someone else to do it for him. He didn't have time to consult the curate over the morality of killing scoundrels.

Rafe and Captain Huntley joined him in the stable, leaving Fletcher to mind the grave and guard the innocents in the house.

"The lane to Stratford curves around hills and floods in low spots," Damien told the others once they'd mounted and he led them into the back field. "Through the pasture is shorter and more solid." Or used to be, fifteen years ago.

The fields may have changed, but this was Gravesyde. Change didn't happen often. "A carriage will have to take the lane slowly. I don't recommend jumping stiles in this mud, but even stopping to open gates, we can cut them off before they reach the main highway." Where they might turn toward London or the north and never be seen again.

Fear forced his rage back to a simmer. Temper only exacerbated his aching head, and he needed to *think*. He'd never been a soldier, but these men beside him had. They had nerves of steel and could plan in times of action. Damien lacked that experience.

He'd chosen a profession in which violence was unnecessary. He might be fearless *talking* in a business meeting and the halls of Parliament. He'd pulled his sword on occasion in self-defense but never wielded the pistol he carried. He had no idea whatsoever how to stop a carriage without causing harm.

He had to do it or never live with himself.

Brydie depended on him. And poor Kate. . . the sister he'd never had. And the boy he wanted to call brother. . . He'd lost everyone. He couldn't bear to lose them too.

He'd think about that astounding revelation later.

He concentrated on leading his small band across muddy sheep pastures and overflowing brooks in the blinding downpour. The sun hadn't set, but the gloom was dark enough for evening. And the icy rain was turning to sleet.

Brydie was out there, riding in this misery, inexperienced and on an unfamiliar mount. She'd never had more than an old farm nag to ride. What did she think she would do when she caught a carriage?

Brydie was incapable of doing nothing. He *knew* that. He pushed his gelding harder.

In the gray dimness of rain and winter twilight, he located the curve the carriage had to traverse to reach the highway. Damien whistled to draw the attention of his companions and pointed at a nearly hidden gate. "I'll go out here and hope to follow behind him. There's another gate in the next field. If we're fortunate, you'll be in front to cut them off. Whistle when you're there, and I'll find a way to distract the driver."

They all knew they could be riding into gunfire, but for Lynly—they had little choice. It was now or never. Damien unsheathed his sword, opened the gate, and checked the narrow, hedge-lined lane. All clear. He waved the others on.

He wished he knew for certain where the carriage was. It could have lost a wheel, turned over in a flooded stream. . . If they met in the middle with no sign of the vehicle, they'd have to turn back and look—while Terwilliger made his escape if he was ahead of them.

Damien fought his red rage. *Think.* People did endlessly stupid things. He couldn't afford to lose his temper and become one of them. Cutting off heads would be satisfying but not beneficial. How did he stop a carriage and kidnapper?

To his relief and horror, as he raced toward the London highway, he caught sight of Brydie ahead, nearly sliding off a galloping, unsaddled horse. That meant he'd judged the distance right and the carriage was ahead. She'd once rode the fields with him, but in a sidesaddle on an old nag with proper stirrups, on sunny days. Not in icy muck with a strange horse and almost no equipment. She was mad.

Of course, she was. She had every right to be. Since her father's death, she had probably tackled everything herself, which was why she worked at an inn. Damien hadn't been there to help, as a good friend and neighbor should. He hadn't been there for anyone, ever.

A man had to start sometime.

He rode up beside her, catching her as she tilted. Her bare fingers looked blue and barely clung to the reins. She had no scarf and her cloak hood scarcely covered her wild hair, which had fallen to curl and frizz on her shoulders.

"How far ahead?" he asked curtly, terrified of keeping her safe while chasing down. . . what, a wizened old financier? Or did the financier have a killer with him? Why the devil had they taken the child?

"Not far, thank heavens," she muttered through chattering teeth. "Go. I'll keep up."

He doubted that, but he wouldn't argue. "Rafe and Hunt are headed toward us. We need to distract the driver in case he's armed. Let me slow him down, then you can ride up on his other side, confuse him."

She wrapped the reins around her wrists so they didn't slip and nodded. A Brydie who didn't talk or order him about was a terrifying experience. He'd commandeer the damnable carriage and dump Terwilliger on the road if necessary to get Brydie and the little girl back to the inn.

A fire and a whiskey sounded good. Tempering his rage with concentration, Damien took the lane quietly, using the spongy verge until he spotted the ancient barouche ahead, around a curve. The rear half-hood, raised against the storm, swayed and bounced as the driver drove his horses far too fast for the road conditions. That wouldn't do. He needed that carriage in one piece.

He slowed his mount and rode up by the rear wheel. The driver couldn't see him behind the hood. He heard no voices, had no idea how many passengers. Glancing behind him, he saw Brydie approaching, looking pale as death. Rage demanded he slice reins, flatten the driver, smack Terwilliger over his boney head. . . He was furious enough to punch Satan. But for

Brydie. . . He swallowed hard and impatiently waited for his meager army.

A sharp whistle indicated Rafe and Huntley approached and saw the carriage. *Now* he could unleash the fury demons.

Damien galloped beside the carriage, startled the horses, and yanked a rein loose with his sword before the driver could gather his wits. In panic at losing control, the driver screamed, but no one shot at Damien. He hauled on the leather, slowing the horses.

Roaring like furies, Hunt and Rafe rounded the bend, grabbing reins, leaping from their mounts, and shoving the driver aside. In seconds, they'd halted the barouche and subdued the only occupant. . . Terwilliger.

His rage slaked and fully focused, Damien leaped into the carriage. Where was Lynly? His mother's ancient, empty trunk had shifted from under the cover of the hood, into the downpour, but appeared to be intact.

Before he could open the lid, Brydie practically fell into the carriage with him. She collapsed in his arms, then struggled to reach the trunk, tearing at the lid.

By then, Rafe had Terwilliger on the road, arms behind his back, and Hunt was trussing him up. The skinny financier shouted protests, but when the lid came off the trunk, he shut up. Lynly did not pop out.

Brydie gently lifted her frail niece, hugging her, then turning big, pleading eyes to Damien. "She's unconscious."

She didn't have to say more. Rafe shoved a handkerchief into Terwilliger's mouth and flung his trussed carcass on the floor, next to the trunk, leaving the covered seat for Brydie and her niece. Damien emptied the quilts on top of them. Brydie protested something about papers getting wet, but he didn't listen. She was practically blue with cold. He added his cloak on top of the quilts and ordered her to bundle up.

Swinging into the driver's seat, he gathered the reins and gestured for the others to take up his and Brydie's horses. Wheels were slow in this muck, but Brydie and her niece needed to be out of the worst of the weather. He turned the barouche around at the gate and began the slow progress back to the manor, where a physician waited.

The living were more important than skeletons or filthy old men. He scarcely heard Terwilliger's muffled protests over Brydie's weeping.

Fear replaced Damien's rage, fear that he'd failed, fear that she'd blame him, fear. . . that his world would never have sunshine again.

TWENTY-EIGHT

BRYDIE

Ensconced within the manor's warm walls Friday evening, Dr. Meera Walker examined Brydie's no-longer numb fingers. "Mr. Sutter is pacing the hall."

When the small physician pressed Brydie's hand between her warm, plump palms, pain shot from Brydie's blue fingertips, and she bit back a moan.

"We need to restore your circulation. I can have Mr. Sutter hold your hands while I look after Lynly," Dr. Walker continued. "Are you ready for your boots to be removed? He can do that better than I."

And see her breeches? Brydie shivered beneath the lovely fleece blanket the physician had wrapped around her. The warmer she became, the more her feet felt as if they were on fire. "Will she be all right?" she whispered rather than agree.

"I suspect a congenital heart condition," the lady said frankly, handing her a warm, not hot, cup of tea and wrapping Brydie's fingers around it. "She woke, but she was agitated, and I gave her something to make her sleep so her heart has time to calm down.

Your sister is with her. She's fine. *You* need to concentrate on warming your extremities before they ulcerate."

Frozen through and only starting to unthaw, Brydie's relief drained her tension and what little energy held her together. She doubted she could move a finger. Despite appearances—Dr. Walker was wearing a shapeless, colorful wrap that didn't belong in a drawing room—the brown-skinned physician wasn't a servant and had far more vital tasks than fighting boots.

At the doctor's invitation, Damien stalked into the manor's infirmary, and Brydie pulled the blanket over her head and ears. Even covered in mud, he was every inch a citified gentleman. Sitting here in her muddy rags, she couldn't possibly look at him. Her ears burned with embarrassment as much as her fingers and toes hurt with cold.

Without hesitation, he kneeled at her feet and began gently wiggling her short boots free. Pain shot up her foot, and Brydie bit back a squeal. She knew the boots had to come off. Thankfully, he made no comment about the breeches. When he gripped her legs, she told herself the extra fabric provided good protection from his marauding hands.

"I recognize your hand in this stitching." He worked the leather over her ankle. "Your boot-making ability has improved."

She winced. So much for concealing her leather theft. Unless he thought she'd bought it on her own. Unlikely.

When she said nothing, he turned to Dr. Walker, who was busily crushing herbs at her workbench. "Frostbite?"

"Frostbite requires freezing, like water and ice, and it's not cold enough to snow yet. No, this is chilblains, at the very least, although from the severe discoloration, I'd say there is an underlying condition. How often do your fingers turn blue, Miss Calhoun?" The physician didn't seem overly concerned.

Brydie shrugged and clung to the warm cup, even though the heat caused such prickling discomfort that she nearly dropped it. "I have chilblains all winter unless I wear gloves. I don't like being cold. My mother had the same and developed severe arthritis, so I do try to avoid it."

"Yet you rode out after Lynly without even donning gloves!" Damien angrily yanked the first boot off, then cradled her toes in his warm hands. "Shall I remove the stocking?"

She'd given her gloves to Arthur. She didn't owe anyone explanations. Brydie yanked her foot away from his invasive fingers. . . and heated touch.

"We don't know what causes arthritis, but you can get it without chilblains. Go ahead, remove the stocking." Meera continued mixing. "If your extremities often turn blue, then white, with cold, there is a condition I've seen occasionally, usually with young women like ourselves. It's not chilblains. I have no remedy except to tell you to keep warm. I will mix a cream that might ease your skin and prevent sores, but I need a few ingredients first. Here's a mild pain killer. I'll be back shortly."

After the physician handed Brydie the drink, she scurried off on her mission, leaving Brydie alone with Damien. Lynly and Kate were just on the other side of the curtained wall behind her. Anyone could enter the reception area in front at any time. No one could cry indecency, except Brydie, as Damien slid her stocking off to examine her bare toes. She thought she might shrivel up in humiliation.

"Your toes look better than your fingers. We need to find you some wool socks to go over the stockings."

She wanted to kick him but lethargy claimed her. She hid behind her warm mug. "Then I'd need new boots to fit over the socks. Just tug off the boot, Damien, and stop molesting me."

He grunted and yanked his hands away.

"I come bearing hot soup and rolls and Hunt's request for anyone who can explain who he is locking up and why. And are there more scoundrels he should send men after?" The aristocratic voice emanated from the entrance.

Brydie peeked from her cocoon to see the captain's lady wife setting a tray on the long counter dividing the anteroom from Dr. Walker's work area where Brydie sat.

"The captain needs to lock up Terwilliger for kidnapping and possible theft," Damien said firmly, rising to take the tray. "We have reports that Tom Butler was with Terwilliger at the inn, but he wasn't in the carriage."

"I saw him ride toward the camp. I haven't seen him since I was a child and didn't recognize him." Brydie finished Meera's mixture so Mrs. Huntley could hand over the hot mug of soup to wrap her hands around. All this pampering would make her lazy, but she had nothing more intelligent to contribute.

Mrs. Huntley left the tray sitting on the bench where Brydie could reach it. "They found Butler trapped by the bridge. The river flooded and took out half the stones. He couldn't go further. Since he was the only man out in this deluge, they hauled him in, but Hunt doesn't know what to charge him with."

"Not certain I do either," Damien admitted. "I'll tell the captain what I know shortly. The ladies are in no condition to speak."

And didn't know enough to speak, Brydie concluded. Butler had been at the inn, but she couldn't put events together with Mrs. Sutter-Butler's death or the earl being pushed or Damien being hit over the head or even Lynly's kidnapping. If no one knew about the quilts. . . Thoughts swirled with no conclusion, but she had seen Terwilliger with the trunk, so she supposed she could contribute that much.

"Definite theft and kidnapping for Terwilliger and possibly for Butler," Brydie said, surprised to learn she could still think coherently. "Be very careful of those quilts we carried in. They are likely to be Damien's inheritance, or what remains of it if Butler took any."

Mrs. Huntley glanced at the reception area floor on the other side of the counter. "If you mean these muddy rags they had wrapped around you, they're still here. Everyone is at dinner.

Should I have someone clean them?" She rightfully sounded dubious of their value.

"No, please, don't. I hope the filler hasn't been destroyed by the rain. Damien, go, do, take your quilts and talk to the captain. I will remove my own boot." Somehow. Her fingers were too stiff to bend, although the soup was spreading a slow warmth through her midsection.

"Tell the captain to eat his dinner in peace. I'll be out when I can." Damien started wiggling the other boot loose.

"Oh, I do love to tell Hunt to shut up and sit down." The lady left, laughing.

"Gravesyde has changed," Damien muttered, yanking off the boot.

Brydie almost managed a smile at that. "The late earl's family is almost all female. Against all convention, the earl arranged for them to inherit the manor, and they're enjoying being in charge."

And then she remembered poor Rob, abandoned at the inn? "Kate, can you hear me?"

Her sister emerged from the infirmary, holding Lynly in her arms. "I can't bear to let her go. Meera says I'm to keep her warm."

"Did you leave Rob with Verity?" Brydie turned to Damien. "And Arthur? Where is he?"

Shrugging instead of answering, Kate exchanged knowing looks with Damien. "Brydie likes to run the ship. Can you handle that?"

Damien proceeded to pull off Brydie's stocking and warm her toes with his hands. "I have it on good authority that strong partners are the best kind."

What the devil did he mean by that? Unable to summon the energy to argue, Brydie let their foolishness fly over her head and waited for an answer about the boys.

Damien tickled the bottom of Brydie's foot until she kicked him with her aching toes. He finally replied, "I believe Arthur is with the curate, who is showing him the difference between good wood and bad."

The curate made coffins. Remembering why Arthur had raced into town, Brydie gulped and quit fighting Damien. He needed the distraction. And perhaps she did too. His hands were warm on her numb foot. Or the painkiller was taking effect. "So, I am to take it Rob is in good hands, also?"

"He's a little older than the boys in the manor's schoolroom, but Mr. Birdwhistle can manage them. He thinks Rob might be a good influence. He's wanting his students to mix with Verity's once she learns who needs what. We're hoping the tower stairs will be safe soon so they can open a schoolroom here instead of in the pub." Kate settled wearily on the bench next to Brydie and rocked her youngest with a wistful expression.

"Birdwhistle?" Damien inquired, glancing up with interest, as if recognizing the name.

"The tutor. Reid boys are eccentric and inclined toward getting themselves killed, so everyone keeps a close eye on the last of them. Rob will be fine in their care. Are you going to look at your inheritance?" Kate asked inquisitively, studying the rags just visible beyond the counter.

Dropping the subject, Damien finally gathered up the quilts, but instead of looking at them, he wrapped them around Brydie's now-bare feet. She tried to kick him away and show him what the patches contained, but with a grave expression, he turned his attention to Kate.

"We found my father's grave, Kate. Did Butler do it?"

Why would Kate know anything about a skeleton. . . ? Brydie sank against the wall and pulled the blanket over her head again.

"Not that I know," Kate whispered. "Your mother. . ."

"Took a tack hammer to his head. It wouldn't have been the first time, but he was usually prepared to fight her off. This time, he wasn't, was he?" Damien asked softly but matter-of-factly.

Brydie peered out in time to see Kate shake her head. Her sister had her eyes squinched shut as if blocking out a memory.

"I don't want to ask, Kate," he said softly. "Would you rather tell Captain Huntley? He could have Tom Butler hanged. My mother couldn't have dug that grave."

"Tom wasn't there," she said firmly. "He may have come later. Your mother saw me home. But I saw. . . There was a lot of blood. And I was glad she'd hit him. He gave me something in the tea and I fell asleep. . . I was too ignorant to understand. . . until much later, after everyone had vanished."

Oh, lordie, no. . .

Brydie leaned over to cuddle her sister in the same way Kate cuddled her youngest. Her strong, wise, older sister turned into Brydie's shoulder and wept. She didn't know what to do. She was supposed to be the one who knew all the answers. She'd blamed Damien for years, and she'd been so very wrong. Perhaps, she should shut up and mind her own business.

"The quilt, Damien," Brydie reminded him, redirecting the conversation. So much for keeping her mouth shut. They needed a dose of good news. "Quit wrapping the soggy mess around my feet and tell us if it holds a future for Arthur."

There, she'd said it. Kate had been miserably used by the Sutter family but the result was not her nephew's fault. He might be a product of violence, but he was a Sutter, just as Damien was.

Frowning at her quizzically, Damien unfolded the old patchwork rag. The papers inside crackled. He located one of the loosened seams and pulled out the wrinkled paper lining to study it.

"Jacques had another one of those papers. What happened to him? He was unconscious when we found him, and the paper was gone." Brydie tried not to think of that scene—the trunk and Lynly vanished, Jacques sprawled on his back, and the men shouting at each other in the yard. She'd taken far too long to recover from shock and grasp what had happened.

"Your valet is in the kitchen, regaling the staff with his courage and brilliance in uncovering a treasure chest. He is sporting a lovely purple jaw." Dr. Walker reappeared with a jar of cream.

"You need to put this on your fingers and toes. It will feel good, I promise."

Setting aside the paper as if it were old trash, Damien took the cream and began rubbing it into Brydie's blue toes. "Tell us what happened. Why would Terwilliger kidnap Lynly?"

That was all the reaction he had to the certificate? Perhaps it was worthless after all.

Sipping her lovely warm soup, Brydie gave up fighting his hands. They felt too good. "Lynly was crowing about finding hidden treasure when I left her with Jacques. They may have even uncovered more papers while I was gone. Terwilliger was upstairs, and possibly Butler. They probably heard the excitement. Once they realized your mother had hidden possibly valuable documents. . . Lynly is a Calhoun. She probably wouldn't let her treasure go."

"They must have punched Jacques, then threw the quilts in the trunk, slammed it on Lynly to shut her up, and raced for the door. I can almost see it. Carrying that trunk would have taken both Butler and Terwilliger. That makes him an accessory to theft, at the least." Damien rubbed his head, smearing cream across his brow before he removed the soup cup and started on Brydie's hands.

"I won't ask why Lynly and Jacques were playing with filthy old rags," Kate said with a sigh. "Meera, is there somewhere Brydie can sleep so Damien will put the captain out of his misery?"

"I'll carry the heroine of the hour. Just lead the way." Damien hauled Brydie off the bench before she could protest.

She snuggled her frozen nose against his neck and let him break his back carrying a big lummox like her. She didn't think she'd actually saved his fortune or Lynly, but she'd take what credit was handed out. She didn't receive it often.

Tomorrow, she'd remember she wasn't a pampered princess.

SATURDAY

TWENTY-NINE

DAMIEN

Last night, after massaging Brydie's long, slender feet and hugging her against him as if he had the right to do so, Damien had had to place a distance between them. He used the excuse that the captain wanted him to attend the trial, and he needed clean clothes in the morning if he were to appear in whatever form of court Hunt put together.

Then he and Jacques had spent half the night at the inn taking apart quilts and realizing the full extent of his mother's brilliance.

This morning, Damien wore a crisply starched neckcloth with a tailored frockcoat and trousers more fashionable than those of any of the gentlemen present, including the duke, although his boots might never be the same. He had impressions to make. His future depended on it.

"Brilliant job cutting off that kidnapper," Hunt said in greeting. "We all need to know the terrain better than we do."

"I wouldn't have even known to go after him if Brydie hadn't sent a warning," Damien corrected.

Lynly might have been lost, and the quilts with his inheritance would have certainly disappeared if Brydie hadn't acted swiftly. She probably would have killed herself trying to find Lynly, and he'd have had to leave Gravesyde forever in shame and despair. Her trust gave him hope he had yet to earn. "I suspect she would have followed Terwilliger to Hades if we hadn't arrived in time."

"Clare wants to find Brydie a more suitable position, but we don't know her talents, other than riding hell for leather bareback." Hunt stopped to watch as the prisoners were marched into the central corridor of the manor.

Looking worse for their night in the manor's prison cells, Terwilliger, Evans, and Butler glared balefully. Damien had a hard time imagining any of them killing his mother. It simply didn't make good sense—unless one of them knew about the certificates. Since the quilts had been thrown out like trash, he had to assume no one had known her hiding place, until Jacques and Lynly uncovered the papers. Had any of these men even known she'd possessed stock? Women generally didn't. Husbands and bankers and trustees invested for them.

Zebediah Johnson had been summoned to appear. Damien hoped he would. The preacher couldn't be completely oblivious to the misdeeds of his flock. One of them had shot at him—possibly more than once—for a reason.

And how the devil did the earl fit into any of this? Had Weston known about the investments? Damien had recognized most of the companies and consortiums, knew they were sound, but he hadn't had time to study all their financial aspects or owners.

"Brydie is good for boot and trouble-making," Damien answered dryly. He knew she'd made those boots she was wearing last night. She'd been in his father's shop.

The Earl of Weston arrived to hear this last. "Will your Amazon join Johnson in demanding the vote? Two troublemakers in one town ought to be entertaining."

"Johnson isn't interested in *women* voting. And Brydie doesn't have time for electioneering, although, give her an opportunity —" Damien acknowledged the possibility.

"She'd make a good politician's wife?" the captain asked with interest, knowing the earl was on the hunt.

Damien was nearly as tall and wide as his younger companions. He could, presumably, knock their heads together. But they painted an interesting picture. . . And he damned well wasn't losing her to Weston.

The ornate clock on the stair landing struck five. Damien checked his pocket watch just to be sure he wasn't dreaming. Still almost nine. The manor apparently ran on its own time.

Hunt interrupted his musing. "Sutter, you're a lawyer, aren't you? I'm tired of being judge, jury, and prosecutor. Be the prosecutor for me. Lead the questioning and let me lean back and look wise and authoritative." Not waiting for assent, he shoved Damien toward the two-story, vaulted great hall where the ladies filled the sofas and gentlemen milled on the sidelines, whispering among themselves.

Daylight barely illuminated the towering, leaded-glass, gothic windows. No one had lit the massive overhead iron chandeliers. The dimness gave the hall a medieval atmosphere. He could practically hear monks chanting.

Except the place had been decorated for a wedding. A long table swagged in what was probably silk drapery occupied the place where the monks' altar must once have stood. A lectern from the library held a large open book, probably a Bible or prayer book. Enormous silver candelabra adorned either end of the table, along with vases of greenery and the last autumn flowers. All the sofas and chairs had been turned to face the altar—convenient for a courtroom.

"I'm a solicitor, not a barrister," Damien protested, but he had a dozen questions he wanted to ask, and Hunt was offering an opportunity.

"That's fine. This isn't a real trial. You don't have to wear a wig." Hunt stalked down the middle of the room to the makeshift podium.

Weston followed on Hunt's heels, and Damien reluctantly took up the reins Hunt had dropped into his hands. "Weston, did your fellows drag Zeb Johnson in?"

"Most of his camp folded and moved into a barn. He's still looking for a pulpit, though. Didn't take much persuasion to lead him here." The earl saw the duke and strayed off to stand guard over his father.

"I won't call the women," Damien warned Hunt as he reached the front. Kate had been through enough. No one needed to know her secret. "But if any of them want to speak, will you allow it?"

Hunt all but cackled. "Allow? Do you think I could stop them? Stay in Gravesyde. Learn how women *really* think." Hunt diverted from his path to consult with his steward, who sat at a desk with pen and paper, apparently prepared to write down testimony.

Leaving Damien looking for Brydie. He needed a future. She deserved a better one. He couldn't imagine how it would all work out, but he had a notion that she was his lodestone. No matter where he wandered, he would always return here, to her.

Entering through the double doorway, Zeb Johnson created a stir by flinging back his cloak to reveal his all-black attire—a gloomy thundercloud on a clear day. Brydie's lips quirked in amusement at the preacher's drama—which set off Damien's sense of mischief.

When he'd left Gravesyde, he'd abandoned his boyhood. He'd taken law and business seriously and had no time for play. If he was considering staying in Gravesyde—*was he?*—could he find the boy he'd once been? Could he keep his temper reined in and start over?

If he followed his impulse—all Hunt could do was take away his new title of prosecutor. Damien grinned. He may as well start the way he hoped to continue. To survive, he'd had to be polite, but now he had the means to more than survive. He wanted to find his childhood audacity and possibly expand it to outrageous.

Damien approached Johnson, who loomed over the audience like a six-foot specter of death. "The magistrate has asked me to act as prosecutor. I am inclined to separate the prisoners and force them to give their stories without consulting one another. They might cooperate more if you stood as their defense."

Johnson looked incredulous. "Me? You are allowing *me* to stand before a duke and earl and a courtroom full of. . ." He sneered at the gossiping gentry filling the chamber. "My congregation should be here."

"Well, I asked." Damien turned to walk away.

Johnson grabbed his shoulder. "If you're prosecuting the death of your mother, you are scarcely impartial."

"If you are looking for who shot at you, neither are you. And Weston is convinced you pushed him into the river. He wants your head." Damien shook off the Grim Reaper's bony hold.

"And you don't?" Johnson' glare was as black as his eyes.

"My mother didn't tolerate fools. She wouldn't have followed you if she thought you were a killer." That was an utterly inane thing to say, given that she was capable of murder. But, if it took one to know one, as the adage went, she would have known if Johnson had murderous tendencies. Or a dangerous temper.

The preacher looked startled at Damien's assessment—probably because he'd never thought twice about a woman's opinion. . .

Which was how his mother had hidden her stolen wealth for so long, Damien realized. Johnson would never have understood her brilliant investments—just as his father probably hadn't. Those certificates represented some of the best investments money could buy, which led Damien to a new set of questions and conclusions as he approached Hunt with his request to keep the prisoners separated.

Hunt studied the motley trio Rafe had chained in different corners of the medieval hall. "We always keep them in separate areas, although, at this rate, I'll have to start building walls in the crypt to create cells. Who do you want to see first? I'll send the others out."

"Tom Butler." He'd had to explain the skeleton in the woodpile to Hunt, as magistrate. He'd warned him that his mother had probably killed his father. He hadn't explained why. "I know he helped my mother escape. He's been protecting her. Let's test his honesty."

"Rafe says he's been to prison for theft. You don't see him as a killer?" Hunt frowned.

"I'll keep an open mind. Enjoy the show. I've set Johnson up as defense." Damien walked away before Hunt could heave him out for his temerity.

Rafe had no difficulty hauling Terwilliger and Evans away. Praying his memory of his mother wasn't corrupted by sentiment, Damien called Tom Butler to the front.

"I didn't do anything," Butler asserted before the first question was asked.

"You helped a killer escape and *buried the evidence*." Cold logic appealed more than beating the man into pulp. For now.

Once he registered that Damien spoke of the past, not the present, Butler seemed to melt inside his coat. His half-blind sister, wearing her Sunday best, stood and shouted, "He didn't do anything! Tom is a good man."

Brydie pulled her down to her seat and shot Damien a speaking look.

He practically read her mind, that's how well he knew her, even after all these years. Women had no place in court, but he nodded agreement. The sister needed questioning. Butler first.

"A good man helps the woman he loves." Damien waited for a reaction.

Shabbier than ever after a night in the crypt, the portly older man had lost a lot of hair. He was no longer the scary figure of his youth.

"Your mother was a good woman. Not a saint. She did what she had to do." Butler glanced at his sister before continuing. "True, I helped her. She was a hard woman to love, but she took care of us in the only way she knew how."

Out of his element, without knowledge of Damien's parents, Johnson merely frowned in confusion.

"A good woman, but a hard one, who held her funds in an iron fist?" Damien suggested.

"She didn't have all that much, and what she had was hers. I helped her find someone to sell her bits of paper. Terwilliger introduced us to Mr. Johnson, and she liked what he had to say. I had to keep her safe somehow, so it made sense to join up with him. Every oncet in a while, she'd sell another bit of paper to help with renting fields or buying food. It wasn't what she was used to, but she didn't complain. There warn't no reason for anyone to shoot her, I tell ya. You got that all wrong. It's Mr. Johnson what they're arfter."

Damien turned to Zeb Johnson, who simply spread his big hands in agreement.

This would go much faster if he could prove Johnson shot his mother, but Dr. Walker had confirmed that the shot hadn't been close range. Besides, no one had found a pistol on Johnson—and they'd found that fancy rifle on the hill.

And if Butler really believed the avaricious woman he lived with had only a few funds. . . The man had to be blind, deaf, and stupid.

"On the day of the shooting, you were seen walking away from your wife. A rifle was later found in that direction. Are you saying that weapon wasn't yours? That you did not kill Margaret Sutter Butler to keep her from revealing what was hidden under the woodpile?"

Damien hadn't wanted to mention the woodpile, but if there was ever a motive for Butler to kill, his mother waving at Damien should have been it. Guilty consciences made men do dangerously stupid things.

The sister stood and shouted before Johnson or Butler could speak. "Tommy can't shoot worth spit. He can't see much better than me!"

Ah, literally blind, not just stupid.

"And those papers belong to Tommy now! He's her husband. I know our rights!"

Pity little sister was also blind or he'd look at her as a suspect. Damien turned to the stunned preacher. "Shall we let Miss Butler lead in her brother's defense? I don't suppose you want to explain to her that you're not an ordained minister and your ceremonies are not legal in a court of law?" He was starting to enjoy himself.

Flustered, Johnson gestured helplessly.

Damien turned back to the audience. "Miss Butler, would you like to take the stand?"

THIRTY

BRYDIE

THE ALMOST ALL FEMALE AUDIENCE GASPED AT DAMIEN'S AUDACIOUS suggestion that a *woman* testify. In his judge's chair, one-eyed Captain Huntley merely sat with his boot propped on a low table. Brydie thought he might be hiding a smirk.

She'd been shocked to realize the familiar man who'd visited Terwilliger was Tom Butler. She remembered him as a lean man with dangerous eyes, but she'd only been fifteen at the time, and she hadn't seen him more than once or twice working in the Sutter's stable. Now that Brydie recognized this graying, portly old man as Miss Butler's brother. . . It was all quite confusing.

Miss Butler sank back in her chair, daunted by Damien's request that she stand as witness in front of an audience of all her new neighbors.

Clare Huntley leaned over and whispered to Brydie, "Give her a shove. Gravesyde can set a precedent—women allowed to testify!"

Brydie didn't need more encouragement. She clasped Miss Butler's arm. "I'll take you up there. Your brother needs a witness on his behalf." She left no room for argument but tugged the reluctant witness to her feet.

Damien gallantly produced a chair for the frightened spinster to sit on. "Thank you, Miss Butler. Mr. Johnson, perhaps you'd like to question the witness? As you have remarked, I cannot be fair in asking if my mother was a good woman who didn't deserve to die."

Captain Huntley covered his mouth as if yawning, but Brydie was fairly certain he hid a grin at this very leading question. *Damien* was directing the trial, and possibly its outcome, and not a man objected, including the duke and earl. Only a proper assize court could decide a man's guilt. They probably viewed the whole ordeal as entertainment, which it was, even if lives might depend on the outcome.

Miss Butler robbed Zeb Johnson of any chance to preach by speaking directly to Damien, uncowed by his tailored elegance or polished speech.

"Like you said, your mother was a hard woman with an iron fist but she didn't deserve to die! Men fritter funds on fancy notions about souls and voting, leaving women to figure out how to feed hungry bodies. After her husband died and she married Tom, Meg told us she had property where we could settle for free, but Tom and Mr. Johnson would have none of it. Mr. Terwilliger now, he understood and argued that we could grow our own food and save our money for good causes."

Returning to her seat, Brydie listened in fascination.

"Your brother didn't want to return his wife to Gravesyde and I followed his wishes," the preacher protested, turning to the suspect. "Why wouldn't you let your wife come home?"

"Because she were my wife and I had to take care of her! Wasn't good for her to come back here. You saw what happened when we did. And now I'm up here being blamed for taking care of her! By my own sister!" Butler was obviously incensed.

"Might I suggest it wasn't good for *you* to return, Mr. Butler?" Damien asked.

"She didn't know." Bunching his fingers into fists, Butler responded belligerently, if not coherently.

Mrs. Sutter hadn't known she'd killed her husband? Brydie's eyes widened.

"Meg thought the neighbors kilt him and that's why he didn't come arfter us. I knew better. I was just protecting her."

Zeb Johnson was rightfully lost, as was most of the audience, but Brydie understood. Meg Sutter had knocked her husband unconscious, gathered her things, and run away, expecting Kate to tell her father about the rape and that charges would be filed, at the very least. Mrs. Sutter had fled to avoid humiliation—and her husband's rage. Butler had known differently.

Apparently also ignorant of what he spoke, Miss Butler stuck to her position. "Tommy took care of Meg. She wouldn't let him know nothing about her coin, but I knew. I heard her and that Terwilliger talking. They were hiding a fortune from us. And once her last husband was declared dead, she wanted to go home, so they were conspiring. It's time we got the money." She stood.

Johnson pointed her back to her seat. "What fortune? What the blazes are you talking about? Terwilliger and Mrs. Butler found us funds when we needed them and shared generously. There was nothing to hide."

"No, they didn't share," Miss Butler said in scorn. "They hoarded. They was playing with what they called *markets*. It's like gambling. Sometimes, they lost. They didn't want you to know but I overheard. Everyone thinks I'm deaf as well as blind."

Brydie wouldn't make that mistake, not after this.

Johnson's expression veered between confusion and apoplexy. Before he could speak, Damien returned to his interrogation. "So, Mr. Terwilliger was aware that Mrs. Butler concealed a fortune? Did he share that knowledge with anyone else, investors like Mr. Evans?"

Johnson objected. "You are treating this as if your mother was the intended victim, when we all know Weston wants me dead. Shouldn't we be looking for who he paid to do his dirty work instead of beleaguering honest men who did no more than support our righteous cause against the oppressors?"

Damien turned back to Butler. "Tom, did any of your men have extra funds recently? Ride off, never to be seen again?"

Butler shrugged his rounded shoulders. "Not that I know. They all got women and children starving out in that field."

Brydie realized how slow she'd been to grasp what Damien saw. Huddling in her shawl, she curled her fingers inside her gloves—the towering room was freezing—and waited.

Damien returned to the self-centered preacher. "*You* didn't have anything worth killing over. Weston scarcely knows you exist as more than an annoying fly. My *mother* was the one hiding a fortune, for which men might murder. Can you verify that Mr. and Miss Butler lack the eyesight to shoot from a distance, since they thought themselves likely to benefit from her death?"

"She's nearly blind. He can't see to write." Johnson pursed his mouth as if he'd swallowed a pickle. "Although, if the Butlers were shooting at *me*, that might explain how I survived."

"We can't solve a mystery with a closed mind, sir." Damien reprimanded him curtly. "Open yours to see beyond yourself."

"Call Weston up and let me interrogate him," Johnson countered. "We'll see whose mind is closed."

Damien faced the audience. "Weston, where were you the day Meg Sutter Butler died?"

"Fishing," the earl replied, lounging in a chair beside the duke. "With half of the wedding guests. If I wanted someone dead, they'd be dead. Ask anyone. I'm an excellent marksman."

"He hired someone—" Johnson started to protest.

Damien faced Butler. "Were there any strangers about that day?"

Butler shook his head. "Just us'ns. I walked up the grounds and only saw men I know. We was roasting mutton and Terwilliger was there for that, but he's the only one don't camp with us."

"Miss Butler?" Damien turned to his witness.

"No strangers that I noticed," she admitted, chin held high. "That doesn't mean one of our own people wasn't playing with a shotgun."

Brydie admired her courage. Like a hound on a trail, Damien intimidated with his piercing questions and refusal to be diverted., but Miss Butler held her head high.

"Or a stranger hiding in the shrubbery," Johnson argued. "It's not as if the Butlers could see everyone! Someone fired shots at me earlier. Ask about then."

"We'll call witnesses from your camp if it becomes necessary," Damien offered. "Let's see where my line of questioning goes."

Damien sent Miss Butler back to her seat and returned to questioning her brother. Brydie now realized that instead of a scheming villain, Tom Butler was merely an uneducated man who had fallen on hard times, as everyone in the village had. But in times of trouble, he'd done what was best to protect the woman he respected and possibly loved, right or wrong. He'd struggled to take care of her and his sister in the only manner available to his limited abilities. He'd actually done an excellent job under the circumstances. They hadn't been homeless or hungry. Well, part of that was Damien's mother.

She regarded the stout old farmer with a little less suspicion.

Damien returned to his interrogation. "You were visiting Mr. Terwilliger at the inn yesterday, were you not?"

Brydie winced. So much for hoping Butler hadn't consorted with a kidnapper.

Butler rubbed his receding hairline in resignation. "Aye, I was. He'd got some bee in his bonnet about us staying on your farm and investing in a shoe factory with that city fellow. I hadn't heard about you finding them bones or I'd have left sooner. I went to the inn to talk Terwilliger out of it."

Whispers circulated after mention of the bones. Rumors had been flying, but so far Damien had kept Kate out of it. Let them believe Mrs. Sutter had killed her husband in a fit of rage. It was the truth.

"You argued?" Damien prompted, while the preacher gave up and listened in puzzlement.

"Aye. Terwilliger claimed he had Meg's money and I could make a good profit on the investment." Butler shook his head in disbelief. "I told the old scoundrel any money belonged to her son, not me. I'm no thief and I'm not entirely stupid. I'm not going back to prison."

Brydie wanted to stand up and cheer. Instead, she patted Miss Butler's shoulder and whispered, "Your brother is a very good man."

Miss Butler nodded curtly. Even though she frowned, she emanated pride and resignation in the way she faced forward, chin up.

"Terwilliger wanted to invest in a *shoemaker*?" Johnson asked, still obviously lost. "He didn't consider that Meg would want *us* to have the funds?"

"He's a money man," Butler retorted. "O'course he don't give to charity. You wouldn't listen when he told you how to raise funds from those what ain't got it, so he was only about when you collected blunt from your rich friends. Otherwise, he only came around 'cause of Meg."

Damien regained the floor before a quarrel could ensue. "So, you argued with Terwilliger. What happened then?"

Butler shrugged his sagging shoulders. "He said he was leaving. He'd dragged Meg's trunk into the hall, claimed you didn't want it, so he was using it for his books and things. I helped him carry it to the carriage and hoped I'd seen the end of him. The trunk wasn't worth nothing even if he was stealing it. It was worth seeing the back of him."

"He lied about stealing the trunk, but you are correct, the trunk itself had no worth." Damien bowed politely at his witness, then turned to Johnson. "Do you have questions?"

"Other than why the hell I'm up here?" Johnson practically

snarled. "You tell me I'm useless rubbish, that a woman was worth more than me, that my right-hand man is reasonably honest but blind and stupid, and the financier I trusted with our futures is a liar, and I'm supposed to question your evidently superior experience with immoral scoundrels?"

Damien shrugged. "I do not wish to be called one of your oppressors because you're too ignorant and self-absorbed to notice the people around you. The men you call oppressors gained their wealth and power—or hold it—by observation and paying attention to details, then using what they learn. Yes, they may start with multiple advantages, but the rich are just as capable of profligately wasting their assets as the poor. The ones you despise use what they were given to their advantage."

And not to the advantage of others, Brydie thought, but Johnson said it for her.

"And make themselves rich and more powerful instead of helping others," Johnson retorted. "The Bible tells us that *it is easier for a camel to go through the eye of a needle than for a rich person to enter the kingdom of God.*"

Damien shrugged again. "I daresay I agree, but I'm not in charge of the world. I'm simply saying you are as much at fault for what happens under your nose as any perceived oppressors. In your self-absorption, you never asked how a woman came into funds. You never asked Butler why he didn't wish to take advantage of free land. You never questioned Terwilliger's presence. You just assumed everyone was there just for *you.*"

Johnson's pale face reddened in outrage, but he had the sense to hold his tongue.

Damien turned to face Hunt. "And my own error in judgment should be brought forward next. If Mr. Butler agrees to remain silent, may he stay while Mr. Evans testifies?" Unlike the preacher, Damien appeared unfazed by his admission that he'd been wrong about his business associate.

Humility looked good on him—but his avenging warrior stance as he waited for Evans to be led in seemed more natural.

211

Damien had never been one to back down from a fight, even with his larger brother. If Evans had killed Damien's mother—or tried to kill Weston—

Brydie hoped Damien wasn't carrying a weapon. He did have a temper.

THIRTY-ONE

RAFE

RAFE WAS INCLINED TO LOCK UP SNEAKY, LYING BUTLER SIMPLY FOR burying a body and concealing murder. But he knew more about innkeeping than the law and bowed to greater knowledge over the prisoner's disposition.

He supposed if he were more forgiving, he might conclude Butler had thought he was rescuing a lady. Men shouldn't be hung for stupidity.

At Damien's request that Butler stay in the great hall, Rafe stationed two of Hunt's ex-soldiers, swords at their sides, next to the prisoner's chair in a distant corner from the witness stand. Accusations of murder did not bring out the best in men, and this day was long from over.

He glanced sympathetically at tomorrow's bride. Her groom was building a coffin for still another funeral, presumably on her wedding day. Modest Miss Peniston appeared resigned and did her duty comforting the distressed Miss Butler. Fortunately, none of Johnson's followers had chosen to attend, except for Butler's sister, who worked for the inn now and had apparently decided to join the community.

Rafe had been having second thoughts about opening the inn before it was ready, but now he was starting to enjoy being recognized as a part of the village. The army had given him an appreciation for the camaraderie and respect of his fellows.

Despite his night in a prison cell, Evans, Damien's former business partner, adopted an arrogant stance when Rafe retrieved him from the study. The former factory owner straightened his wrinkled frockcoat, brushed off his once-fine trousers, and ran his fingers through his gray hair to tidy it. He couldn't conceal the red puffiness of his eyes or his wince at the loud voices emanating from the hall.

Still, he held himself like a statesman as he entered the intimidating great hall. Rafe couldn't help but admire his temerity. Evans only wilted a little and rubbed his probably aching head when confronted by the sight of wide-shouldered Damien in tailored clothes and immaculate linen dominating the front of the room.

"I didn't do anything wrong," Evans declared, before Rafe shoved him into the witness chair.

"You stole my deeds and the list of my mother's investments," Damien countered. "You broke into my house and ransacked it looking for investment certificates. Tell me how that wasn't wrong?"

Rafe hovered behind the businessman. It was rich city men like Evans who had arranged to divert the highway away from his father's inn so they could develop their own properties. His hardworking father had lost everything, while his wealthy neighbors had become wealthier, as they always did. The preacher's argument that men grew richer by taking advantage of others rang true. Rafe had been resentful as a lad, but war and marriage had mellowed him. The wealthy didn't live happier lives for their gold. They just ate better and died like everyone else. And had hangovers.

With age, Rafe had learned that what a person did was what mattered. Making the world better left a mark, not funds stashed in a bank, doing nothing more than accumulating numbers on paper. Since he figured he'd never have enough funds to prove his theory, he could live with using his few coins and his brawn to improve what was around him. It made him happy. The once-wealthy businessman didn't look real happy.

Evans responded to Damien's question with irritability. "You told me we'd be partners, that I could turn your unused property into a manufactory that would someday replace the one the army shut down. I could employ some of my former workers and pull myself out of debt. Then you took it all away! What was I supposed to do, beg in the streets?"

A new manufactory sounded good to Rafe, better than stashing cash. He knew a lot of fellows with nowhere to go now that the war was over.

But Preacher Johnson crossed his arms and glared. "He's one of the war-mongering oppressors who made fortunes off the backs of ill-treated factory workers. Must I defend him?"

Damien turned his palm up. "Give it a try, practice looking at the world from his perspective. I am definitely prejudiced." He glanced up at Hunt. "Would you like to interrogate the prisoner?"

"Let's hear the facts first," Hunt suggested. "Rafe, what can you tell us of Mr. Evans?"

Him? Rafe refrained from snorting at a rough man like him standing up in front of nobles and being heard. But like any good sergeant, he gathered his thoughts and spoke with care. "Damien Sutter arrived Monday around noon, said he was here on business, and offered good coin to open up rooms for him and his valet, said his valet would take care of him since I didn't have staff. Mr. Evans arrived after dark, offered gold, and said Mr. Sutter's valet would suit him fine. Mr. Johnson gave one of his speeches that night. Mr. Evans wondered if their business plans had been discovered and if Johnson was speaking against the factory. He and Mr. Sutter discussed it but decided there wasn't no reason for concern."

Johnson propped his hip on Hunt's table without speaking. Damien nodded, so Rafe figured he was doing all right.

"Next day, Tuesday, Mr. Johnson claimed the earl shot at him, so I had to look into that. I couldn't find no evidence, and since Mr. Evans and Mr. Sutter were outside the inn where they could see anyone riding by, I asked if anyone rode out. They hadn't seen no one, and they took off to look at property. When they returned, they said there'd been intruders at the shoe shop, but they didn't seem to expect me to do anything. They asked for a room to go over papers. I left them in the library. As far as I'm aware, Mr. Evans was still working on those papers when Mr. Sutter rode off with Brydie Calhoun to visit Johnson, where he saw his mother shot." Rafe wrinkled up his brow attempting to remember the hectic events.

"Mr. Evans stayed at the inn during the shooting incident?" Hunt asked.

Rafe shrugged. "As far as I know. He didn't call for his horse while I was there, but he could have walked off, and I'd not know otherwise. The inn has several exits and I'm not always about."

Hunt nodded. "Understood. Go ahead."

Rafe reorganized his thoughts to who was where and when. "When Mr. Sutter returned from seeing to his mother late Tuesday evening, Evans was working in the library because they called for tea and writing paper. Wednesday, I was busy looking into Mrs. Sutter's death and didn't pay him no mind, although I think they took more writing paper that morning. My staff took up tea. And then later in the day, the earl got shoved in the river. As far as I recollect, Evans didn't join the search party. I don't remember seeing him all afternoon or evening. My wife reported that after the earl was found and Mr. Sutter returned to his room, there was an altercation between the gentlemen." He glanced at Damien.

Damien grimaced. "We argued over my mother's papers. Evans thought I was wealthy after my mother's death and that I could afford to finance the shop entirely. I told him I had nothing but the land and expected him to pay his fair share. He'd been drinking, and it became apparent he didn't have the funds he'd told me he could summon. I won't deal with drunks. We argued. He stormed out."

Rafe nodded. "Evans' horse was gone Wednesday night. He didn't attend the funeral of Mrs. Sutter on Thursday, but after the funeral, Mr. Sutter got hit on the head and had his keys stolen. Thursday night, while I was out at the camp questioning folk, the Morgan lad came riding in to say the Sutter's farm was being robbed. Mr. Sutter rode out with the lad, and they caught Evans ransacking the property. He's been locked up since then."

"So, it is not impossible that Mr. Evans could have shot Mrs. Sutter *and* pushed the earl in the river?" Hunt asked.

"*What?*" Evans shot up from the witness chair. "What do you think I am? All I want to do is start a boot factory. I'm a successful businessman. Why the devil would I kill a woman and an earl I never met?"

The preacher actually beamed, an evil beam, perhaps, but definitely a different expression than his usual morose one. "You hoped Mr. Sutter's mother would leave him the property free and clear and perhaps leave him funds to finance your factory! And you knew the earl was offering for the property, and you wanted him out of the way."

The great hall broke out in excited chatter.

"You're supposed to be defense, not prosecution," Damien said in exasperation as the audience grew louder.

Rafe rolled his eyes and roared, "Enough! We're not hanging anyone 'cause they mighta, coulda done. Anyone got proof that Evans went anywhere either of those days? Because his nag stayed right there in the stable until late Wednesday evening."

"The river is walking distance," Johnson helpfully pointed out, undeterred by his presumed position of defense. "Your stable houses many horses. He could have borrowed one. And you said yourself, you weren't there most of the time. Evans could have ridden off and back and you'd not have known."

And the rifle they'd found could only belong to someone who

had funds and access to the latest weaponry. Having worked for the military, that would be Evans. Rafe still thought the notion far-fetched.

Even the earl and duke frowned, until Damien stepped into the fray. "Evans, tell them what you were doing Tuesday afternoon when my mother died and Wednesday afternoon when the Earl of Weston was shoved into the river."

The businessman sank back into his chair and rubbed his stubbled jaw as if in pain. "I lost *everything* when the boot factory went under. I'm in debt to men who are bleeding me dry. My family left me. This opportunity was my only hope."

"And you thought I was green enough to let you bleed me dry in return?" Damien asked in derision.

"I wasn't thinking about anything except getting on my feet again." Unable to face anyone, Evans studied his polished boots. "While you were off visiting the camp, I found your father's deeds and some of your papers and copied your signature. I thought with the deeds in hand, I could talk someone into loaning me the funds I needed to start up again. I rode back to Stratford Wednesday night and spent Thursday going from bank to investors, looking for funds. Without numbers to prove I could be successful, I was refused. So, I risked my life riding back that same evening, in the dark, to go over the books I'd seen in the shoe shop office, hoping to put together a list of buyers and suppliers and manufacture some financial papers."

Rafe glanced up at the captain. "We can verify that with the bank, can't we?"

Hunt nodded and waited for Damien to take up the reins again. Johnson just slumped against the table, unable to attack a man who had few morals but no apparent connection to anyone but Damien.

Damien glanced to the audience. "Weston, did Evans at any time attempt to ask you about investing in his factory?"

The earl didn't bother standing. He just bowed his noble head of thick dark hair in acknowledgment of the question. "I had our steward make inquiries about your property and make an offer. Evans became aware of it and wrote to him. Our financial man discouraged us from investing in a bankrupt who wanted to run a boot factory."

Damien winced but didn't question further. Rafe was beginning to see that owning property and possessing funds meant toying with the lives of others, whether or not one intended the consequences. The path to riches required one to develop a thick skin and a hard heart. He was almost glad he had nothing.

Damien paced up and down, obviously unhappy. "At his own admission, we have Mr. Evans for drunkenness, theft, forgery, assault, and potential fraud, but he had no motive for murder. I'd advise holding him until all matters are resolved, but you're the magistrate."

"Would pummeling Evans for hitting you over the head suffice as punishment?" Hunt asked in amusement.

Damien eagerly looked up, then glanced back at the women in the audience, and shook his head. "As much as I'd like to plant him a facer, laying him flat won't teach him anything. He did no more than muddy waters."

"Just displayed his selfish wickedness," Johnson said bitterly. "This is how rich people advance, not any noble use of their brilliant abilities."

Deciding if everyone was allowed to speak, he could, Rafe took Evans's arm to lead him away. "I've seen half the world," he told the preacher. "The rich don't have a corner on selfishness and evildoing. People are people, no matter what clothes they wear. They come in good and bad and everything in between."

What mattered most to Rafe was his wife's eyes gleaming proudly as he led the prisoner away. Verity was a learned lady who had suffered at the hands of a real villain. She knew right from wrong. If she approved of what he said, then he wasn't doing too badly.

Evans yanked his arm free and eyed the door—but the captain's large cousins blocked the exit. The prisoner wilted into the corner Rafe shoved him into. Rafe left Fletch, his brawny silent partner, guarding him. The war had left his friend with wounds no one could see. Fletch's massive fists would floor Evans without compunction.

The skinny preying mantis of a financier was next. Maybe they ought to let Brydie interrogate the insect. Obviously realizing who came next, she glowered as if she'd eat the man alive.

THIRTY-TWO

BRYDIE

LADY ELSA, THE MANOR'S COOK, ARRIVED WITH SERVANTS TO DELIVER trays of crumpets and tea, offering a break to the tense morning. To Brydie's surprise, Kate and Lynly entered, followed by Jacques. Eyes wide at the spectacle of the great hall, the valet positioned himself in the draperies where he wouldn't easily be noticed. Kate and Lynly took a sofa and Brydie joined them.

"Why are you here?" she whispered, ignoring the tea to take her niece on her lap and hug her. "It's Saturday. I thought you'd be at home with the boys."

"Arthur is helping the curate finish the coffin, and Rob is in the schoolroom, working on some project with Mr. Birdwhistle. Lynly is feeling much better, and we wanted to see what happens with Mr. Terwilliger. Jacques didn't know if he'd have to testify, and he was wearing himself out pacing, so we asked him to come along as our escort. Can Terwilliger be sent to assizes for a failed kidnapping?" Kate anxiously watched the gentlemen gathering around Hunt.

"He didn't exactly fail. He stole the trunk with Lynly in it and knew it." Brydie handed her niece a biscuit from one of the trays being passed around. "And he stole valuable certificates. Hunt will have to send him to assizes and let the judges decide. The problem is that we don't have any evidence to tie any of the prisoners to *murder*. Damien is vexed."

"He's looking a little worn. This has to be hard on him. You mean Mr. Butler didn't kill Mrs. Sutter?" Kate asked.

Kate had always been fond of the Sutter brothers. Did her comment indicate she was seeing Damien anew? Now that they all understood about Arthur, perhaps there was hope Damien might stay? Kate was sturdy and stubborn enough to survive on her own, but she had children. She really needed a man's support to keep a roof over her family's heads, and the children needed a father.

Brydie would simply have to move to the inn if they married.

She redirected her thoughts to the front. "Unless Damien can prove everyone is lying about Butler's eyesight, and maybe come up with witnesses saying he carried a fancy rifle, I'm afraid we'll never know what happened to Mrs. Sutter."

Brydie feared a tired Damien would eventually give in to his temper, but she was thoroughly impressed by his ability to winkle information out of the culprits in an orderly fashion. "And they really haven't even started on who would want to push the earl into the river. This could be a long day."

"We'll just stay to see about Terwilliger," Kate assured her.

"I want the quilt back," Lynly protested. "Can't Mr. Sutter let me have the quilt?"

Brydie hid a smile as her sister tried to hush her. Kate didn't understand why her daughter was so insistent on the quilts. They'd have to rescue them from Damien after Jacques opened all the blocks. The quilts contained finer fabric than any in their basket. They just needed washing.

The audience settled down after Lady Elsa and the servants swept out with the trays and Rafe returned with the last prisoner.

Lynly cowered in Brydie's arms as Rafe and the Comte Arnaud Lavigne, Hunt's artist cousin, marched the financier to the front of the great hall. Graying hair, gray coat, unshaven gray stubble, too scrawny to fight, Terwilliger didn't appear dangerous. That Rafe had found it necessary to ask the count, instead of a servant, to help with an old man must mean the prisoner had tried to escape. Running away did seem to be his habit.

"Since you are familiar with the suspect, perhaps you would like to question Mr. Terwilliger first, Mr. Johnson?" Damien suggested courteously, leaning against the table as the preacher had done earlier.

"About what?" Johnson didn't appear to be happy with his place in the court. "I have no notion of his misdeeds. He dealt with Mrs. Butler. She understood filthy lucre better than I ever did."

Brydie really thought the preacher made the best suspect. Was Damien trying to lead him into admitting guilt—at least in the attempt on the earl's life?

Damien shrugged and straightened up. "Mr. Harlan Terwilliger of Birmingham?"

"Aye," the older man answered in suspicion.

"And you make your living doing what?"

"Helping gentlefolk to invest their earnings for a better future," he said promptly.

"And in what ways do you help them to invest?" Damien asked in boredom.

A deceptively bored Damien was a dangerous one, Brydie knew. She hugged Lynly and set her back on the cushions between them as a precaution. Kate would protect her youngest. Brydie was as large as half the men in here, and with her hands free, she could guard her family.

"I help people buy into prosperous companies that pay them dividends while the value of their investment increases. What does it matter what I do?" Terwilliger's gnarled fingers rubbed at the arm of the chair he'd been placed in.

"I'm asking the questions, sir. You are saying that you'll take money from the likes of Johnson here, or Mrs. Sutter Butler, and give them pieces of paper in return?"

"Those certificates are *receipts*. All their shares are properly recorded with the company, their bank, and in my broker's books. There isn't anyone can say I've ever turned a dishonest dime!"

The preacher frowned but obviously had no more understanding than Brydie. Why wasn't Damien questioning the insect about Lynly's kidnapping and the theft of the quilts? Jacques was right over there. Shouldn't Damien be calling witnesses to name Terwilliger as the guilty party? She waited for enlightenment.

Damien paced a few steps back and forth as he formed his questions. "No one is questioning your honesty. I simply wish the court to understand your business. Let us say Mrs. Sutter came to you with those receipts, as you call them, and asked you to sell them. Could you do that?"

"Of course, it's a commonplace transaction. I write to the company and the bank holding their books, and we consult the brokerage for the current market rate, and the bank issues a note for the value, all proper and aboveboard, I assure you."

The ladies in the audience rustled restlessly, leaning over to whisper among themselves. They'd all thought this case would be a quick one. Everyone knew he'd kidnapped Lynly and stolen the certificates, after all.

"And you earn your money by taking a percentage of those sales and purchases, correct?" Damien returned to leaning against the table, arms crossed, staring absently over the audience.

Where was he going with this? Was attempted kidnapping and attempted theft not enough to convict the prisoner? Brydie gnawed at a fingernail, knowing Damien must have something in mind.

"People pay for my knowledge, otherwise they wouldn't have no idea how these things work. Noblemen and bankers are my clients. I'm well respected in the business. Mrs. Sutter was right to come to me to sell off some of her investments when she needed funds."

Having never had money to invest, Brydie had little compre-
hension, but it seemed to her it would be easier to go to the bank
or company directly. She was obviously naïve.

Of course. . . Banks didn't like to do business with women. But
Terwilliger would? Now Brydie caught a glimpse of where this
was headed—Damien wasn't just seeking Lynly's kidnapper.

"But Mrs. Sutter didn't just sell old investments, did she?
We've heard testimony that she bought new ones as well. Were
they doing well?" Damien feigned interest in the reply. Brydie
could see his knuckles whitening. He couldn't beat up an old man
physically, but the university had apparently taught him verbal
means.

"They were, they were," Terwilliger said nervously. "She had a
sharp mind about her. Always a pleasure working with her."

"And she kept those certificates, didn't place them in bank
boxes or anything?"

The brooding preacher narrowed his black eyes at this question but stayed silent.

The financier nervously bobbed his balding head. "I had no
notion what she did with the paper. Most people leave them with
us or a solicitor or the bank and just collect their dividends, but
she always had the certificates for the ones she wanted to sell on
hand, and I gave her the ones she bought, plus banknotes for her
dividends, all legal. She didn't much trust anyone, including
banks."

"If I take those certificates to a bank or brokerage, will they
give me full value?"

Brydie bit back a gasp. He thought his inheritance was
fraudulent?

"If they're the ones I gave her, most certainly. What are you
insinuating, lad? I am an honest man." The financier attempted to
look indignant.

"An honest man does not steal certificates and kidnap little
girls," Damien replied scornfully. "At what point did my mother
decide you weren't as honest as she believed?"

Terwilliger pushed out of his chair, red-faced. "That's not true! She never said a word against me, never!"

The audience gasped. Brydie clenched her fists in preparation for anything.

Despite his red hair, Rafe had no temper. At twice the old man's size, he easily returned the prisoner to his chair. "One more outburst, and I'll tie you down."

An audible sigh of relief swept the room.

"Perhaps Mrs. Butler asked you to sell some of her investments so she could move back home?" Damien suggested, taking a new line of questioning, although Brydie couldn't see where this one led.

Miss Butler, however, made a muffled noise. The half-blind spinster *heard* things. Brydie leaned over her chair back and whispered, "Is there something you should tell them?"

Bespectacled, faded, and wrinkled with hardship, the prim maid wrung her hands and shook her head. "It's not mine to say. I don't know if I should. . ."

Wanting Terwilliger locked up, Brydie didn't hesitate. She rose and instantly drew Damien's attention. Another time, she'd be flattered that he noticed. For now, she wanted justice. "Miss Butler heard almost everything that happened in that caravan. Perhaps you should call on her again?"

Damien's eyes had darkened to angry green, but he turned to the older woman and bowed respectfully. "If you would be more comfortable remaining where you are, Miss Butler, could you add anything to our knowledge?"

She rubbed her gloved hands in her skirt, wrinkling it, then hesitantly stood. "Meg cried a lot after she heard of her son's death. She wanted to go home, so Tom brought her here, told her there wasn't nothin' here. But when we got here, she still insisted she wanted to go home, to see her younger son. She and Tom had a row. She wasn't always reasonable when in a snit. Mr. Terwilliger was there, and she brangled with him, too, ordering him to sell some stocks. He told her prices were down, that she shouldn't sell any, that she didn't need funds if she owned the land. She said it was her money, and she wanted to fix things right with her only son, that he'd handle her investments if Mr. Terwilliger wouldn't."

Brydie bit back a gasp. A whisper of speculation floated around the room. Damien looked pained. She wished she could hug him, help him understand that just because his mother suddenly felt guilty about abandoning him, none of this was his fault. . .

Meg had a temper—as did Damien. Brydie watched him almost visibly close up. He'd learned to control his anger, not necessarily for the good if it created a powder keg. She studied him warily for signs of explosion.

"This was when, ma'am?" Damien asked tightly but keeping his voice calm.

"The day she died," Miss Butler whispered, barely loud enough to be heard.

Damien turned to Johnson. "I don't suppose you'd like to step in now? My mother was one of your flock and proposing to take her money and run. What havoc did that create?"

"I knew *nothing* of her funds. If you think I killed her to prevent her leaving, I will warn you that I have friends in high places who will vouch for me." Johnson glared.

"I have friends as well." Damien said wearily, gesturing toward the duke and earl. "All I want is truth. Do you have a better way of learning it?"

Johnson glowered. "You just want me to testify. Very well then. I did not oppose Mrs. Butler returning home and taking people with her. I heeded Tom's objections, no more. Out of respect for the lady, I even went against those objections after her death, because I had been told we had funds to do so."

Johnson turned to Miss Butler. "Did Mrs. Sutter Butler agree to sell her stock after all the argufying?"

"Not that I know. The tempest died, like it always did, and she let Mr. Terwilliger talk her into waiting until she returned to her old home and saw what she needed. She was packing to leave. That's all I know. All was quiet when I left to help with the cooking." The maid abruptly sat down.

Johnson turned his glare on Terwilliger. "You told me it was imperative that we keep Mrs. Butler happy by considering that property for our church. I went against Tom's will to look into it, even after her death. I thought it might be respectful to offer her son a fair amount. You had said we could afford to lease it. Can we?"

Terwilliger tugged at his high neckcloth. "Not if the investments go to her son and not Tom. I thought they were proper married and the funds were his. I wished to save them for your church."

"You argued with her not to sell her stocks *before* she died. Did you change your mind *after* she died, because you thought they belonged to Butler, who had no notion of their value?" Damien asked cynically when Johnson gave up with a frown.

Brydie struggled to string together the pieces. Tom Butler hadn't wanted to return to the farm because he feared someone finding those bones. That, she understood.

Johnson *said* he wanted the farm, ostensibly for his church and maybe even out of respect for Mrs. Sutter, but he hadn't tried very hard.

Evans had been willing to commit fraud to obtain the property and open a shoe manufactory.

The earl had offered for it to keep it out of Johnson's hands. Was this all about *land*?

Or. . .

Terwilliger didn't know about the bones, didn't care if Meg returned home, but had argued with her about selling her stock before she died.

Then after her death, as Damien implied. . . Terwilliger had agreed that Johnson might buy or lease the land—because Butler and Johnson had no understanding of the value of the certificates?

And they most likely would allow him to continue handling them?

"A memorial," Terwilliger stuttered, apparently realizing his story wasn't quite holding up. "We wanted a memorial."

"To be built on my property, with the investments that I inherited? Would you care to elaborate, sir?"

Lynly wriggled impatiently out of Brydie's lap and shouted, "He said the quilts were *his*! He called Mr. Jacques a bad name and stole them!"

That cut through the briars right enough. Kate gasped and tried to pull her daughter back to her seat.

Brydie noticed a motion against the dark curtains and turned to glimpse Jacques fisting his fingers and easing out of hiding, as if waiting for Damien to call on him?

He did. Damien gestured for Kate to hold onto her daughter and glanced to Jacques. "Will the court accept the testimony of a Frenchman?"

Hunt irritably pounded his walking stick on his table. "If we didn't, we'd be idiots."

Hunt's cousins were French and stood guard over the prisoners as they spoke. Gravesyde had learned to accept that people were people: no more calling the enemy *frogs* because they were different. Brydie respected that acceptance.

Damien gestured for his valet. Jacques stood before Hunt with hands behind his back and waited expectantly.

"Mr. Jacques Rousseau, will you state your business on the day of the alleged kidnapping?"

"On Friday, as my employer, you said you were to be away for the day and I was to do as I liked. Me, I straightened the wardrobe and ironed the linen. Then, it was raining and I could not go out, so I looked at the contents of the trunk your mother left for you. I found Miss Lynly Morgan snipping at a quilt. She said she had approval because. . ." He glanced over the audience. Brydie held her breath, hoping he wouldn't give away Lynly's secret.

Damien gestured for him to continue.

229

Jacques gathered his thoughts. "She worked on a project for her aunt. I helped her. Miss Calhoun checked on her niece. We discovered paper in one of the patches. The ugly little room had no light, so Miss Calhoun, she took the paper to study it. We found more paper."

Lynly stirred restlessly, kicking her feet and sulking. She wanted to be the center of attention. Brydie smiled and tapped her knee to stop the kicking. She appreciated that Damien was trying to do this without a child's testimony.

Jacques wrinkled his sharp nose. "A new guest at the inn," he nodded in Terwilliger's direction, "spied on us, saw what we did, and tried to steal our work. I told him the papers did not belong to him and stood on them. That is when he hit me with his stick. I fear I cannot say what happened after that."

"Thank you, Mr. Rousseau." Damien grimaced, apparently realizing that wasn't enough to convict anyone. Gesturing for Jacques to step aside, he turned and seemed to question Kate, who nodded. "Miss Lynly, would you like to stand up here and tell us what happened?"

Wearing a fierce frown on her elfin face, tiny Lynly slid from her mother's arms and off the sofa to stand fearlessly in front of the intimidating audience. Damien assisted her to stand on a wooden chair so people could see her.

"What happened the day you were kidnapped, Miss Lynly? What did you hear Mr. Terwilliger say?" Damien used reassuring tones, backing off so as not to loom over her.

Wide-eyed and pale, she faced Terwilliger. "That man saw the papers Mr. Jacques was holding and shouted *mine*. Mr. Jacques stepped on them so they couldn't be taken, and that man got angry and *hit* nice Mr. Jacques in the face real hard with a walking stick and *stole* them. I tried to scream for Aunt Brydie, but he shoved me into the trunk and threw quilts on me and I didn't hear more. I'm sorry."

Because the child's heart had stuttered and she'd passed out. Brydie wanted to leap up and smack Terwilliger with a walking stick, *hard*, just for that alone. Anyone who would beat a servant and mistreat a child. . .

The financier leapt from his chair, and before anyone could react, reached for Lynly—

Faster than the big men around her, Lynly lashed out with her tiny boot and kicked him. . . in his manly parts, what there were of them.

Terwilliger howled, crumpled in agony, and tottered into Fletch.

Then the old fake snatched Fletch's dagger from his belt.

THIRTY-THREE

DAMIEN

Instinctively, Damien clenched his fists, prepared to knock the old man flying, but he froze as the dagger appeared under Lynly's chin. Behind him, Jacques gasped and Hunt's chair scraped against the old floor. The audience burst into an uproar.

The huge chamber was filled with men who could easily snap Terwilliger in two, but no one dared endanger the child by moving. Big gray eyes wide with terror, the prisoner's vulnerable shield protected him too well.

And then Lynly fainted. The dagger nearly pierced her exposed throat before the old wretch adjusted his hold. Damien's knuckles whitened, but the child was still breathing. Small-boned Jacques clung to Fletch's huge arm, preventing the furious soldier from doing anything stupid. Damien had to be the one to figure this out.

"I'll set her down once I have my carriage. Back away, send for my horses." The scoundrel edged toward the big double doors leading into the main corridor. Freedom was only the length of the chamber away.

Damien focused on the child and didn't see Hunt's signal, but a footman dashed out.

Lynly needed her mother and a physician. The wretch would take her from this room over Damien's dead body.

Or Brydie's. Damien nearly had an attack of the heart as he followed Terwilliger down the wide aisle meant to allow a bride to reach the altar—and Brydie shoved her way through the horrified audience to meet them.

He knew that look. Towering Vikings must once have glowered like that and terrified their smaller neighbors into retreat. Except Brydie had no sword or ax, just herself.

Just her beautiful, sunny self, trampled once more by his family's avarice and violence. Her lovely full lips tightened, her eyes narrowed, and she should have frightened any sane man into dropping the child—except the fugitive dismissed womanly curves to watch the armed gentlemen guarding the door. Stupid.

She glanced to Damien, thank all the heavens and a few hells. *She remembered.* She wasn't taking matters into her own hands but still trusted him as she had when they were children.

"Right," Damien said in a tone that might have sounded like agreement and shouldn't alarm the rogue in front of him.

To Brydie, it was a signal and a warning. Terwilliger held the weapon with his right hand, on the side where Brydie stood. Lynly was on his left side. It wasn't an ideal situation, but as he well knew, Brydie was flexible.

It had been over fifteen years since they'd last paired up against his big brother and brought him down for stealing her apples. A knife, however—that was trickier than a bully's fists.

Until Jacques slipped up silently behind Damien, holding Damien's pistol. Bless his quick-witted valet—who had come prepared. Jacques had not always led an easy life.

"Evans," Terwilliger shouted, passing Brydie without a second look, "take their swords. I have a ship waiting. You're welcome to join me. Americans need boots." He inched down the length of the chamber. An eight-year-old child, no matter how frail, was an awkward burden.

Damien held his breath as Evans glared at him, then away. A drunken coward, perhaps, but one with a conscience, Damien hoped. Evans had children of his own. He didn't jump at the offer.

The financier slowed down to adjust Lynly's awkward weight slumped over his arm. Brydie eased up until she was almost parallel with them. Damien would rather have any of the men endangering themselves than Brydie, but men seldom saw women as dangerous. Terwilliger didn't even acknowledge her presence. Besides, she was the only one who understood how Damien had maneuvered his bigger brother when Harry had his hands full of apples or whatever else he had teased them with.

Everyone focused on the open doors of the exit, where Evans stood uncertainly. Hunt must have signaled his cousins to drop their swords. The two broad-shouldered Frenchmen didn't look happy.

Evans didn't appear precisely delighted at his freedom either. "I have family here," he argued. "I can't just sail away."

"You have debtors here," Terwilliger countered. "I can finance you over there. Run out and see if they're preparing the carriage."

One more step. . . Damien signaled Brydie with a nod.

No delicate miss, she emitted a wail of despair and fell head-long against Terwilliger's right shoulder, incapacitating his knife-holding arm, causing him to loosen his grip and the angle of the weapon.

Only a length behind, Damien snatched the pistol from Jacques's hand. He had always used his fists in this maneuver, but Lynly was more precious than apples. He couldn't take chances. With Terwilliger distracted into attempting to fling Brydie aside, Damien fired at the scoundrel's left shoulder. Terwilliger screamed, dropped the knife, and grabbed for his injured arm.

Leaping forward, Damien caught Lynly's limp form just as he'd once grabbed a basket of stolen fruit.

His brother usually turned on him at this point, but despite having his arms full of a small, brave girl, Damien avoided being knifed for his audacity. Brydie kicked away the weapon. Jacques jumped on Terwilliger's back, leaned over his scrawny shoulders, and began beating the prisoner's face with small fists and a load of fury.

The delay was long enough for Fletch to reach them. He yanked the wiry valet aside and jerked Terwilliger's wounded arm behind his back until the scoundrel howled, while Hunt shouted for the physician. Ladies pressed around Jacques in gratitude as the angry ex-soldier marched his prisoner toward the door.

Damien transferred Lynly's limp form to Brydie. Cuddling her niece, she rested her tear-stained face against Damien's shoulder and accepted his support while she wept. He let the crowd's confusion fade into the background while he wrapped his arms around the most beautiful, courageous woman he'd ever known. With Brydie in his arms, he experienced a fragile moment of peace. Anger vanished, and even Kate's terrified, tearful scolding didn't register, not with Brydie babbling gratitude, *thanking* him for letting her and her niece nearly be killed.

Kate gathered up her daughter. Men pounded him on the back and nattered, but Damien didn't listen. He had Brydie in his arms again. Free of his burden, he held her, relishing ripe curves and relinquishing the guilt and recriminations that haunted him.

"I never want to let you go," he murmured idiotically.

She tilted her head back to stare at him in disbelief. "I'd break your back."

Laughing, Damien buried his face in her wild curls, enjoying the rose fragrance she used in her soap. "I carried you upstairs, goose. You have no notion of how much I hated to put you down. We're good together, Brydie."

"Us?" She seemed bewildered. "Not Kate? She's the pretty one."

Before Damien could disabuse of her that idiocy, Rafe arrived to glare forbiddingly at the two of them.

"If you'll quit molesting my best worker, Hunt wants a written report to send with the prisoner. He reckons a lawyer knows the right words."

Brydie hastily stepped away, blushing a beautiful pink as she straightened her gown. Damien grabbed her hand before she could flee. They had things to discuss, and he wasn't letting her go easily this time.

"We don't know anything yet," he argued. "We can't accuse Terwilliger of killing anyone simply because the coward keeps running away."

Rafe snorted. "You don't know the captain. You have ten minutes to grab a drink while Meera patches up the hole in the prisoner's back. That tiny bang-bang of yours is barely good for shooting roaches."

The ginger-haired bailiff and innkeeper bowed an apology to Brydie. "It's important, sorry," then turned back to Damien. "In the study, just past the library. The curate's arrived. He'll stand witness to anything said."

"Deuced insane way to hold a trial," Damien muttered. But then, shooting the prisoner to make him talk was highly questionable as well. He squeezed Brydie's hand and glared down at her. "Don't go away. Look after your sister and niece. I'll come for you when we're done."

He was being presumptuous, he knew. Brydie's narrowed eyes told him that. He'd make up for it somehow. He'd waited too damned long to grow up. He signaled Jacques, who extricated himself from his admirers, appearing worried.

"I owe you," Damien told his valet. "We'll talk later."

Leaving his valet with a relieved expression, determined to be a proper citizen for a change, Damien followed Rafe to what had once been the earl's private study, where the gentlemen gathered to sip the manor's aged brandy.

Weston poured drinks, then produced a document from his pocket. He handed it to Damien, while speaking to Rafe. "I wrote to our steward about that rifle you found at the encampment. As you said, it's recent military issue, not many available to the public. I'll happily buy it from the owner. But the reason I wrote. . . I thought I recognized the design. The manufacturer wanted us to invest in his company and brought us drawings some time back."

Damien grimaced as the picture cleared. "I assume Terwilliger's brokerage was the one selling stock in the company to obtain financing for the manufactory."

The earl shrugged. "It's a good brokerage, good company."

A rare rifle few would own, in the hands of a man who represented the maker. . .

His mother had been shot from a distance and that rifle was designed for sharpshooting.

Would the judge accept that as sufficient evidence to tie the old rogue to the murder weapon? They needed to prove Terwilliger knew how to fire it. *Motive*, however. . . If the financier had killed Damien's grasping mother for the stock she'd stolen from his father—irony at its worst. Released from the red haze of anger and guilt, he supposed he was almost ready to accept that.

But why push Weston into the river? Revenge? Anger?

After finishing his brandy and consulting with his cousins, Hunt settled behind an ancient, battered desk in the earl's old study. Damien had begun to sort one dark-haired French cousin from the other. The one who owned the tavern stayed in the study, but the larger one, the artist, left and eventually returned with Terwilliger, who looked grayer than ever. Someone had provided fresh linen, but he wore his bloodied frockcoat over his injured shoulder. Damien wanted to feel sorry for an old man, but that rifle returned his fury.

They tied the prisoner to a heavy chair, then led in Evans. Obviously uncomfortable, the boot manufacturer took a second chair in front of the desk, although they didn't tie him up. Damien would have locked up the bastard under general principles, but that was temper speaking. He was trying to be better than that. Wisdom forced him to recall that Evans might be a desperate drunk, but he hadn't run or helped Terwilliger when the opportunity offered.

Paul Upton, the curate hoping to marry in the morning, had taken a comfortable wing chair in a corner behind Hunt, near the blazing hearth. The warmth was welcome after the chilly great hall. The poor man was probably hoping for a quick end to this case so he could enjoy his wedding day in peace.

Gravesyde had a chapel and a pastor now. If Damien stayed. . .

He set that possibility aside as the Earl of Weston settled into another wing chair and indicated that Damien take the one beside him and behind the prisoners. "Didn't know you could shoot, Sutter," he murmured while Hunt pointed at Rafe to take a seat.

"I can hit a target with an arrow. Pistols are too easy." Because they were too easy to cause harm, his family had never kept firearms. His brother had chosen cavalry because he could swing a sword and wield a bayonet, not aim a rifle. Damien had learned to keep a pistol on the road but preferred not to carry one otherwise. Firearms and hot tempers did not pair well.

He glanced at Terwilliger, who stayed upright, not looking at anyone. The damage to his shoulder couldn't have been extensive. Damien's gut still roiled with anger at what the scrawny coward had done, *twice*, to little Lynly, but he'd never wanted to put a man in the ground—until he'd learned about the rifle.

"Lynly?" Damien whispered to Fletch as he lounged in the chair on his other side.

"Awake and ready to kick the old goat again. Has spells, the women say. Feisty mite. Apologize for the knife. Didn't think the worm had it in him." Rafe's partner straightened like the good sergeant he'd been as Captain Huntley lay down his pen and screwed the top on his inkpot.

"Mr. Sutter, would you care to present Mr. Terwilliger with Weston's letter identifying the weapon that killed your mother?" Hunt sat back to watch the prisoner squirm.

Damien stood to face the scoundrel again. "Mr. Terwilliger, have you ever served in the military?"

The old man didn't even look up. "Made sergeant when I was a lad." He turned a glare to Hunt. "Killed a lot of rebels."

"Fellow countrymen," Damien corrected. "Captain Huntley's family descends from the Earl of Wycliffe. So, you'd say you're a good rifleman?"

The prisoner grunted. "Didn't have rifles in them days. Old Bess did what it needed."

"If you could hit a target with a musket, then one of the new rifles should be even easier, shouldn't it?" Damien swung Weston's letter at his side, not reading it aloud.

Terwilliger looked anywhere but at him. "Needs some practice."

"Oh, then you're saying you're out of practice? Did you practice by shooting at Mr. Johnson early Monday? Or were you aiming at Mrs. Sutter then too?"

The preacher wasn't in the room. Terwilliger just scowled.

"All right, let's put it this way. I have sent inquiries to your brokerage and to several of the companies whose stock certificates were in my mother's possession." Damien didn't believe in geese with golden eggs. He trusted no one until proven honest, even a broker who swears he was. "Will they verify that those shares belong to my mother and honor their sale?"

Terwilliger slid down in his seat. "Bringing our troops home collapsed business. No one wants rifles and uniforms when there's no war. You saw what it did to Evans. I told her to hold onto them, that they'd reorganize and find new markets."

"So, she didn't know that you had already sold them?" Damien suggested.

"I woulda paid her back! They're good companies. I sold high and woulda bought again low if she'd just waited!"

Skimming the profit for himself. As the man handling a woman's investments, how often had he done that?

Damien's gut tightened at the monetary loss. He had never counted on being wealthy, but it would have been nice to offer

239

Brydie comfort. His mother mattered more. He pressed on. "What did you do with the money?"

"Tucked away a tidy sum and bought shares of new companies. She didn't want to risk the unknown, said she was getting too old to gamble. She wanted to retire in comfort. I coulda talked her around, but then *you* showed up."

Damien let the guilt roll away at this accusation, and as it did, the anger went with it. He would have taken his mother with no money at all. *He* hadn't told this wretch to play with other people's money. *He* hadn't told him to kill to eliminate the evidence. Damien didn't give a damn about money he'd never known he might have had. He simply wanted justice so he could move on with his life.

"You killed my *mother* because she would have sued over her stolen funds and ruined your reputation! You deserve to hang, sir." Damien returned to his chair and left the rest of the proceedings to Hunt.

The past was over and done and he couldn't change a bit of it. All he wanted now was Brydie and a future he still couldn't quite envision.

THIRTY-FOUR

RAFE

Rafe watched his elegantly-garbed guest in his fancy frockcoat and pristine neckcloth go white-lipped at the realization his mother's money had been stolen and his mother murdered by a scrawny grasshopper planning to make a future across the sea.

The scoundrel needed to swing, but would a court convict a prosperous, respected broker over the death of a poor woman who'd run away after killing her brute of a husband? For enough money, a good barrister might persuade the judge to let even Judas go free, as Rafe well knew.

When Damien rubbed his jaw and settled into his chair, satisfied he at least knew what had happened, Rafe glanced at the quiet curate, who raised his eyebrows and nodded encouragement. Mr. Upton had been here longer than Rafe, investigated cases worse than this. He understood what was needed for conviction.

Hunt turned expectantly to Rafe. All righty then. . .

Rafe stood and donned his perplexed countryman expression. "So, you're saying Mr. Terwilliger has sold Mrs. Sutter's stocks, and her certificates are worthless, because the bank books show them sold? And he kept the funds, so he's guilty of theft?"

The captain beamed approval. "We'll have to write the issuer of the certificates for verification, but yes, we'll hold the gentleman on theft and fraud."

Terwilliger muttered but bound as he was, he couldn't escape this time.

Rafe nodded while both Walker and the curate jotted notes. Hunt's bad eye prevented him from writing clearly. "And am I understanding correctly that when Mrs. Sutter wished to sell the stock she no longer owned, Mr. Terwilliger panicked and shot her?"

The prisoner scowled. "My attorney will see you in court. You have no proof."

"You have the right to remain silent," Damien said with a shrug from his chair. "That doesn't mean I won't beat you half to death before you reach your attorney. This isn't London."

Under Rafe's bailiwick, he meant the law to be *better* than the city, but he was fairly certain the gentleman didn't mean what he said. He intervened, just the same. "I'll see the prisoner makes it to assizes. I just want facts straight in my mind. I'm thinking Mr. Terwilliger, here, was unhappy with Mrs. Sutter, but he had no reason for pushing an earl into the river, correct? He had Mrs. Sutter's funds and could have bought the property, but he'd rather not. So he didn't care if the earl bought it."

The mood in the room immediately shifted. Rafe didn't like his conclusions, but foxes didn't become chickens overnight because someone said so. He inched closer to his suspect. "Mr. Evans, here, was the one what wanted the land and the funds for investing, if I'm understanding rightly? Did he approach you about financing the purchase, Mr. Terwilliger?"

The financier glowered belligerently. Evans squirmed. The earl sat up straight, his fists clenching—the first time Rafe had seen the idle nobleman express more than boredom or mild amusement. Intrigued, Damien merely raised his dark eyebrows.

Apparently seeing a way to shift blame, Terwilliger shrugged. "He did. I've known Evans for years. He's clever at pinching pennies, and manufacturing is the future, but he had nothing for me to invest in except an old idea. Selling boots to backwoods farmers won't show a profit for decades. I have no idea if he asked Mrs. Sutter about investing after I turned him off."

"Don't think you can shift the blame to Evans," Damien said angrily. "*You* are the one who knew my mother. Evans didn't arrive until Monday night. At the time, we had no notion that she lived. He wasn't desperate until *after* her death, when I had second thoughts about selling."

The earl's eyes narrowed at Evans. Big men curled tense fingers into fists.

Rafe blocked Evans with his bulk. Hunt's cousins guarded the only exit. Hunt had chosen the windowless study for a reason. This would be settled here and now.

"I never knew Mrs. Sutter existed," Evans protested nervously, obviously judging the mood of the room. Was it guilt that prevented him from glancing over his shoulder at the earl?

Using Damien's casual tactic, Rafe settled his large posterior on a corner of Hunt's desk, crossed his arms, and glared at Evans. "But you knew *Weston*, didn't you? Had you approached him before about funding?"

"Weeks ago," the earl growled, answering for the prisoner. "We'd invested in his boot manufactory in the beginning, then sold out before it collapsed. We knew production would slow with the war's end, and we gambled on Wellington winning."

"But Evans didn't approach you while he was here this week?" Damien asked, acknowledging that he was in a better position to interrogate earls than Rafe.

"He sent up a note." Weston shrugged the shoulders of his tightly tailored frockcoat. The earl didn't possess the muscular build of men who worked for a living, but his attitude commanded attention. "We'd refused him once. Didn't see a reason to respond again."

"And you were desperate, Mr. Evans, weren't you?" Rafe asked in his most neutral voice. "Desperate enough on Wednesday, when you saw Damien was having second thoughts, to seek out a nobleman in the pouring rain? If I ask around, will the servants tell me you had inquired into the earl's whereabouts?"

When Evans sat tight-lipped, Rafe glanced at Hunt. "I've already interviewed the household servants. He must have inquired in the stable. Could you call in your land steward? He'd most likely—"

Evans shrank into his seat and studied his boots. "I asked, yes. Weston trusts Damien—Mr. Sutter. I thought I could make the earl see that if he bought the Sutter property, I could rent it, paying him increasing sums as profits grew. Land is a good investment. I wanted to own it, but at least I'd be back in business."

Hunt leaned forward, a dangerous gleam in his eye. "So, you sought Weston out on the river?"

"It was an accident!" Evans shouted, leaping up and eyeing the exit, still blocked by two brawny Frenchmen. "I slipped! The rain was damned blinding out there by the time I reached the river, and the fool was standing on the edge! I'm not a countryman accustomed to climbing hills. I stumbled, caught my foot in the rocks, and the next thing I knew, Weston was in the water! I can't swim. I had no idea what to do—"

And Rafe hadn't been at the inn to see him return, soaking wet. No one would have if he used one of the rear exits. They wouldn't have even known the earl was missing.

"Let the judge decide," Weston declared, going to the back of the room for the brandy bottle. "I'd like to throttle him, but I believe his story. I was fighting that deuced fish. My footing wasn't good on the moss. It wouldn't have taken much to push me over. And he had no real motive to kill me. We hadn't even argued."

An honest nobleman. Rafe appreciated that. Back when he was shooting at Napoleon's army, he hadn't anticipated a day when he'd have Frenchmen on his side and a nobleman at his back. Gravesyde Priory was another world, a better one, he hoped.

He unhooked the rope from his belt and tied up Evans, all neat and tidy, giving prayers of thanksgiving that he wasn't a judge.

THIRTY-FIVE

BRYDIE

Brydie was unaccustomed to idleness or being surrounded by delicate ladies in beribboned muslins and servants who hovered. She wanted to go home and feed the chickens and start the week's bread and mop floors.

Except she was as eager as everyone to learn what was happening in the study. She wasn't waiting for Damien. Definitely not. All the hugs and kisses in the world didn't change the fact that he was a restless grasshopper. He meant to sell his home and ride away, unburdened by family ties. She certainly couldn't blame him. Gravesyde held nothing for him.

But she was the ant who needed her cozy home and family. She couldn't follow.

The great hall had to be returned to its purpose of seating wedding guests, then decorated for the curate's nuptials. The vicar had traveled a long way to visit this tiny parish, and the village was eager to meet him.

So, she allowed herself to be drafted into the wedding preparations. She was *not* waiting for Damien. A thirty-year-old spinster had no illusions. She was very tall and stronger than half the men in Gravesyde. And smarter and better read and bossy. . .

Damien was bigger and smarter and better educated and bossier than she. And older, with gray hairs, she reminded herself. She liked him, that's all. He'd always listened to her, which was a pleasant change.

And he'd held her as a man does a woman and she'd liked it much too well. She should go home.

"They *will* find the guilty parties and we won't need this courtroom anymore," Miss Peniston declared mulishly, while she shoved chairs about. Her petite size didn't slow her down. "They sent Paul and Walker away. That must mean they're done."

If words could make it so. . .

"Do you think Johnson and his followers will leave?" Brydie welcomed the distraction as she helped move a sofa twice the weight of the librarian shoving at it. "Winter is no time to be sleeping in fields."

"We need people to rebuild Gravesyde." The librarian aligned two chairs precisely and eyed the row. "I believe Captain Huntley was talking to them about some of the cottages. I don't know how that turned out."

Brydie had always considered the manor as a castle the peasants never entered, but even if she didn't appreciate the drafty grandeur, she was enjoying the opportunity to talk with the curate's wife-to-be. "Johnson wanted a church where he could preach the gospel according to him. Perhaps he'll buy Damien's land after all."

"It wouldn't hurt to share the chapel. The stained glass is lovely, but I suppose he considers the windows ungodly or some such fustian. I would have loved to marry there, but everyone has worked so hard. . ." She gestured helplessly at the newly-waxed oak paneling that would shine magnificently once they lit the chandeliers.

"The village is truly looking forward to your nuptials," Brydie assured her. "There were nothing more than funerals until the manor opened again, with no one to minister to the grieving. We are eager to show our gratitude for our new curate and celebrate his marriage. We're hoping that means Mr. Upton will stay, even though the village can't offer much. Besides, Lady Elsa's feast will prevent a few from going hungry another night. This isn't just about the grandeur or your special day, it's about community."

The modestly garbed librarian bride-to-be sighed. "I know that in my head, but I have never been the center of attention. It is quite uncomfortable."

"Whereas your intended is always the center of our attention," Brydie warned. "Perhaps a large wedding ceremony is necessary to divide the two stages of your lives."

Deep male voices and loud bootsteps resounded in the corridor. The trial had ended. Brydie tried not to glance too eagerly at the doorway through which the other ladies left to join their spouses.

Pensively, Miss Peniston didn't heed their exit but followed her own thoughts. "You are quite right. Marriage is very permanent. I am marrying the parish as much as its curate. My life of roaming has ended, and now I will finally have a home of my own."

She suddenly grinned. "I can use my grandmother's dreadful china for target practice in the backyard, if I like."

With that, she lifted her skirt and hurried toward the double doors, where the curate hovered anxiously. He broke into a huge smile as his betrothed raced into his arms, swinging her up in the air, and ushering her into the noisy crowd gathering in the central corridor. Brydie sighed at the sight of such devotion.

A home of one's own, with a good man at one's side who appreciated. . . what? She didn't have any china to shoot. She didn't even own a trousseau. She had no dowry. The farm was in trust to Arthur. Women were meant to be chattel who brought their husbands advantages they needed. She had nothing but her strength. Maybe she could find a sickly husband who required. . .

Damien entered the dim, empty chamber and slammed the double doors closed.

She gulped. Even in the dim light, she could see those broad shoulders and brawny arms that had the strength to lift her great gawking length. He didn't need her ax-wielding abilities.

"It's over?" she managed to ask in something less than a whisper. Attempting normalcy with Damien's green gaze fastened on her as if she were his last meal required concentration. Remembering how his arms had embraced her—had all the blood rushing from her head. Giddiness did not aid concentration.

"It's not over until a judge rules and Terwilliger is hanged, but we've done all we can." He halted less than a foot away, their toes almost touching.

He was telling her that the financier had killed his mother, but that seemed less important than what else he hadn't said.

His starched linen was still immaculate. From this position, with her nose at his chin level and her breasts nearly brushing his neckcloth, she could see how well his tailored superfine displayed the breadth of his chest and shoulders.

"That's not what I want to talk about while we have these few minutes of privacy," he informed her.

"This is highly improper." But she couldn't back away as she should. She'd always loved his masculine scent, so different from her own. Her insides swam in circles. "Kate will yell."

"You are a grown woman, and Kate has her hands full. Besides, she knows I'd never harm you." A shadow flickered across his angular cheekbones. "At least, I hope she does, after the violence she has suffered at the hands of my family. Do you think she will ever forgive me for what they did?"

Now she wanted to comfort him. . . "Not your fault any more than it is mine. Kate was at the shop in secret, wanting new slippers for a dance, the first she'd ever attended. None of us knew. . ."

Damien brushed one of her pesky curls behind her ear. "Your sister is brave. Her children are wonderful. I am proud to take

Arthur as the brother I've missed. But you, Brighid Calhoun, you are the sun I want to start my day. The star I want to light my night. It's always been you. I never thought I deserved the sun and stars."

Brydie felt his words all the way to places she didn't acknowledge and blushed up to her hairline. She had to be sensible. A fine sight she must make in her dusty apron and ugly brown wool, with her hair all about from moving furniture. "I might be big and bright enough to be a sun or star, but there is nothing special about me. I have nothing, sir, except a family that needs me."

Not laughing at her objection, Damien ran his hand into her hair, smoothing it. "And I am very likely a poor man, unless we can squeeze my mother's stolen funds from Terwilliger's bank and brokers. That could take years. I'm a lawyer with no clients, and a landowner with no farming skill. But I have learned my lesson. Life is short and we can't count on tomorrow. I fear I still can only offer myself and my property, if we must discuss business. I am only interested in acquiring one asset, Brydie, and that's you."

He didn't give her time to argue, not that she'd found her tongue to do so. He dug his hand into her hair and brought his mouth down on hers, and the world slipped away.

Until the double doors slammed open and Rafe shouted, "Sutter, is that you? Use your words and stop Fletch from dismantling a clock worth two fortunes!"

"I knew my smooth-talking tongue had a purpose, " Damien muttered, refusing to release his grip on her.

"Yes, I think you displayed that quite adequately." Dizzily, Brydie pushed him away. Tongues could do that?

Recovering her senses somewhat, she followed them out to where Rafe's partner had angled the towering medieval hall clock halfway around to examine its back.

"He gets like this when he's mad and wants a drink," Rafe offered.

She shook her head in disbelief at the things men did—and said—and went in search of Kate.

She needed her wise sister's advice before she fell victim to a smooth-talking gentleman far out of her league.

SUNDAY

THIRTY-SIX

RAFE

THE NOBILITY AND GENTRY OF WYCLIFFE MANOR STOOD IN RESPECT as their housekeeper's son—their penniless curate—walked down the aisle of the great hall with his new bride, the descendant of earls, who had spent half her life in tents and the other in libraries.

It was a spectacle not often seen and the audience rustled with anticipation. Rafe couldn't see who started the unusual clapping, but as the newly-wed couple reached the village folk near the exit doors, the entire crowd stood and applauded heartily. The fancified vicar who'd conducted the ceremony frowned.

The curate's sister, who sang in her husband's tavern, let her beautiful soprano ring out in a cheerful melody that was definitely not a hymn. The newly-tuned pianoforte played by the captain's wife accompanied her. The vicar was probably having a fit.

But the beauty and song were enough to bring tears even to an old soldier's eyes. Rafe bent over his weepy wife and kissed her brow beneath her ridiculous hat. "I should have given you a wedding like this."

Verity's small gloved palm scarcely registered when she smacked his bicep. "Pomp and circumstance are for royalty and bored nobles, not for practical people like us. Our names in the parish register for all to see is. . ." She studied his rough-hewn face with her big brown eyes. "It's hard to describe how proud it makes me feel to have you tell the world I'm yours and you're mine. And to make us a part of—" She gestured to include the hall's occupants—which represented almost all of the village.

Rafe puffed with pride and reckoned he understood. He felt like that about his inn. He just didn't have a way to express feelings the way his wife did. Instead, he nodded to where Damien stood with Brydie and her family. "He says he's staying. Hunt's looking for a way to pay a lawyer out of the maintenance trust, but it's hard to call a lawyer maintenance."

Verity laughed quietly as the nobles started filing out. Neither of them had ever been this close to an earl and a duke before coming to Gravesyde. Having seen wealthy nobles in mud-splattered hunting clothes this past week, they weren't quite as impressed by their jeweled pins and fashionableness now.

"If maintenance includes fighting for ownership of the cottages, perhaps that would cover his wages. Although I fear the banker will disagree. What will we do without Brydie if she marries Mr. Sutter and sets to restoring his old house instead of the inn?"

Rafe shrugged, put his hand at her back, and steered her into the aisle with the others. He was starving, and there was a wedding feast waiting. "Miss Butler may not see well, but she hears enough to keep the rest of our staff on their toes. Until we have more guests, we don't need much. I just liked having Brydie about while you worked with your students."

He didn't have to mention that Verity was small but Brydie had the strength to handle troublesome students.

"Mr. Birdwhistle thinks they'll have the tower stairs ready to reach his schoolroom by the first of the year. I may not be about as much if I'm teaching at the manor."

The tutor wasn't large, but large enough to handle the trouble makers.

Verity halted when they reached the corridor. They both raised their eyebrows in surprise.

Instead of setting up tables outside for the villagers as usual, the staff had placed buffet tables down the central, gaslit corridor, allowing nobles and village folk alike to stay out of the weather while mixing and mingling. Rafe could tell they hadn't set out the best china, but he was fine with that. He pushed Verity into line behind Damien, Brydie, and her family.

Damien leaned back to Rafe to ask, "What is your partner's fascination with ancient timepieces?" He nodded at the landing above the marble staircase.

Fletch was again studying the case clock that never kept time —but not molesting it this time.

"Father was a clockmaker," Rafe explained. "Fletch used to drink. We all did. War requires it. Then one day, we rolled into a French village, drove everyone out, and he stumbled into a clock-maker's shop."

Rafe filled his plate from the first table while Verity explored different dishes. Damien and Brydie hung back to hear the story while keeping worried eyes on Fletch toying with the lock on the glass front.

"He walked out of that shop with a box of broken automa-tons," Rafe finished. "Hasn't been drunk since. Whenever he feels like drinking, he takes one apart and makes it work again."

"Everybody has a story," Brydie murmured. "Someone ought to write them down."

"Not me," Rafe and Damien said at the same time.

Laughing, they finished raiding the buffet.

THIRTY-SEVEN

DAMIEN

D ECIDING T ERWILLIGER OWED HIM MORE MONEY THAN HE'D EVER SEE
again, Damien appropriated the financier's carriage and horses to
drive Brydie and her family home after the celebration.

The afternoon sun still peeked through the clouds as he
handed the women out and Arthur proudly led the horses back to
the stable. Damien held Brydie's hand and tugged her away from
the only home she'd ever known. He'd not done this properly the
other day. He'd been overwhelmed and worried about his decision to stay. He couldn't expect her to fall into his plans the instant
he thought of them.

He understood some of her reluctance to accept his
unorthodox proposal, but he didn't think his brave childhood
companion had changed a great deal underneath her newly-prac-
tical adult self.

"Give me a reason to stay, Brydie." He'd wasted too much
time as it was. He needed to know he had hope. He led her across
the lane to the derelict yard and manor house hidden behind
overgrown trees and bushes. "I can't live in that house of horrors
by myself. I want to be rid of it, but it isn't as if Gravesyde offers

better. I want to quit traveling, settle down, look after Arthur. . . and you, if you'll let me."

She didn't drop his hand or run. He considered that promising. Her wayward auburn curls peered out from beneath her bonnet, glimmering in the sunlight. Her animated face reflected the joy of the day and maybe, just maybe, his company? Her gray eyes gleamed nearly silver as she contemplated the prospect of restoring a crumbling old stone farmhouse. The locals called it a manor, but he knew better. His home had been a hovel of horror for all his life.

"I don't need anyone looking after me," she told him bluntly. "I can look after me and my family. Sending Arthur to school is the right thing for you to do, but you don't need me for that. I've been thinking about what you said and realize I am unmarried for a reason. It's not just because I'm tall or hardheaded or that I don't have a dowry. It's because men who might be my equal aren't interested in a woman who doesn't need them." She shrugged her cloaked shoulders. "And I simply haven't found a reason to settle for someone who isn't my equal."

Damien wanted to laugh at his Brydie's brilliant confidence, but she was telling him something very important, and he needed to listen and heed her words. He held her hand tighter, studied the dreaded shop that was his heritage, and let her words sink in.

"I am not a student of equality," he admitted, sorting his thoughts slowly. "I use people. I earn a living by bringing together wealth with creativity, intelligence, and ability. They all need each other because no one man is equal in all areas, not that I've met, at least. I've never really considered women. None has ever come close to comparing to you and they're irrelevant in the business world that I inhabit. But you, Brydie. . . I have never ever stopped thinking about you. I stayed away because of you, because I had nothing to offer you. I had hoped. . . well, no, selfish beast that I am, I didn't *want* you to marry anyone else. But I hoped you might find happiness."

She strolled further into the yard, finding a late-blooming rose among the brambles, caressing the petals. "You broke my silly, childish heart, Damien. I knew you were a grown man who needed to make his own way, but you didn't even ask me to wait for you. You just rode off, leaving me with a sister who cried every night, and a father who was too ill to work, and then we had a baby none of us knew how to care for. And life went on. After your parents disappeared, I almost commandeered the workshop and started my own shoe business, but I kept hoping you'd return."

"The shop is yours, if you want it." He waved dismissively at the building. "I never had any interest in it. If you don't, I mean to offer it to Jacques, although he knows nothing of what a rural community needs, so you might be partners. I wish I could apologize for my actions, but I really thought you'd be better off without me. You would have hated traveling and never having a home of your own, but it was the only way I could make a living and earn the respect I never had here."

"Jacques will love that shop," she said with a laugh. "He just needs to make work boots, although I suppose the gentlemen might ask for fancy riding boots. I don't know if there's enough work for a manufactory. That part is up to you." She put her hand around his elbow and wandered further into the yard.

Damien swallowed hard and tried not to rush her. He could talk rings around anyone, but he wanted Brydie's honest opinion. His didn't count right now.

At his silence, she tilted her head so he could see her lovely face beneath the hat brim. "I loved you as a child, you know. We're not children any longer."

A tear seeped from the corner of his eye but he ignored it. "I turned my back on what you offered, I know, I'm sorry. You had reason to hate me. I'm not sure it's possible to make amends. But I never stopped loving you, Brydie. Whatever you decide, I think I'll stay here. This empty pile of stone isn't my home. You are. For you, I'll stay."

Tears brightened her eyes as she smiled up at him. "Those are the words I'm waiting for, Damien. I don't care about houses or shoes. Houses are easy. The difficult part is finding someone to love, someone who loves bossy, dowerless me. If you tell me that, we'll paint the walls red and yellow and fill the house with people and laughter."

For a brief moment of pure relief, Damien closed his eyes. Then, as joy surged through him, he clasped his beautiful bossy Brydie in his arms and kissed her as he'd dreamed of doing almost every night of his life.

GRAVESYDE'S COUPLES BY BOOK

GRAVESYDE MANOR MYSTERIES

Book #1 *The Secrets of Wycliffe Manor* Captain Huntley and Clare
Knightley
Book #2 *The Mystery of the Missing Heiress:* Jack de Sackville and
Lady Elsa
Book #3 *The Bones in the Orchard:* Patience Upton and Henri
Lavigne
Book #4 *The Question of the Wedding Pearls:* weddings of #1 and #2
couples
Book #5 *The Case of the Purloined Pages:* Minerva Peniston and Paul
Upton
Book #6 *The Dilemma of a Dead Scholar*: Arnaud Lavigne and
Dorothea Talbot

GRAVESYDE VILLAGE MYSTERIES

Book #1 *The Villain's Fatal Plot:* Verity Porter and Sgt. Rafe Russell
Book #2 *The Scoundrel's Deadly Deed:* Damien Sutter and Brydie
Calhoun

GRAVESYDE VILLAGE MYSTERIES

The Villain's Fatal Plot
Book One

Bestselling author Patricia Rice brings you another small-town mystery in Regency England. . . He's looking for a future - she must escape the past. . . if only they can survive the present.

In the derelict village of Gravesyde Priory, newly-arrived Verity Palmer discovers her beloved former governess poisoned, her dying breath a whispered confidence. Shaken and alone, cautious Verity fears trusting total strangers with a dangerous secret.

Seeking work and a roof over his head, bluff ex-mess sergeant Rafe Russell accepts the position of bailiff, tasked with uncovering the truth about the governess's untimely demise. Caught in a web of suspicious characters, he discovers an unexpected ally in his best suspect, perspicacious Verity. She possesses a sharp mind that cuts through nets of intrigue, while hiding behind a cloak of mystery.

With no choice but to share a cottage—and a kitchen that quickly becomes his, not hers—Verity and Rafe piece together clues to save lives, including their own. As violent incidents escalate, Verity has to confront her own past and learn to trust if they are to expose the shadowy villains stalking their every move.

If they're to have any hope for a future, they must unveil the truth before the killer strikes again.

Buy The Villain's Fatal Plot

GRAVESYDE PRIORY MYSTERY

The Secrets of Wycliffe Manor
Book #1

Be wary of what you wish for. . .

In Regency England:

The descendant of adventuring—dead —aristocrats, Clarissa Knightley supplements a modest inheritance by penning gothic novels that cost more than they earn. Upon learning that she has mysteriously inherited a share of an earl's estate, she rashly packs up her household. In remote Gravesyde Priory, she hopes to find a safe haven and family who will welcome her and her young nephew.

Instead, she discovers a drunken American army captain, his African servant, and ancient, surly caretakers. Terrified, prepared to flee, Clare is lured to linger by the prospect of secret diaries, hidden jewels, and an increasingly intriguing man. Then a killer strikes.

The crumbling manor's ominous and baffling history offers

fascinating fodder for Clare's horror novels—if only she can survive real-life madmen and a spectral murderer who may seek the jewels at any price.

Buy The Secrets of Wycliffe Manor

❦

The Mystery of the Missing Heiress
Book #2

Wycliffe Manor, a magnet for murder...

On a long-delayed errand to remote Wycliffe Manor, ex-Lieutenant Jack de Sackville stumbles across the murdered body of London dandy, Basil Culpepper, in the hedgerow, a long way from his usual haunts. To Jack's dismay, he discovers the earl's daughter Culpepper ruined hiding in Wycliffe's kitchen.

Disguised as a lowly cook, Lady Elspeth Villiers may have liked to shoot Culpepper for ruining her life, but she dropped out of sight for more immediate reasons than an old scandal —her wealth has become the focus of greedy men. The arrival of Jack, the man she's adored since childhood, along with Culpepper's corpse, mean her hiding place is no longer safe.

But once Lady Elsa reveals herself to the unconventional inhabitants of Wycliffe Manor, they become the protective family she has never known. Outraged to learn the beautiful woman he once loved and lost has become a target of greed, Jack joins the investigation into Culpepper's death.

With a murderer on the loose, the amateur sleuths must unravel a deadly tangle of kidnappers and counterfeiters or the

Manor's eccentric inhabitants will be in as much danger as their cook.

Buy The Mystery of the Missing Heiress

❦

The Bones in the Orchard
Book #3

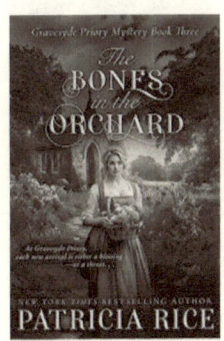

At Gravesyde Priory, each new arrival is either a blessing—or a threat. . .

Wycliffe Manor has been neglected for decades. Its new heirs are determined to create a welcoming home. Yet soon after the latest family moves into the nearby parsonage, bones are uncovered in the orchard. . . and odd strangers arrive.

When her curate father returns his family to Gravesyde for the marriages of the manor's heirs, gawky spinster Patience Upton has high expectations—until her father is murdered. Shock at learning her father had a mysterious past, leads to alarm that the killer may have been after his notebook, which she now possesses.

After the chapel is ransacked and a witness killed, it's clear the murderer isn't done. Desperate to find the truth, Patience accepts the aid of Henri Lavigne, Wycliffe Manor's smooth-talking rake. Intent on saving his new home and family from danger, Henri is drawn to the clergyman's guileless daughter but wonders if she hasn't reason to conceal the killer's identity.

Before there will be any courting, much less marrying, the inhabitants of the manor realize if they want a chance at a future, they must hunt the killer themselves. But are they hunting one murderer. . . or more?

Buy The Bones in the Orchard

∿

The Question of the Wedding Pearls
Book #4

Will death ruin the perfect wedding?

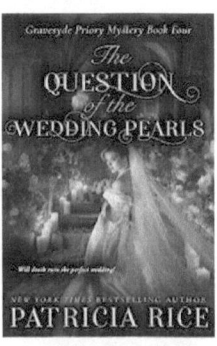

Bestselling author Patricia Rice brings you another haunting country house mystery in Regency England. . .

Spinster and secret novelist Clarissa Knightley and her gruff American engineer, Captain Huntley, along with their friend and cousin, the Honorable Jack de Sackville and Lady Elspeth, are to wed at last! In anticipation of the double wedding, friends and family are gathering at moldering Wycliffe Manor—until a dying stranger is discovered on the neglected grounds.

Despite the tragedy, aristocratic wedding guests, and their retinues, foreign and domestic, continue to arrive, not all by invitation. Compounding the bedlam, tales of missing pearls and ghostly encounters precede a second alarming death. Fearing that a killer lurks inside the manor walls, Clare and Hunt are swept up in a whirlwind of secret bigotries, deceit, and increasing peril. Before their family's joyful plans veer into heartbreak, can they put an end to mayhem and catch a killer?

Buy The Question of the Wedding Pearls

∿

The Case of the Purloined Pages
Book #5

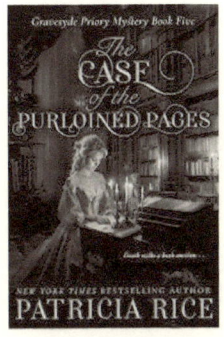

Death stalks the library. . .Bestselling author Patricia Rice brings you another haunting country house mystery in Regency England. . .

Minerva Peniston, intrepid spinster and booklover, is determined to capture the villain who tried to shoot a duke at a book auction— imperiling her father's position and the only home she's ever known. And now the same wealthy biblio-philes are gathering at Wycliffe Manor. . .

Paul Upton, over-educated and impoverished curate, has volunteered to assist the residents of Wycliffe Manor in preparing for a book auction to save the village and the manor's future. When an intriguing wallflower drags him into aiding her quest to find a potential killer, he agrees for her safety, and to keep trouble from upending the long-awaited nuptials of the manor's owner.

Despite their efforts, Minerva's chatty book-collecting friend is strangled before the auction begins. A killer on the loose threatens to upend both sale and wedding. Paul and Minerva must deter-mine what secrets the garrulous victim revealed. . . and to whom. . . before the murderer strikes again.

With valuable manuscripts at risk and a half dozen more potential victims on hand, only an unlikely white-knight and mousy spinster can save the auction and the wedding. As much as Minerva adores books, even she knows they aren't worth dying for.

Buy The Case of the Purloined Pages

❧

The Dilemma of a Dead Scholar
Book #6

At Wycliffe Manor, a legendary pirate treasure draws danger... .Bestselling author Patricia Rice brings you another haunting country house mystery in Regency England. . .

An heiress haunted by ghosts, Dotty Dorothea knows her family believes her mad. Fearing fortune hunters who would lock her and her awkward little brother in an asylum, she flees behind the ancient walls of Wycliffe Manor.

A French artist and émigré, his soul bearing scars from a French prison, Comte Arnaud Lavigne has lost everything to war. His only foreseeable future is restoring bad artwork in his cousin's decrepit manor. Mad heiresses aren't his concern, until the day a mathematical scholar is murdered. The deceased leaves a coded journal that might lead to Wycliffe Manor's lost treasure—inside the sealed tower the terrified heiress swears is haunted.

Ghosts don't exist as far as Arnaud is concerned, but killers and thieves are real, especially when stolen treasure is involved. How is he to work with the dotty heiress when neither of them trusts the other—or themselves? But the inhabitants of Wycliffe Manor, young and old, are in peril unless a heartless killer and thief is caught. . .

Buy *The Dilemma of a Dead Scholar*

ABOUT THE AUTHOR

With several million books in print and *New York Times* and *USA Today's* bestseller lists under her belt, former CPA Patricia Rice is one of romance's hottest authors. Her emotionally-charged contemporary and historical romances have won numerous awards, including the *RT Book Reviews* Reviewers Choice and Career Achievement Awards. Her books have been honored as Romance Writers of America RITA® finalists in the historical, regency and contemporary categories.

A firm believer in happily-ever-after, Patricia Rice is married to her high school sweetheart and has two children. A native of Kentucky and New York, a past resident of North Carolina and Missouri, she currently resides in Southern California, and now does accounting only for herself.

ALSO BY PATRICIA RICE

The World of Magic:

The Unexpected Magic Series

MAGIC IN THE STARS

WHISPER OF MAGIC

THEORY OF MAGIC

AURA OF MAGIC

CHEMISTRY OF MAGIC

NO PERFECT MAGIC

The Magical Malcolms Series

MERELY MAGIC

MUST BE MAGIC

THE TROUBLE WITH MAGIC

THIS MAGIC MOMENT

MUCH ADO ABOUT MAGIC

MAGIC MAN

The California Malcolms Series

THE LURE OF SONG AND MAGIC

TROUBLE WITH AIR AND MAGIC

THE RISK OF LOVE AND MAGIC

Crystal Magic

SAPPHIRE NIGHTS

TOPAZ DREAMS

CRYSTAL VISION

WEDDING GEMS

ABOUT BOOK VIEW CAFÉ

 *Book View Café* LLC (BVC) is an author-owned cooperative of professional writers, publishing in a variety of genres including fantasy, romance, mystery, and science fiction — with 90% of the proceeds going to the authors. Since its debut in 2008, BVC has gained a reputation for producing high-quality ebooks. BVC's ebooks are DRM-free and are distributed around the world. The cooperative is now bringing that same quality to its print editions.

BVC authors include New York Times and USA Today best-sellers as well as winners and nominees of many prestigious awards.